James Grant

The Secret Dispatch; or, the Adventures of Captain Balgonie

James Grant

The Secret Dispatch; or, the Adventures of Captain Balgonie

ISBN/EAN: 9783337091132

Printed in Europe, USA, Canada, Australia, Japan

Cover: Foto ©Andreas Hilbeck / pixelio.de

More available books at **www.hansebooks.com**

THE

SECRET DISPATCH;

OR,

THE ADVENTURES OF CAPTAIN BALGONIE.

BY

JAMES GRANT,

AUTHOR OF "ROMANCE OF WAR," "SCOTTISH CAVALIERS,"

ETC. ETC.

NEW EDITION.

LONDON:

CHAPMAN AND HALL, 193, PICCADILLY.

PREFACE.

I NEED scarcely inform the reader of history, that most of the events narrated in the subsequent pages actually occurred in the manner stated; and I have done much to soften, or subdue, the actual barbarity of the story, though such barbarity was consonant enough to the days of her, whose "lust of power and contempt of all moral restraint" won her the name of "the Semiramis of the North."

For the betrothal of the young Lieutenant of the Valikolutz Infantry to his cousin, it may be mentioned that a dispensation was necessary, as the Russian Church—like the Catholic—forbids all marriages within four degrees of relationship.

As stated in the text, the little song of the gipsy is one of many current enough in Russia, where the destruction of the Crescent is always fondly predicted; but never so confidently as during our late Crimean War: and even at this very time, an aged Muscovite, named Alexis Alexandrovitch, after a seclusion of many years in the district of Samara, has come forth as a prophet on the same subject, and is now proceeding from place to place, like another Peter the Hermit, foretelling and preaching the downfall of "the sick man" at Stamboul, and the speedy substitution of the Russian Cross for the Turkish Crescent on the dome of St. Sophia.

26, Danube Street, Edinburgh.

CONTENTS.

CHAPTER XII.

THE SECRET DISPATCH.

CHAPTER I.

THE LOST TRAVELLER.

"Heaven aid me! where am I now—which way shall I turn—advance or retire?" exclaimed Balgonie, as his horse came plunging down almost on its knees, amid wild gorse and matted jungle.

A cold day in the middle of April had passed away; a pale and cheerless sun, that had cast no heat on the leafless scenery and the half-frozen marshes that border the Louga in Western Russia, had sunk, and the darkness of a stormy night came on rapidly. The keen blast of the north, that swept the arid scalps of the Dudenhof (the only range of hills that traverses the ancient Ingria), was bellowing through a gorge, where the Louga poured in foam upon its passage to the Gulf of Finland, between steep banks that were covered by gloomy pines, when the speaker, a mounted officer in Russian uniform, who seemed too surely to have lost his way, reined up a weary and mud-covered horse on the margin of the stream, and by the light that yet lingered on the tops of the tall pines, and gilded faintly the metal-covered domes of a distant building on the opposite bank, looked hopelessly about him for the means of crossing the dangerous river.

"Where am I?" he repeated, almost despairingly; for, as Schiller sings in his "Song of the Bell,"—

"Man fears the kingly lion's tread;
Man fears the tiger's fangs of terror;
And still the dreadliest of the dread
Is man himself in error!"

Though clad in the uniform of the Russian Regiment of Smolensko, which was raised in the famous duchy of that name, the traveller was neither Muscovite nor Calmuck, Cossack nor Tartar, but a cool, wary, and determined young Briton, one of the many Scottish officers whom misfortune or ambition had drawn into the Russian service, both by sea and land, from the time of Peter the Great down to the beginning of the present century; for many Scottish officers served in the Russian fleet with Admiral Greig at the famous bombardment of Varna: and it was such volunteers as these that first taught the barbarous hordes of the growing empire the true science of war and the necessity for discipline.

The rider's green uniform, faced with scarlet velvet and richly laced with gold, was covered by a thick grey pelisse (like our present patrol-jackets), trimmed with black wolf's fur: he wore a scarlet forage cap with a square top, long

boots that came above the knee, and a Turkish
sabre that had once armed a pasha of more tails
than one.

"Swim the river I must," he muttered, after
having traversed the valley in vain, looking for
a bridge, boat, or raft of timber; "but, egad,
death may be the penalty. Well," he added,
with a gleam of ire in his dark grey eyes and
a bitter smile on his lip, "there was a time,
perhaps, when I little thought that I, Charlie
Balgonie, would find a nameless grave in this
land of timber, hemp, and salted hides, where
caviare is a luxury, train-oil a liqueur, and the
air of Siberia deemed healthy for all who have
any absurd ideas of political freedom, or are silly
enough to imagine that a man may be the lord of
his own proper person."

To add to his troubles and discomfort, though
the month was April—usually the most serene of
the year in Russia—snow-flakes were beginning
to fall, rendering yet greater the gloom of the
gathering night.

"I was to have found a bridge here. Can that
Livonian villain, Podatchkine, have deluded, and
then left me to my fate?"

He knew that in his rear, the way by which
he had come, lay half-frozen morasses, heathy
wastes, and forests of spruce, larch, and silver-
leaved firs—vast natural magazines for supplying
all Europe with masts and spars—the haunt of
the wolf and bear; he knew that to linger or to

return were worse than to advance, and that he must cross the stream and seek quarters and guidance at the château, the name of which was yet unknown to him.

This was, if possible, the worst season for passing the Louga, which is always deepest and most navigable in spring. It rises in the district of Novgorod; and, after traversing a country full of vast forests for more than 180 miles, falls into the Gulf of Finland.

Balgonie buttoned tightly his holster-flaps, hooked up his sabre, assured himself that an important dispatch with which he was entrusted was safe in an inner pocket, and prepared seriously for the perilous task of swimming his horse across the stream.

Again he looked anxiously at the château, the abode evidently of some wealthy noble or *boyar*. Its outline had almost disappeared in the increasing obscurity; the last faint gleams of the west had faded away on the onion-shaped roofs of its turrets, and a central dome of polished copper, which was cut into facets like the outside of a pine-apple (for there is much of the Oriental in the old Russian architecture); but lights were beginning to sparkle cheerfully through its double-sashed windows upon the feathery and the funeral-like foliage of the solemn pine woods.

Could those who were comfortably, perhaps luxuriously seated within, but know that there was a poor human being on the eve, perhaps, of perishing helplessly amid the dark flow of that deep and roaring river!

"Courage, friend Charlie!" said the rider to himself; and then he hallooed loudly, as if to attract attention, but did so in vain. The night was becoming a very severe one; the flakes of snow fell thicker and thicker on the gusty and cutting blast.

"Ah! if I should perish here—such a fate!" thought he, shuddering. "Shall I be swept down this black and horrid stream, the Louga, to be cast a drowned corpse upon its banks, to be found stripped and buried by wondering but unpitying serfs and boors; or shall I be torn and mangled by bears and wolves; or borne even to the Gulf of Finland, far, far away, having thus an obscure and wretched fate, without winning the name I had hoped to gain—forgotten even by those who wronged me in Scotland, the land that never more shall be a home to me!"

He did not say all this aloud; but certainly some such painful surmises flashed upon him as he forced his snorting and reluctant horse, by a vigorous use of the spurs, through the thickly interwoven brushwood that grew on the bank of the river, the dull and monotonous rush of which, encumbered as it was by large pieces of ice, was sufficient to appal even a stouter heart than that of this young Scottish soldier of fortune.

With a brief invocation on his lips, he gave

his horse the reins and gored it with the rowels. A strong, active, and clean-limbed, but somewhat undersized animal from the steppes of the Ukraine, with a fierce and angry snort, it plunged into the torrent, and breasted the icy masses bravely.

The slippery fragments that glided past, struck at times both horse and rider, forcing them to swerve down the stream ; others were dashed by the whirling eddies against the projecting pieces of rock or roots of old trees; but after twice nearly despairing of achieving the passage, and believing himself lost, his horse trod firmly on the opposite bank. It emerged, panting, snorting, dripping, and trembling in every fibre, from the flood, and then Captain Balgonie found that he had escaped with life, and had safely passed the swollen waters of the Louga !

Leading his sturdy little steed by the bridle and caressing it the while, he made his way up the opposite bank, guided only by the lights in the mansion (or castle) ; but he proceeded with extreme difficulty, for the underwood was thick and dense as that which grew round the Palace of the Sleeping Beauty ; ere long, however, he reached a plateau, the border of a park or lawn, and saw the snow-whitened walls and turrets of the edifice towering before him.

Rising from a balustraded terrace, with an arched porte-cochère in front, the façade was square, and three storied, having a central dome like an inverted punchbowl, and several little angular towers, tall and slender like minarets; these cut the sky-line, and were surrounded each by a broad cornice or gallery, and terminated by a bulbous-shaped roof, exactly like an onion with its acute end in the air.

The lights in its many windows, the red and yellow coloured curtains within, all indicated warmth and comfort; while with the snow flakes freezing on his sodden and saturated uniform, his limbs benumbed, and his teeth well-nigh chattering, Balgonie hastily led his horse under the porte-cochère, and applied his hand vigorously to the great brazen knocker on the front door.

It was speedily opened, and a white-bearded *dvornick*, or porter, wearing a long flowing *shoubah*, or coat of fur, lined with red flannel, admitted him with many humble genuflections, at the same time summoning a groom to take charge of his horse.

By the bearing of these lackeys, one might almost have thought that the Captain had been expected, or was a friend of the family: but a uniform has ever been an all-powerful passport, and an epaulette the most mighty of all introductions in Russia, where everything is measured by a military standard; thus, in an incredibly short space of time, the wants of rider and horse were alike hospitably attended to.

CHAPTER II.

Captain Balgonie, of the Regiment of Smolensko, soon found himself in a comfortable bed-chamber, where the genial glow of a *peitchka*, or Russian wall-stove, diffused warmth through his chilled frame, and where every current of the external atmosphere was carefully excluded by double window sashes, adorned with artificial flowers between.

When he chose to repose, a couch draped with snow-white curtains, and having a coverlet of the softest fur, awaited him ; and above it hung a little holy picture of the Byzantine school, a Holy Virgin, with a halo of shining metal in the form of a horse-shoe round her head, if he chose to be devout and offer up a prayer.

A valet, after supplying him with hot coffee and a good dram of *vodka* (which somewhat reminded him of his native " mountain dew "), said that the Count, his master, would rejoice to have the pleasure of the visitor's society, after he had made a suitable toilet, and exchanged his wet uniform for a luxurious robe-de-chambre, in the pocket of which he took especial care to secure his dispatch unseen.

Hospitality such as this, was not merely then a characteristic of the people, but was the result, perhaps, of a meagre population, and the absence of inns; thus the arrival of a stranger, especially an officer on duty, at this Russian mansion, created little or no surprise among its inmates.

He was ushered into the presence of Count Mierowitz, whose name at once inspired him with confidence and satisfaction; for, by one of those singular coincidences "which novelists dare not use in fiction, but which occur daily in actual and matter-of-fact life," he had arrived at a mansion where he was not altogether unknown.

"I have to apologise to your High Excellency for this apparent intrusion," said he; "but I have been misled or abandoned by my guide. I am Captain Balgonie, of the Regiment of Smolensko, and have the good fortune to number among my friends your son, Lieutenant Basil Mierowitz, the senior subaltern of my company."

"For Basil's sake, not less than your own, Captain, are you most welcome to the Castle of Louga," replied the Count, lifting and laying aside his cap.

He was a man well on in years; his stature was not great, neither was his presence dignified; he stooped a little and was thick set, with a venerable beard, undefiled by steel; for, like a true old Muscovite, he contended that man was made in the image of God, and should neither be cut or carved upon. His eyebrows were white, but his eyes were dark, keen, quick, and expressed a spirit of ready impulse, for laughter or for ferocity—one, who by turns could be suave or irritable, especially when under the influence of wine, which generally made him fierce and stupid; for never, in all his life, had he suffered control or had his will disputed.

His silver hair was simply tied behind with a black ribbon; in his hand he carried a little cap of black wolf's fur, adorned by rudely set jewels; he wore a queerly cut coat of dark red cloth trimmed with fur, and wore breeches of the same stuff, and lacked but a dagger and pistols with brass Turkish butts at his girdle, to seem what he really was, in disposition and character, a type of the boyar of the old school, who preferred quass to champagne, ate his pancakes with caviare, and was proud of being a specimen of the old Russian noble, as he existed in the time of Peter the Great, when his class first united some of the vices and luxuries of Western Europe to their native lawlessness and hardy ferocity.

Such was Count Mierowitz.

"When did you last see my son?" he asked, in tone more of authority than of anxious inquiry.

"Some three months since, Excellency: he has been detached on the Livonian frontier."

"And you, Captain—"

I am proceeding on urgent imperial service from Novgorod where my regiment is stationed in the old palace of the Czars."

" To whither ? "

" Schlusselburg."

The host changed countenance and almost manifested signs of discomposure on hearing of that formidable fortress and prison—the veritable Bastille of St. Petersburg, and he said:

" A name to shudder at—by St. Nicholas it is ! "

" And, but for the feather in the wax of my dispatch," resumed Balgonie (showing a red government seal in which a piece of feather twitched from a pen was inserted, the usual Russian emblem of *speed*), " I had not, perhaps, tempted the dangers of the Louga, but sought a billet on the other side, if such could be found."

" You know not, perhaps, that my woods are full of wolves ; but this is not the way to St. Petersburg."

" Yet I was so directed, Excellency."

" You have been misled, and are only some seventy versts or so from the place you have left."

" You amaze me, Count," exclaimed the perplexed Captain ; for in the Russian service, an error becomes a crime.

" Captain, you should have gone by Gori, Oustensk, Spask, and so on."

" That devil of a Podatchkine, an orderly of General Weymarn, who sent him specially with me, has either deluded or abandoned me."

"Yet we must thank your Podatchkine, in so far that he has procured us the pleasure of your society in this lonely place—my daughter and my niece, Captain Ivanovitch Balgonie," continued the Count, introducing two young ladies who came through the curtains of a species of boudoir, "Natalie and Mariolizza Usakoff. Our visitor, Natalie, is that Ivanovitch Balgonie of whom Basil has spoken so much and so kindly."

Without being a vain man, Balgonie felt at that moment considerable satisfaction in the conviction that he was—as his glass had often informed him—decidedly a good-looking young fellow, with regular features, fine dark eyes, curling brown hair, and a smart moustache; for Natalie Mierowna, like her cousin Mariolizza, was one of the most attractive women at the dangerous Court of the Empress Catharine II.; for it was during her reign that the story and the atrocities we have unfortunately to record took place; when among us, in more civilised Britain, the grandfather of her present Majesty, old George III., was king, and the arts of peace and war grew side by side.

"The friend and comrade of my brother Basil is welcome," said Natalie, presenting her hands (very tiny and delicate they were) to Balgonie, who bowed and touched them lightly with his lips; "he has often written to us concerning you and your adventures together in Silesia."

"I am but too fortunate to be remembered thus."

"Nay." rejoined Natalie, "we could scarcely forget that daring act of yours, which won you the rank you hold at present. Ah, Basil told us all about that when he was last here," she added, with a beautiful smile, of which she knew that many had already felt the power.

"You mean my reconnoitring the enemy's position and avoiding being taken by them?"

"Yes, pray tell me about it?" said Mariolizza, her blue eyes dilating with pleasure; "my brother was there too—Apollo Usakoff, a lieutenant in the Regiment of Valikolutz."

"It was a very simple matter," replied Balgonie, bowing to each of the cousins, and not sorry to have a good personal anecdote to relate of himself, one which was certain to make him appear to advantage in the estimation of two very attractive women. "It was only a *ruse de guerre*, and occurred when our Regiment of Smolensko was with the combined armies in Silesia, and before the King of Prussia attacked Count Daun at the Heights of Buckersdorff. An exact account of the Austrian position was required by our general, who had not then received the orders of the Empress to fall back upon the Russian frontier. The task was one of extreme peril; so I being a soldier of fortune, having all to win, and nothing to lose——"

"Save your life!" interrupted Natalie.

"One in my position, among a foreign army, must not value that too much," said the Captain, in a tone not untinged with melancholy.

" Well ? "

" I volunteered for it, despite all that your son, Count, my friend could say to dissuade me. Well armed, at midnight, I set out upon my solitary mission, unattended and alone, without relinquishing my uniform ; for if taken prisoner when otherwise attired, I would infallibly be hanged as a spy ; but ere long I found, that in such a dress, there were insuperable difficulties to making the reconnoissance required.

"At the cottage of a Silesian boor, near the base of the Eulanbirge (or mountain of the owls), I stopped to make some inquiries. The fellow proved to be partially tipsy ; the contents of my pocket-flask, potent vodka, completed his happy condition, and after a few jests I prevailed upon him to change dresses with me. He donned the green coat, epaulettes, and boots of the Regiment of Smolensko ; I, the ample canvas caftan and girdle of a Silesian boor,—a fur cap, and a visage daubed with grime, completed my costume. Thus attired, and retaining only my pistols, I reconnoitred safely and unheeded the Austrian position, noting the defences, trenches, fascine batteries, cannon, and general disposition ; but I had a narrow escape, for when returning to the cottage of my new friend the boor, a party of Count Daun's Imperial Cuirassiers, who had been patrolling the Eulanbirge, overtook me, and at once perceiving I was not a Silesian, questioned me rather closely and curiously.

"I succeeded in passing myself off as a Pomeranian, and pointing to the cottage, told them that there was concealed an officer of the famous Regiment of Smolensko. They at once galloped off and surrounded it, while I stole away to a thicket, and climbed into a tree, from whence I could see the poor boor, clad in my uniform, and still labouring under the influence of his late debauch, dragged a prisoner — despite all his bewildered protestations and denials — towards the camp of Count Daun, while I, under cover of night, reached in safety the lines of the allies, and made my report to General Weymarn, then commanding our division of the army.

"It proved of no use to us, as we fell back next day; but it enabled our ally, the King of Prussia, to storm with signal success the Heights of Buckersdorff, to drive back Count Daun, and invest Schwiednitz. He offered me rank in his army; but I declined, on which the Empress sent me the commission of Captain in her Regiment of Smolensko, thus enabling me to rank as a noble of the ninth class."

"May you soon rank as one of the sixth," said the Count, patting the Captain on the shoulder frankly.

"Ah, Excellency, it may be long ere I become a colonel; yet," he added, almost as if talking to

himself, " when I got the letter of the Empress
addressed to me, Carl Ivanovitch Hospodeen*
Balgonie, I could not but smile at the thought
of how such a title would have sounded in the
ears of my good father, old John Balgonie, of
that Ilk ! "

" Let me repeat that you are most welcome,"
said the Count, who totally failed to understand
the meaning of the last remark; " and luckily
you have arrived just as the ladies and I were
about to proceed to the supper-table."

To Balgonie it had become apparent that each
time he mentioned the name of the Empress, the
proud pink nostrils of Natalie seemed to dilate,
and that a decidedly dangerous expression glittered in her splendid dark eyes.

Natalie Mierowna, whose beauty had caused
such jealousy at Moscow and St. Petersburg
(two duels are spoken of concerning her), had
ever shone brilliantly in the " follow-my-leader"
kind of dance, now so well known among us as
the Mazurka,—the old Sclavonian measure, in
which all succeeding couples have to imitate the
motions of the first ; and the chief Russian pecu-
liarity of the dance consists still in the circumstance of the ladies selecting their own partners
—the brilliant Natalie, we say, having twice
sportively, or in a spirit of coquettish bravado,
chosen a handsome young aide-de-camp, whom
the Empress was supposed to view with favour,

* Equivalent to Monsieur or Esquire.

led to her abrupt exile from Court, and to the detaching of Captain Vlasfief, of the Imperial Guards, to irksome and secluded duty at the state prison of Schlusselburg. This unmerited affront filled her brother, Basil Mierowitz, with such fiery indignation, that but for the dread of compromising his whole family, he would have cast his commission at the feet of the imperious Catharine, and quitted the Russian army; but flight or exile must at once have followed the act.

As it was, though detached and distant on the Livonian frontier, he was now conceiving a scheme for vengeance, much more perilous to himself and to all concerned, and which actually aimed at the dethronement of the Empress Catharine!

CHAPTER III.

NATALIE.

THERE are few Russian ladies now, who do not speak with equal facility, German, French, and English; but Natalie Mierowna and her cousin were then each mistress of them all,—and this was in the comparatively barbarous time of Catharine II.

Thus their acquaintance with European literature enabled them to excel in an easy and well-supported conversation of which the old bovar, their kinsman, could make nothing; and which they could embellish by their wit and power of quotation, and with an exquisite *finesse d'esprit* peculiarly their own. When this dangerous charm was added to the great beauty of Natalie, she could not but prove a perilous acquaintance for the young Scottish wanderer.

Her loveliness was indeed great.

She was a large, showy, and snowy-skinned beauty, almost voluptuous yet very graceful in form, with fine dark eyes, that were dreamy or sparkling by turns as emotion moved her; long-lashed they were, and perhaps too heavily lidded. Her hair was of the darkest brown, almost black;

her lips were full, but flexible, small and pouting when in repose, almost too large when she smiled, which was frequently.

It was when she spoke of the Empress, that her white bosom heaved, and a fiery expression seemed to pervade her whole features. She said little, and that little was generally said with assumed gentleness or real reserve, for language cannot be too guarded in Russia; but her dark eyes flashed, her delicate nostrils dilated, her short upper lip quivered, she threw back her proud head, and more than once Balgonie saw her white hands clenched; for all the dove-like softness of her nature seemed to depart, when she thought of the affront that exile from Court had put upon her, and her whole family, even to delaying the marriage of her cousin Mariolizza to her brother Basil, to whom she was engaged — solemnly betrothed by a religious ceremony.

She took the arm of Balgonie, and led the way to the dining-room, which was lit by brilliant crystal girandoles, and heated, of course, by a peitchka, the greatest luxury of civilised life that can be found in a cold climate, and which warms a house more effectually than any grate of coals can do. Built on that side of the large, lofty, and magnificent room which was farthest from the windows, it was formed of solid stone, with several carved apertures, and lined with white shining porcelain; within it, blazed a constant fire of billets and faggots, under the care of the dvornick, or house-porter, and these were furnished by the Count's serfs or woodsmen from the adjacent forests.

All made a sign of the cross in the Greek fashion, and seated themselves; but weary and exhausted by his long ride and recent immersion in a swollen and icy river, Balgonie found it almost impossible to partake of the supper that was pressed upon him : caviare on slices of bread to begin with,—" caviare from the roe of the sturgeons of the Don," as the Count informed him,— roasted capon and jugged hare, dried figs and conserves, prunes, and *pastilla* of fruit and honey compounded, together with the champagne, Rhine wine, and vodka, in silver tankards and goblets of jewelled Venetian crystal.

The jaded traveller could make only a pretence of eating; but he could drink deeply, for he was athirst; and more than one foaming goblet of sparkling Moselle was filled for him, till he became giddy and confused. Were the fumes of the wine mounting to his head? What was the Count saying in an undertone? Was it of him that the cousins were talking in some strange language, and covertly exchanging smiles with their beautiful eyes? " Courage, Charlie," thought he, " this is a bad beginning !"

Though people were not very particular as to a bumper more or less in those days anywhere, in Russia least of all, an emotion of shame came over the young Scottish officer; he felt his cheeks and

forehead burn, and he made a vigorous effort to
rally his senses, but in vain : he heard the voices
of Natalie and of Mariolizza ; but he knew not
what they said or what he replied, for he felt as
one in a half-waking dream. They were talking
merrily, however, in French, which is always spoken
well by the Russians ; perhaps because the tongue
that can master Russ may achieve anything.

After a time he mustered sufficient energy and
sense to beg that he might be permitted to retire,
as he had his journey to resume betimes on the
morrow; and he was escorted to his chamber by
the Count in person. Its four corners seemed to
be in rapid pursuit of each other now, and the
floor and the ceiling to be incessantly changing
places; then his senses reeled, and the light
departed from his eyes. He found himself fainting.

The sudden and rapid journey from Novgorod,
the lack of food and the toil he had undergone
for one night and two entire days, while wandering with the treacherous Podatchkine, the crossing
of the Louga, and the bruises he had unconsciously
received from several pieces of floating ice, had
all proved too much for his system, and brought
on a relapse of an old camp fever from which he
had suffered once when serving with the army in
Silesia,—and in the morning he was delirious.

Though weak, bewildered, scared by the prospect of loitering thus when proceeding on urgent
duty (for obedience and discipline become a second
nature to the soldier), enduring a raging thirst

and a burning pang that shot with each pulsation through his brain, stiff in every joint and covered with livid bruises, he had still strength left as dawning day stole through the double sashes of his windows, to stagger from bed, and search for the dispatch, which, on the hazard of his life, he was to place in the hands of Bernikoff, the Governor of Schlusselburg.

He hurriedly, and with a tremor that increased, examined each of his pockets in succession, then his sabretasche, and lastly the pocket of the robe-de-chambre; but the dispatch—the dispatch of the Empress—entrusted to him as a chosen man by Lieutenant-General Weymarn was gone!

Lost, or abstracted, it was irretrievably *gone!*

Was he the victim of treachery or of a snare? Was it a dream that the voluptuous and beautiful Natalie, with her snowy skin, her dreamy eyes, and her fascinating smile, had been hovering about him—a dream or a reality?

Alas! he knew not; for again the walls and windows were whirling round him in wild career, and he sank on the floor insensible.

Poor Charlie Balgonie knew not that the morning on which he made this alarming discovery was that of the second day since his arrival at the Castle of Louga.

CHAPTER IV.

CORPORAL PODATCHKINE.

SCARCELY had Charlie Balgonie achieved the passage of the Louga, and, in the dark, forced his panting horse up the wooded bank towards the lighted windows of the castle, than his guide and orderly, Corporal Michail Podatchkine, who, for reasons which were his own, and which shall ultimately be explained, had decoyed him many, many versts to the southward of his proper route and then abandoned him, while he still cautiously followed, and watched him plunge into the perilous stream—watched him in the hope that he might perish in its icy current; Corporal Podatchkine, we say, had barely seen that the officer's safety was certain and assured, than he turned his horse's head, and with a hoarse malediction on his bearded mouth, rode away in an opposite direction.

The lighted windows of the Castle of Louga soon darkened and vanished in his rear; the snow-flakes came thicker and faster on the icy blast, whitening his round bearskin cap and fur shoubah or cloak, and the untrimmed mane of his shaggy little horse; but with his long lance slung behind him, his knees up to his saddle-bow, and his fierce, keen eyes peering out the way before him, the amiable Podatchkine, who, though a Livonian by birth, had the honour to hold the rank of corporal in a corps of Cossacks, rode on through the dense fir forest as unerringly as if every tree therein had been planted by his own warlike hands.

Ere long, with a grunt of satisfaction, he struck upon a track that led to the right and left, and he unhesitatingly pursued the latter. There were then none of those verst-posts, about ten feet high or so, such as may now be found by the side of the Russian roads through the forests, or along the open steppe; but Podatchkine rode steadily on, pausing only now and then to unsling and grasp his spear, or give a fierce gleaming glance around him, while the nostrils of his thick snub-nose dilated, when a prolonged and melancholy howl, rising from the woody depths into the chill drear sky of night, announced that some wolf was rousing itself in its lair among the grass, or in its den beside the river.

Anon he came to a place where the forest was partially cleared, and there stood a little hut built of squared logs. The walls of this edifice were whitened artificially; but the roof was rendered whiter still by a coat of the fast-freezing snow. A single ray of smoky light streamed from the opening (which passed for a window) near the door, on which Podatchkine, without dismounting, struck three blows with the butt of his lance.

"Nicholas Paulovitch," he exclaimed, "are you within?"

The door was soon unfastened, and thereat appeared a figure, not unlike an Esquimaux, bearing a pine torch. He was a man of great stature and muscular development, clad in a caftan of coarse, thick, and warm material, girt by a broad belt in which a long and rusty knife was stuck; he had on bark shoes and long leggings of sheepskin, which, like Bryan O'Linn's breeches, had "the skinny side out and the hairy side in;" and he cultivated one long lock of grizzled hair behind his right ear in the old fashion of the Black Cossacks; but this appendage was concealed by the hood and tippet of fur which he wore. This man, however, did not belong to any of the nomadic military tribes, but was a species of Russian gipsy, a half-breed.

He held up the pine torch, and its flaring light tipped with a lurid, weird, and uncertain glow his fierce, tawny, and repulsive visage, causing his cunning and almond-shaped eyes to gleam redly, like two carbuncles, from under their thick and impending brows, which were nearly as shaggy as the moustache that blended with his greasy and uncombed beard; and in the same light the head of Podatchkine's lance and the hafts of his sabre, dagger, and pistols glittered at times, being the only bright parts of his remarkably dingy costume.

"Is it you, Michail Podatchkine—and *alone ?*" he asked surlily.

"Yes; even so, alone. Dost think I have the evil eye about me that you stare so, Nicholas Paulovitch ?"

"God forbid !" replied Nicholas with a shudder, for this idea is the grossest and the greatest of all Russian superstitions ; " but I expected two— yourself and another."

"Who told you so?"

"Olga Paulowna, my sister, who yesterday saw you at Krejko."

"True, I remember. Now listen, old friend and comrade——"

"Hush, the girl is within and may hear you."

"Well," said Podatchkine, lowering his voice, while the other extinguished his torch, half closed the door of his hut, and drew nearer the speaker, " by order of General Weymarn, Governor of St. Petersburg, General of the Cavalry, Director-General of the Canals, Bridges, and High-ways——"

"And the devil knows all what more !" said the other impatiently. " Well?"

"I am ordered to guide this Carl Ivanovitch Balgonie, who is a stranger, to the gates of Schlusselburg, as he bears to Bernikoff a dispatch of importance; but I have been promised a heavy sum——"

"Ah! how much say you?"

"I have said nothing yet."

"But you spoke of a heavy sum."

"Two hundred silver roubles."

"Two hundred silver roubles!" exclaimed Nicholas, opening his avaricious eyes with wonder, and then closing them again, so that they looked like two narrow slits.

"Yes, every *denusca*, if I, by fair means or by foul, prevent the delivery of that paper into the hands of old Bernikoff."

"He whose dagger tickled the throat of Peter III.: and by whom are you offered this, friend Podatchkine?"

"I can trust you: well, by the Lieutenant Apollo Usakoff."

"The grandson of the Hetman Mazeppa!"

"The same; and by Basil Mierowitz——"

"Well, and what the devil have I to do with all this?" growled the half-breed.

"Much: fifty roubles will be yours, Paulovitch, if you will assist me," said Podatchkine in a husky whisper.

"Let us talk over this: dismount, and come in."

"Nay, there is Olga Paulowna: then I have other work to do; but give me a drink, for I am sorely athirst."

The other speedily brought him a painted bowl full of foamy quass, which the Cossack Corporal, for so we may term him, drained to the dregs;

though it is a liquor, to any but a Russian, horrible as the water of Cocytus.

"Let us be wary, friend Podatchkine," said the woodman : "the knout is not an angel, but it teaches us to tell the truth alike of ourselves and of others."

Refreshed by his bitter draught, the Corporal shook the gathering snow-flakes from the sleeves of his fur shoubah, and resumed somewhat garrulously :

"My next instructions are, that the dispatch, which is from the Empress herself (whom God and our Lady of Kazan long preserve!), and which bears the imperial seal, shall never be delivered; but must be obtained by me for Basil Mierowitz and the Lieutenant Usakoff, now detached upon the Livonian frontier, and who both know as little as I care, that its bearer is actually their own dearest and most valued friend! I misled the Hospodeen Balgonie, lured him to the river's brink, and left him there, in the hope that he and his horse might become frozen on the steppe or in the forest, where I could rob him at ease ; but the man seems made of iron, and, to my astonishment, I saw him swim the Louga. I thought all gone, he, the dispatch, and my 200 roubles, when he plunged his horse into the river; but he stoutly won the opposite bank, and has made his way straight to the dwelling of Count Mierowitz, where now, I doubt not, he is safely housed."

" It seems to me, friend Podatchkine, that you took a great deal of useless trouble when you had your dagger and pistols," said the other, suspiciously.

" Nay, if he was to perish thus, suspicion might too readily fall upon me, for he is a favourite officer of the Empress, and of Weymarn too. My plan is this: I may get the dispatch to-night in yonder castle of Count Mierowitz."

" And if not?"

" Then I shall again lure and mislead Balgonie, and bring him here in the night."

" What then?" asked the woodman doggedly.

" How dull we are, Paulovitch. We shall drug and drown him; thus shall he die without a wound. I will take back the dispatch to Novgorod; and you can carry the body on his horse to St. Petersburg, where a sum will be given you for finding it. The poor stranger, they will say, has perished amid our keen Russian frosts, and that will be all. Nicholas Paulovitch, the carcass will be well worth twenty roubles to thee."

" And thy fifty?"

" You shall receive when the affair is over, and when you come to me at Novgorod, where I am quartered."

" By the bones of my tribe, and by the sword that flames in the hand of the holy Michail, I am with you, Podatchkine!" exclaimed the half-breed with ferocious joy, mingling his gipsy

cant with that of the Russian church.   Then
they shook heartily their hard and dingy hands
—hands that had wrought many a deed of
merciless cruelty.

"And now, Paulovitch, give me a light for my
pipe, and let me begone."

A few minutes more and these worthy com-
patriots had separated.

Podatchkine rode somewhat leisurely to a ford
that he knew of lower down the river, believing
that in time the whole onus, and perhaps suspicion,
of Balgonie's death (if it was necessary) might
fall on the woodman, whom he had resolved to
cheat of the promised fifty roubles if he could.

"He will play me false," muttered Podatchkine.   "Is not the dog a gipsy?   Beware of the
tamed wolf, of the baptized Jew, and the enemy
who has made it up; why should I not delude
him who will readily delude me?"

Our enterprising Corporal was correct in his
estimate of Nicholas Paulovitch; for, at the same
moment, that personage, while wrapped in his
filthy sheepskin (caring nothing for the comfort
of any other bed than the floor), was considering
how he might drug and drown both the officer
and his treacherous guide, sell both their bodies
at the nearest military post, and, by taking the
dispatch to Novgorod himself, obtain the entire
reward offered for it by the Lieutenants Mierowitz
and Usakoff, or still more, perhaps, by **delivering
it to the Empress!**

There was a third person who had overheard the first savage plot, and who felt her heart stirred with pity and terror for Balgonie, who had given her a silver kopec at Krejko but yesterday, —the gipsy girl, Olga Paulowna, the sister of Nicholas. Paulovitch ; and she resolved to baffle both conspirators if she could.

It was in perfect ignorance of who might be the bearer of that dispatch (with the contents of which a spy had acquainted them) that the two officers, who were then engaged in an extensive and dangerous political and military conspiracy, contrived to have Podatchkine, in the character of a guide and orderly, sent upon the trail of one who was really their most valued friend and comrade ; though, as a foreigner and soldier of fortune, they deemed it proper to keep him as yet in total ignorance of their daring hopes and plans.

CHAPTER V.

It may now be necessary to afford the reader a little historical insight as to what it was that hinged on this important dispatch of the Scottish officer, Balgonie.

When the Emperor Peter II. died of small-pox (just on the eve of his marriage), closing a short reign of three years of stormy trouble and dark intrigue, the whole male issue of Peter the Great of Russia became extinct.

The Duke of Holstein, son of his eldest daughter, was entitled to the throne; but the Russians, for certain cogent political reasons, filled that perilous seat with Anne, Duchess of Courland, daughter of Ivan, Peter's eldest bro-ther. Governed by her favourite Biron, on whom she bestowed the duchy of Courland, she broke through all the limits which growing civilisation had imposed upon the power of the Czars; she engaged in many useless wars, lost vast treasures and more than a hundred thousand men in strife with the Turks, and closing an inglorious reign, was succeeded by one who will shortly be introduced to the reader, Ivan Antonovitch, or

John IV., son of her niece, the Princess of Mech-lenburg, an infant only six months old. This Princess sent Biron, the Regent, to the usual place of Muscovite seclusion, Siberia, and assumed the administratorship during the minority of her son.

This state of affairs was but of short duration when Elizabeth, daughter of Peter the Great, having a strong party, seized the crown, banished the entire family of Mechlenburg, and deposing the infant monach, Ivan IV., confined him for life a prisoner of state in the great Castle of Schlus-selburg, where he had been for twenty-three years, at the period when our narrative opens.

To mention him in conversation, and still more to possess a coin bearing his effigy, incurred the guilt and insured the punishment of treason! More than twenty years after the deposition of this transitory emperor, a German tradesman, who had worked long as a cabinet-maker at St. Petersburg, went to Cronstadt, intending then to embark for his native city, Lubeck. As it was not permitted to carry out of Russia above a certain quantity of specie, an officer of customs asked the German "what he had with him?" "Only a few roubles to pay for my passage," he replied; and on being commanded to show them, one was discovered having the effigy of Ivan IV! In vain did the unhappy tradesman protest that he neither knew he had such a coin, nor from whom he had received it. Death was the penalty; but his goods were confiscated, and he was condemned to perpetual imprisonment in the mines of Siberia.

The Empress Elizabeth died the victim of intemperance; and while poor Prince Ivan, an uncrowned emperor, a prisoner without a crime, was left to pine in the Castle of Schlusselburg, the sceptre was given to the feeble and dissipated Peter III., the husband of the beautiful, voluptuous, and talented Catharine II., daughter of a petty prince, but descended from the ancient house of Servestan,—a woman whom, in three short months after their coronation, he contrived to disgust by his political innovations, and still more by his amatory inconstancy; so it was resolved to get rid of Peter, who was then in his thirty-fourth year.

Peter I. had nearly lost Russia by compelling the people to cut off the tails of their coats; and Peter III. became equally unpopular by ordering them to trim their vast beards, and by putting his troops in the Prussian uniform. Crowned heads should leave such matters to tailors and tonsors; but he certainly abolished the secret tribunal with its contingent horrors, and recalled many a poor exile from Siberia.

A party was formed for his dethronement; so one evening in July, 1762, when he was surrounded by his guard of Holsteiners, and amusing himself with his flower gardens (he was a great botanist), and with some of his beautiful mistresses at the palace of Orienbaum,—particularly the Countess of Woronzow, to whose allurements he had abandoned himself,—the exasperated Empress prepared to strike a final blow for Russia and for herself.

Putting on a uniform of old Russian Guards belonging to her future favourite, Captain Vlasfief, with the most coquettish grace, this young and beautiful, but in some respects terrible, woman borrowed from the nobles around her all the accessories of a complete military toilette: of Basil Mierowitz, a hat; of Count Orloff, a scarf; of Colonel Bernikoff, a belt; of some one else, a sword. Over all, she wore the blue ribbon of the first order of the Empire, which her impolitic husband had laid aside for that of Prussia.

The drums beat to arms: in this strange guise she showed herself to the troops, who were now mustered to the number of twenty thousand men in the great square of St. Petersburg, where the sight of the uniform of the old guard, which had been forced to give place to Peter's cherished Holsteiners, raised bursts of acclamation, quite as much as the appearance of Catharine, who was then "in the full flower of her robust beauty, perfectly elegant in figure, and purely feminine from her shoulders to her feet, which were remarkably handsome, and of which she was very proud." Her nose was aquiline, her eyes blue with black lashes, and her hair, a brilliant auburn, was curling on her shoulders. Thus has an eyewitness described her.

The regiments began to file off against the Emperor, and little knowing the end of the expedition, among the troops on this night marched Charlie Balgonie, with the colours of the Regiment of Smolensko on his shoulder.

Everywhere the rebellious Empress was received with enthusiasm, and the Great Chancellor Woroslaff, who was sent against her, was among the first to join her party.

The Emperor, abandoning his flowers and his fair ones, fled to his yacht or galley, which was rowed to Cronstadt, of which his enemy, the High Admiral Talizine, had already made himself master. The imperial galley (relates M. Rulhière in his "Histoire sur la Révolution de Russie") came under the ramparts in the night, while the great alarm bells rung, the drums were beaten and scarlet rockets ascended in showers from the dark mass of the Castle of Kronslot; and then, all along the line of fortifications, Peter saw two hundred port-fires shedding their weird unearthly glare through the yawning embrasures upon the twilight sea and sky—each port-fire beside a loaded cannon— loaded against himself!

This was at ten o'clock; but ere the great oars of the galley were laid in, or the anchor dropped, a sentinel challenged :

" Who comes there ? "

" His Imperial Majesty the Emperor," replied the Captain of the galley, who was standing on its gilded prow.

"There is no longer any Emperor!" was the stern reply of some one on the ramparts.

"'Tis false! I am here—I, Peter Antonovitch," said the Emperor, growing pale at these daring and terrible words, as he stood up and threw back his cloak to show himself and his well-known Prussian star, by the clear, lingering twilight of the northern evening.

"Sheer off," shouted the Admiral Talizine, "or, by our Lady of Kazan, I will fire on you!"

"We are going—give us but time," cried the Captain hopelessly, through his speaking-trumpet.

At that moment a thousand voices on the ramparts shouted on the still twilight air—

"Long live the Empress Catharine II.!"

On hearing this, Peter burst into tears, and fell back into the arms of his attendants, saying—

"The conspiracy is general—from the first days of my short reign I have seen it coming!"

He was soon after abandoned by all, even by his obnoxious Holstein Guards, who surrendered to the Regiments of Smolensko and Valikolutz; and then he was committed by his wife, prisoner of state, to the Castle of Robsch, in a solitary place, eighteen miles from St. Petersburg. Six days afterwards had only elapsed, when it was suggested that though young Ivan was still lingering a captive at Schlusselburg, and some were not without hopes of replacing him on the throne, tranquillity could not be perfectly restored while Peter lived, though lonely and abandoned now.

His wife's lovers and favourites came to this decision speedily; so late one afternoon, three horsemen arrived at the residence of the fallen Emperor. They were Count Orloff, who had in his breast a laced handkerchief of the Empress, the grim Colonel Bernikoff, and a Hospodeen or gentleman, who announced that they had come to sup with him; and, according to the Russian fashion, glasses of brandy were served round before they sat down.

In that given to the Emperor was poison.

Whether, adds the historian we quote, they were in haste to carry back their dark tidings, or whether the horror of the deed made them anxious to finish it, none can know; but to hasten their terrible work, they insisted on giving him another glass.

Already the subtle poison was diffusing itself through the vitals of the unhappy Emperor; and now, struck by the pallor of their faces and the ferocious expression of their eyes, he started back, refused the proffered glass, and despairingly summoned assistance.

They then flung themselves upon him, and Count Orloff, pulling from his breast the hand-kerchief he had concealed there, threw it over the mouth of Peter, to gag him and stifle his cries. He was dashed again and again to the floor, where he defended himself against his assassins with all the fury that terror of death and despair could inspire.

Two young officers of the guard now rushed in, and, as the orders of all were to slay Peter without a wound, they knotted the handkerchief round his neck to strangle him, while the Count pressed his knees upon his breast.

Still the dying Emperor struggled so fearfully that the ferocious Bernikoff, losing all patience, plunged a dagger into his throat; and thus, poisoned, stabbed, and strangled, he expired without further resistance.

A few hours after this, pale, dishevelled, and covered with blood, dust, and perspiration, with torn garments and disturbed bearing, Count Orloff appeared before the Empress. "She arose in silence," says M. Rulhière, "and passed into an inner room, whither he followed her. Some minutes after, she called Count Panin, who was already named her minister, and informed him that the Emperor was dead, and consulted with him upon the mode of announcing his demise to the people."

It was given out that he had died a natural death.

The wound inflicted by Bernikoff's dagger was carefully sewed up; the orifice was neatly covered by a piece of gold-beater's skin; and the body, in an old green regimental coat, with four wax candles as a funeral state, was exposed for three days to the people. The Russians were permitted to wear their beards; the Empress poured out her afflictions in a ukase, and offered up her prayers, as became a widow, in the church of our holy Lady of Kazan.

And it was in the service of this charming people,

> " —— this new and polished nation,
> Whose names want nothing but pronounciation,"

—a people, who, in the arts of peace, were little better than the Scots when James I. was butchered in the Black Friary at Perth, or the men of " Merry England " when her crook-backed Dick was smothering the royal babies in the Tower— that, by an adverse fate, our hero found himself a soldier of fortune, when, as before stated, old George III. was King of the British Isles, and " the first gentleman in Europe " was a sinless infant on his mother's knee.

After Peter was laid in his grave, and Catharine was firmly seated on his throne, her conduct was cautious and judicious, and, as even her enemies admitted, at times magnanimous; yet frightful atrocities were committed during her reign when she degenerated into ferocity and debauchery.

The captivity of the young and innocent Ivan in Schlusselburg, in charge of the unscrupulous Bernikoff, Captain Vlasfief, and a Lieutenant named Tschekin—three officers in whom Catharine had implicit reliance—seemed more hopeless now than ever when the sceptre was in her firm grasp.

Now that Peter was disposed of, her only dread consisted in the chance of Ivan's escape; so his guards were doubled, and her orders to Bernikoff concerning him were to ensure his detention even by death if necessary: and it was concerning this very dread that Captain Charles Balgonie was proceeding with a dispatch from Novgorod, where Catharine, with some of her favourites and courtiers, was residing for a time in the ancient palace of the Czars.

CHAPTER VI.

THE PALATINE.

CORPORAL PODATCHKINE was an admirable specimen of his own type of Russian,—one who was
more afraid of neglecting Lent than of murdering
his fellow-being, especially if that fellow-being
was a foreigner; "for," saith M. L'Abbé Chappe
at this time, "they do not reckon foreigners
among the number of their brethren."

His thick black scrubby hair was cut straight
across the forehead in a line with the eyebrows,
and at each side it hung perpendicularly down
below the ears, in the old Russian and Mediæval
fashion, and was, moreover, cut square across the
neck behind, just as the English wore theirs in
the days of Richard III.; and he kept alternately scratching and smoothing his rugged front,
nervously and assiduously, when he removed his
fur Cossack cap; and, full of affected concern,
even to exhibiting tears in his small cunning eyes,
presented himself, through the bribed auspices
of the dvornick, to Natalie Mierowna next morning, and besought her to have him "conducted
to the chamber of his brave, his beloved Captain, his comrade and brother, who was, he now

learned, seriously ill, helpless, and delirious,"—
and, in fact, just as the cunning Corporal wished
him to be.

There he found Balgonie, certainly too ill and
weak either to recognise him or understand what
he was about; so the faithful Cossack made a
rapid and skilful investigation of all the officer's
pockets, and especially his sabretasche, for the
dispatch.

Not a vestige of it was to be found.

"What the devil can he have done with it?"
muttered the bewildered Corporal, as he thought
of his 200 silver roubles; " can he have lost it in
the river, or swallowed it?"

The truth is, that Natalie Mierowna had her
doubts about the fidelity of Podatchkine, and
even of some of her own domestics, and aware of
the risk run by the stranger if he lost a dispatch
of the Empress, she had, prior to the introduction
of the Corporal, secured the document, and at that
moment it was hidden in her own fair bosom
until she could secure it in a safer place.

In her bosom! Poor Natalie! Alas, she little
knew its contents, and the horrors they were yet
to produce!

Baffled thus in his attempt to secure it, there
was no resource for the faithful warrior of the
steppes now but to take up his quarters, which
he was nothing loth to do, at the Castle of the
Louga, and there quietly and comfortably to
smoke his pipe by the kitchen stove; await the

recovery or the death, he cared not which, of Balgonie; and to concert further measures with the huge gipsy, Nicholas Paulovitch, whom he saw daily.

It was no feverish dream of Balgonie that Natalie Mierowna had been hovering about his bedside; for she and her cousin Mariolizza had been his especial nurses.

In less than three days the feverish delirium subsided, sense completely returned, and the young Captain appeared to be labouring only under a species of influenza. A cold, as we understand that homely but troublesome kind of ailment in foggy Britain, is almost unknown in the latitude of St. Petersburg. " It is," says Dr. Granville, "indigenous to England, and, above all, to London;" yet we fear Balgonie had a most unromantic and unmistakable cold, consequent on his immersion in the icy Louga, together with an aguish shivering, which rendered the quitting of his couch, and betaking himself to the saddle, as yet quite impossible.

Balgonie had an insatiable thirst: he had visions of iced champagne; but in lieu, got only tea-punch, if we may so call it, being tea in the fashion still taken by the Russians (who hold that milk spoils it), with a slice of lemon or preserved fruit; and as he got stronger, Katinki, a strapping Polish damsel with fine black eyes, who was Natalie's own particular follower, added thereto a dash of rum and then *tsvetochny*, or

flowery tea, with cakes, which the Captain seemed
to relish all the more when he understood them
to be made by the white hands of Natalie: an
appreciation which showed a decided improve-
ment in that young officer's health. But—

"My dispatch," he frequently said aloud,—"I
must begone with my dispatch!"

"Might it not be entrusted to the Corporal
Podatchkine?" asked Natalie one morning, as
she personally gave him his warm and soothing
drink with her own hand, Katinka standing
demurely by with a silver salver.

"Impossible, Hosphoza, for so I may call you:
an officer alone can carry a dispatch of the Empress. Its contents are most urgent: this delay,
over which I have no control, may be visited by
royal disfavour, even punishment; and I fear that
the air of Tobolsk or Irkutsk would ill suit a
Scotsman's lungs, Natalie Mierowna."

"Yet tarry here you must," said she, with a
smile, the beauty of which proved very bewildering: "the Louga is coated with ice this morning, but not so thick, however, that it might not
be broken by throwing a five-kopec piece from
here; but to travel yet would only kill you, Carl
Ivanovitch, and cannot be thought of just now."

Then as she glided away, with her beaming
smile, her white hands and taper arms, her rus-
tling dress of scarlet silk trimmed with snowy
miniver, and all the sense of perfume that pervaded her, Balgonie sighed wearily yet pleasantly,

and half thought that beautiful figure a dream,
as he turned on his soft and luxurious pillow, and
marvelled whether his past or his present existence was the real one.

A captain in the ducal Regiment of Smolensko
and not yet twenty-five! Some ten years ago,
his future seemed to point to a very different
course of life.

Far from Russian steppes and icy streams,
their forests and barbarity, his mind had been
wandering home to Britain's happier shore; and
he might have said with the Bard who sang the
" Course of Time,"—

> " Nor do I of that Isle remember aught,
>   Of prospect more sublime and beautiful,
>   Than Scotia's northern battlement of hills,
>   Which first I from my father's house beheld,
>   At dawn of life; beloved in memory still,
>   And standard yet of rural imagery."

His story is a brief one, and not very startling,
save for its rapid career of injustice.

Charles Balgonie, son of John Balgonie of that
Ilk in Strathearn, had come into the world during that which was perhaps the most stupid,
lifeless, and impoverished era of Scottish existence,
the middle of the reign of George II.; when the
country was without trade, energy, or enterprise,
and when nothing flourished save that which
prospers there more than ever even under the rule
of her present Majesty, and will do so apparently
unto the end of time,—gloomy fanaticism and
canting hypocrisy: more among the laity cer-

tainly, who make a trade and cloak of outward religion, than among the clergy, who dare not be liberal, even if so disposed; for without a public and noisy exhibition of sanctity, few have ever had much chance of place or profit north of the Tweed.

Moreover, Charlie was born at a time when to be a Scotsman or an Irishman was almost a political crime in the eyes of their somewhat illiberal fellow-subjects, and when for either to attain eminence in the service of their native country was nearly an impossibility; and hence the Scots crowded to the armies and fleets of Russia and Holland, and the Irish to those of France and Spain.

By the early death of his parents, Charlie had been cast, in his extreme boyhood, upon the tender mercies of a bachelor uncle, Mr. Gamaliel Balgonie, a hard-hearted, grasping and avaricious merchant in Dundee—one who was a noisy exhibitor of religion, a fervent expounder of crooked texts, and, of course, an Elder of the Kirk; a great quoter of Scripture upon unnecessary occasions; one who always wore garments of sad-coloured broad cloth, with a spotless white cravat, and whose quavering voice and meek but cunning eyes were frequently uplifted against the enormities, the wickedness, and "the temptawtions and tribulawtions of this weary world;" and who was, moreover, a vehement despiser of that which he stigmatized as "its wretched dross,"

but which he left no means, fair or foul, untried
to acquire.

In the lovely vale of Strathearn—one of the
most exquisite tracts of verdant scenery in Scotland—stood the home of Charlie Balgonie. In
his delirium, the present had fled, and the past
returned. He had been a boy again at his father's
knee—a child with his curly head nestling on his
smiling mother's breast; again, in fancy, had her
kisses rested on his cheek, and her soft voice
lingered lovingly in his ear; again had he felt
all that happiness, perfect trust, and security
which the boy feels by his father's hearth, and
the man, in after life, never more!

He heard not the hoarse Louga crashing down
its ice-blocks to the Baltic Sea; but the gentle
murmur of the Earn, flowing from the wooded
hills of Comrie towards the broad blue bosom of
the Tay—the Earn, where many a time and oft
he had lured the brown trout and the speckled
salmon from the deep, dark pools, near the old
battle-cross of Dupplin and the Birks of Inver-
may.   Again he had heard the leaves rustle
pleasantly in the summer woods, where he had
nutted and birdnested when a boy; and he had
seen, in a vivid dream, his glorious native valley
where it narrows at Dunira; and far beyond, the
blue ridges of the mighty Grampians, lifting their
summits, alp on alp, to the clouds, eternal and unchanged as when the foiled legions of Julius Agri-
cola fled along their slopes in rout and disorder.

On the death of his parents his small paternal
estate of a few hundreds per annum would have
become, as all might have supposed, his inheritance; but the relation before mentioned—the
paternal uncle, Gamaliel, a man of the strictest
probity, and of that which was equally valued in
Scotland, extreme sanctimony; one who, on the
funeral day, had shed abundance of tears at the
uncertainty of life, and had excelled even the
minister in prayer and "in warsling wi' the diel"
(*i.e.*, wrestling with Satan)—suddenly produced
a will, by which, to the profound astonishment
of all, the entire estate was left to him as a
return for certain loans and sums advanced to
the deceased, of which, however, no proof could
be found; but it was a veritable death-bed will,
written accurately by a notary, and duly signetted
with the autograph of "John Balgonie of yt Ilk."

Though tremulous and shaky,—strangely so,
—and rather unlike the usual signature of the
deceased laird, three men there were, accounted
good, worthy, and religious men, who solemnly
deposed to having seen "the hand of the dead
man pen those four words."

It was a case which made some noise in those
days, because thirty-six hours after the alleged
signature was given John Balgonie died.

The law of Scotland requires that, after fram-
ing and signing such a deed, the testator must
have been able to go once at least to church or
market. How it came to pass we know not

E

now, but the dispute, though without a basis, was brought before the Supreme Court by some friends of the orphan, for there were not a few persons in Strathearn who alleged that John Balgonie's hand had certainly traced the signature which was sworn to so solemnly as his,—but had done so after death: the pen being placed in the fingers of the corpse, which were guided by those of the pious and worthy merchant of Dundee, who wanted his nephew's little patrimony in aid of certain speculations of his own.

Pending a decision, the bereaved boy was removed to the busy town on Tay side, and was left to solace his sorrows at school, prior, as he supposed, to becoming a drudge in his affectionate uncle's counting-house, when the last of his slender inheritance had been frittered away in the fangs of the law.

One day—poor Charlie never forgot it—his worthy Uncle Gam returned from Edinburgh by the packet. The case had been decided against him, and the Court was about to name trustees to look after the estate of the orphan boy: so that boy learned long after. Mr. Gamaliel Balgonie was unusually grave, stern, and abstracted; but he deliberately seated himself at his desk, and while humming, as was his wont, a verse of a psalm, he penned a letter addressed to the captain of a vessel then lying in the harbour, and gave it to his nephew for immediate delivery, desiring him to wait for the answer.

Charlie remarked that Uncle Gam did not, according to his usual careful custom, keep any copy of this letter, and that it was written in a hand so unlike his usual penmanship as to be completely disguised.

The boy, then in his fifteenth year, started on his errand with alacrity. It was better to be out amid the bustle of the sunlighted quays, than drudging with a quill in the sombre merchant's office in a narrow gloomy alley of Dundee. He soon found the ship, which was moored at some distance from the shore, with her fore-topsails loose, and blue-peter flying at the fore, to indicate that she was ready for sea; yet Charlie had no suspicion of the trap into which he was running, or the cruel fate that awaited him.

The skipper, a rough, surly, and brutal-looking man, eyed the boy keenly, while tearing the letter into minute fragments, after he had perused it, with a grim smile of satisfaction. He then went to a locker, where he poured out a glass of something that seemed to be port-wine.

"Drink that, my lad," said he, "while I write an answer to your uncle."

Charlie, half afraid to refuse, though the skipper's bearing began to inspire him with distrust, drained the glass; but scarcely had he done so when the cabin seemed to be whirling round him; he thought that he was becoming sea-sick, and was in the act of staggering towards the cabin stairs, when he was felled to the floor by a blow from the skipper's heavy hand—a blow dealt cruelly and unsparingly.

He recovered consciousness some time after, to find himself stiff, sore, and bloody from a wound in the temple, lying on deck in the moonlight, with some twenty-five other boys, several of whom were still in the same state of stupor or intoxication in which they had been brought on board. Others were loudly lamenting their parents and brothers or sisters they never more would see, and all were more or less covered with blows and bruises. To his horror and dismay, Charlie now found that the ship was at sea, and running between the dangerous reef known as the Bell Rock and the flat sandy shore of Barrie, and that, through the machinations of Uncle Gamaliel, he had been lured into the hands of one of the most notorious plantation-crimps that ever infested the Scottish coast, Captain Zachariah Coffin of New England, whose craft, a palatine ship, the *Piscatona*, was a letter of marque, carrying twelve six-pounders and fighting her own way.

Many miserable little fellows who had been lured to a certain den in Aberdeen, and there drugged, robbed, and manacled, were brought on board the palatine ship as she lay off Girdleness and burned three red lights, in the night, as a private and concerted signal with the crimps ashore: and some of these same crimps were discovered, in after years, to have actually been the magistrates of the city!

After this, the *Piscatona* was hauled up, in order to go north about by Cape Wrath, having on board nearly fifty boys, who were to be sold as slaves to the highest bidder in Virginia, for nowhere was the infamous crime of kidnapping carried to a greater excess, even during the early years of George the Third's reign, than in the neighbourhood of the Granite City, where, in some instances, whole families disappeared, and their horror-stricken and bewildered parents died broken-hearted and insane.

Among the little Palatines—a name given by Americans to individuals who were thus kidnapped—some there were who pined and wept for home; and some who built castles in the air, and looked to America as a land of promise. Others there were who schemed out vengeance, and were sullen. Among the latter was our hero, who hoped yet to repay his wrongs on Uncle Gam, but meanwhile was knocked about mercilessly by the sullen skipper, and was so repeatedly rope's-ended by him, that he was often a mass of blood and bruises; and then, like a poor little victim, as he certainly was, Charlie would creep away into a corner, or skulk between the lee-carronades, where the salt spray flew over him, and mingled with the tears he wept so unavailingly, for those once tender and affectionate parents who were lying side by side in their graves, in sunny Strathearn, far, far away.

Many times, after being beaten cruelly, he was deprived of food for hours and put in the bilboes, where the captain amused himself by hunting a savage dog upon him.

But his time of vengeance was coming !

Storms came on when the *Piscatona* entered the Pentland Firth ; and four days after Dunnet Head with its flinty brow, four hundred feet in height, had vanished into the wrack and mist astern, a sudden cry of fire caused every heart to thrill on board the lawless vessel.

Whether an act of treachery or not, it was impossible to ascertain ; but it had broken out near the ship's magazine, to which it communicated with frightful rapidity ; for suddenly, while the crew were all running fore and aft with buckets, a dreadful explosion seemed to rend the *Piscatona* in two.   Half of the main-deck was blown away with two of the boats.   A whirlwind of fragments flew in every direction ; and then the flames shot into the air in scorching volumes, which soon set the courses and topgallant sails on fire.

Discipline, or such a system of it as Zachariah Coffin maintained on board, was totally at an end. Some of the crew lowered the only remaining boat, and fought like wild beasts for possession of it, knocking each other into the water without mercy.   Captain Coffin cocked his pistols at the gangway, shot one man dead, and swore with a dreadful oath that he would kill the next who dared to precede him; but he was struck from behind by an iron marline-spike, and falling together with his savage dog into the flaming gulf that yawned amidships, was seen no more.

Some of the crew ultimately pushed off in the boat; others sprang overboard and held on to spars and booms; but these and nearly all the little Palatines perished miserably, after being half scorched. Some were crushed to death by the falling yards and masts. Many held on to the fore and main chains, till these became so unbearably hot, that they had to drop off, with screams of despair, when they sank, faint, weary, and helpless, to the bottom at last.

How it all happened Charlie Balgonie never knew, but hours after the whole affair was over, and the detested *Piscatona* had burned down to her water-line and sunk, leaving all the sea around her discoloured and covered with floating pieces of charred wood and the buoyant parts of her cargo, he found himself adrift in the wide and stormy Pentland Firth; but wedged with comparative safety in a large fragment of the fore-top, to which, the yard being still attached by the sling, a certain amount of steadiness was given; yet his heart leaped painfully, each time, when the fragment of wreck rose on the summit of a green glassy wave, or went surging down into the dark and watery trough between.

To add to the terrors of his lonely situation, the sun had sunk amid gloomy purple clouds, and a rainy night was drawing on. Half drowned perhaps, the poor boy soon became faint and exhausted, and would seem to have dropped into a species of stupor; for when roused by the sound of strange voices, he found himself close by a great and towering ship, which lay to, now right in the wind's eye with her main-yard aback, and her gunports and hammock nettings full of weatherbeaten faces, gazing at him with eagerness and curiosity in the twilight, while a boat was lowered from the davits and pulled steadily towards him by six sailors clad in dark green.

She proved to be a Russian 50-gun ship, the *Anne Ivanowna*, commanded by Thomas Mackenzie, one of the many Scottish admirals who have bravely carried the Russian flag in the Baltic and the Black Sea, the same officer who a few years after was to build the great harbour and forts of Sebastopol, at the little Tartar village then known as Actiare.

His youthful countryman became his *protégé*.

The worthy admiral sought to make a sailor of the rescued Palatine; but the latter had seen quite enough of the sea while on board the *Piscatona*, and while he was clinging like a limpet or barnacle to the piece of drifting wreck; so he became a soldier, and served under General Ochterlony, of Guynd, in the Regiment of Smolensko, where, as a cadet, his superior smartness, intelli-

gence and education, not less than his courage,
soon distinguished him among his thick-pated
Russian comrades : thus, in less than ten years,
he became, as we find him, Captain Carl Ivanovitch Balgonie, the most trusted aide-de-camp
of Lieutenant-General Weymarn, Commander-
in-Chief of the City and District of St. Petersburg.

CHAPTER VII.

THE SOLDIER OF THE CZARINA.

" You can never know, Ivanovitch Balgonie, how much I pitied you—"

" You, lady ? " was the joyous response.

" That is, I and Mariolizza," said Natalie Mierowna, slightly blushing (the Russians always speak thus, putting the personal pronoun first), "when we found you sunk on a fever-bed, in a foreign land, so far from your country, your friends, your mother, perhaps; for you are young enough, I think, to miss her still, at such a time, although a soldier."

" Far indeed, in many ways ! " replied Balgonie, with a bitter smile, as he thought of Uncle Gam and the Palatine ship, or perhaps it was illness that had weakened him. " I have a country to which more than probably I shall never return ; but father, mother, or friends, I have none there : all who loved me once, have gone to the silent grave before me."

" All ? "

" Yes, lady."

" But you are making many friends in Russia," said Mariolizza, cheerfully : " there are my cousin,

Basil Mierowitz and my brother Apollo Usakoff, who both, I know, love you as a brother."

"True; and most grateful am I to them for their regard, for both are polished gentlemen. I have old General Weymarn, too, though I know not what he will think of this delay in delivering the Imperial dispatch."

"Alas, that most tiresome dispatch!" exclaimed Natalie; "but I forget," she added, with a curl of her short upper lip, "those who proceed on the errands of the Empress Catharine, would need seven-league boots, or the carpet of the prince in the fairy tale, which transported the owner at a wish."

"Hush, cousin," said Mariolizza, glancing timidly round: but no one was near save Corporal Podatchkine, who was stolidly smoking a huge pipe at a little distance on the terrace, when this conversation took place two days after Balgonie became convalescent, and fully a week since the night of peril on which he swam the Louga.

"I cannot describe to you, ladies, the relief that came to my mind on discovering that it had neither been lost nor stolen, but was safe—"

"In Natalie's bosom!" said Mariolizza, laughing.

"Certainly the last place, where, for her own sake, I would place a dispatch of the widow of Peter III.," responded the other, haughtily; but Balgonie felt his heart beat quicker as she spoke. Her voice was sweet and low, and had a wonderful chord in it.

The day was mild and beautiful, and truly an April one. The last of the ice had disappeared from the river; not a flake of snow was visible among the woods or on the distant hills; and the bright sun of noon shone clearly and brilliantly from a deep-blue sky flecked by floating masses of white cloud, and cast across the bosom of the Louga the shadows of the great fir trees that spread like a sea of solemn cones for miles along its banks; and amid that woody sea, the most striking feature was a white-walled monastery with its "golden-headed church" and all its metal cupolas glittering in the sunshine.

As they promenaded on the gravelled terrace that lay before the Count's residence, Balgonie could see the domains of Mierowitz that lay for miles around : the patrimonial village of the Count, nestling among the coppice, containing a dozen or so of stone houses, and double that number of quaint tumble-down edifices of wood, and a church with a little gilt cupola, where his serfs said their prayers, and thanked God and him for permission to live and breathe, and to hoard their roubles in secret—for wealth in a serf was a sure source of misery, extortion, and perhaps of torture, if discovered.

In the immediate foreground were wharves, where the wood for masts and spars from his forests were launched, and formed into great rafts for conveyance to the Gulf of Finland. The din of axes and the crash of falling timber, with the cheerful voices of the woodmen and labourers, were heard rising from the echoing woods, as they lopped and trimmed the giant pines for conveyance to the Baltic coast; for his forest trees were one of the chief sources of revenue to Count Mierowitz.

"Your father's mansion is indeed a noble one!" said Balgonie, who after surveying the landscape from the terrace, ran his eyes over the façade of the castle, as it was named, though by no means so well fortified as his patrimonial tower in Strathearn, which dated from the days of the Sixth James.

"So noble that the first Count of our name who built it, when Ivan Basilovitch—Ivan the Terrible—was Czar, put out the eyes of the architect, who was, of course, one of his serfs," said Natalie.

"For what reason?" asked Balgonie, starting.

"Lest he should repeat the work for another," replied Natalie; "but then the Count was a fierce soldier, who had served under Yermack in the conquest of Siberia. I fear you think us very barbarous, Captain Balgonie; but I can assure you, that even in the remote forests of Yakoutsk, on the banks of the Lena, there is more regard for human life and divine laws now, than existed when my father was a boy. He has, indeed, seen terrible things!"

Balgonie did not see much of the Count, who was generally occupied among his people, to whom he was alternately a source of reverence and of terror.

Though infinitely more civilised than the old Russian noble as described by Clarke, " unwashed, unshaven, eating raw turnip and drinking quass" (for according to the Doctor, in 1799, "raw turnips were handed about in slices in the first houses, on a silver salver, with brandy as a whet before dinner"), he was a fair average specimen of a fine old Muscovite gentleman "all of the olden time," who had a cat-o'-nine-tails always at hand ; who generally unbuttoned his vest when the gold cup was brought, in which he drank his pink champagne or rare Hungarian wine, which he always had in equal plenty with his fiery vodka and bitter quass; who reckoned his silver roubles by sacksful, and his Sclavonian souls by thousands ; and who, though by no means a bad fellow, as his imperious and outrageous class go in Russia, had still the somewhat czarish notion, that true nobility "means the privilege of being treated like a human being of intelligence and feeling, and of treating others as if they were nothing of the kind."

Scandal said that in his wild youth he had flogged his serfs to fight with his favourite bear, and flogged them again if they maltreated or bit Bruin too much : Balgonie certainly saw two or

three old serfs who had lost an ear in these com-
bats. And when the Count took his afternoon
nap, if a cock crowed in the village, a dog barked,
or a cat mewed, the whole community were
wont to tremble, when the stout dvornick, or
house-porter, was seen to issue forth with his
cat-o'-nine-tails in search of the proprietor.

A rich sash usually girt the waist of his old-
fashioned tunic, which was of fine cloth, and
trimmed with fur, broad or narrow according to
the season; a square cap of crimson velvet,
tasselled with gold and edged with ermine as
white as his beard, was placed diagonally on his
head, when he went abroad; and then he carried
a long gold-headed cane, with the exact weight
of which most of the shoulders in the neighbourhood were perfectly familiar. On holy festivals
the breast of his best velvet coat was always
covered by orders of the empire; a dozen of
servants usually hovered about him when he
dined; and he always went to church and confession in a clumsy old coach drawn by six
white horses, three abreast, in honour of the Holy
Trinity.

He was proud of being one of the old hereditary
nobles, who are distinguished from the personal
nobility by their right to possess serfs, and to
whose earthly tyranny there was no limit, save the
tomb. All the wretched serf possessed, even his
wife, was the property of his lord. Fear of secret
murder alone protected the latter species of pro-

perty; hence no wonder is it that the land is without a middle class. Even in the present century, Heber, in his Journal, mentions an instance of a Russian noble who, in his profane cruelty and lust of power, nailed a servant on a cross, for which he was only imprisoned in a monastery.

But in the character of Count Mierowitz, there was something of the rough and hardy country gentleman. He it was who caught with his own hands, and in his own forests by the Louga, the famous team of brown bears which, in the marriage procession of the late Empress Elizabeths' jester, drew that jocular personage and his bride, when the newly-wedded couple proceeded to the wonderful palace of ice (which was built on the frozen Neva), all the ornaments of which were icicles, and the appurtenances of which were also ice, even to the cannon which were fired, and did not burst.

" When Peter the Great came to the throne," said he, one day, " he found only two lawyers in all Russia ; so, Captain Balgonie, he hung one as an example to the other. Ah, he was a truly great man, Peter! The English admire him solely because he tried to imitate them ; but, for that very reason, we don't approve of many of his innovations. We look from the north and south sides of the same hedge."

It is not surprising that Charlie Balgonie preferred the society of two beautiful young girls to that of a testy old boyar. To enhance their natural attractions and winning manners, they were always dressed in the most fashionable French *mode*, and wore the rich stuffs which came from Moscow, and even from China.

They and he had many topics in common, on which they could converse, after old Count Mierowitz had dined and dozed off to sleep—such as the theatre erected some years before at Yaroslaff, by Volkoff, whose troupe were now performing the tragedies of Soumorokoff at St. Petersburg, where a government theatre had just been erected by a ukase; while another ennobled the manager, Volkoff, who had died last year, after appearing at Moscow in Zelmira. Their knowledge of French and German opened up the best literature of Europe to the two cousins, which was fortunate; for at the period of our narrative, Russia had almost none, save some barbarous national songs, fabulous ecclesiastical records, and ferocious traditions : nor is she now much advanced in letters, though certainly, two months after publication, Charles Dickens may be read at Tobolsk—that terrible Tobolsk—where, as we have all read in our youth, Elizabeth wept such grateful tears on the bosom of her Smoloff.

Exiled from court, and secluded amid these forests by the Louga, a Russian lady had few resources for amusement then ; so the unexpected visit of Captain Balgonie, with whose name and courage they were quite familiar, proved a most

F

welcome and fortunate circumstance to those two handsome girls, who were merely enduring life, or simply vegetating, in the great old mansion of Count Mierowitz.

But there was one topic in which our soldier of fortune could by no means agree with Natalie Mierowna—her bitter and most unwise hostility to the strongly-established power of the Empress, or, as she styled her, "the woman who now occupied the throne of Ivan;" a prince whom she viewed exactly as the Scottish Jacobites did "the Young Chevalier," and a few old Frenchmen do at the present hour, "Henry V.," the descendant of St. Louis.   These sentiments, however, she had to utter in secret, or when none were by them; and when he gazed into her dark and beautiful eyes, so full of romantic enthusiasm and of dangerous light, he felt thankful that one so peerless and so perilous was not, at all events, his enemy.

She had accompanied the Empress on her celebrated pilgrimage to the ancient cathedral of Rostov, by the Lake of Nero, where the last of the Princes of Jaroslav was murdered in cold blood by Ivan the Terrible.   Her expedition had taken place in the May of the preceding year. Catharine and her ladies walked ten versts afoot daily, and it was at the conclusion of this devotional journey that the final quarrel had taken place concerning the mazurka with the Aide-de-camp Vlasfief.

"That insult shall never be forgotten here!" said she, stamping a little foot, in a prettily-embroidered scarlet shoe, on the carpet of the drawing-room where, fortunately for herself, she was alone with Balgonie: "an insult to me—to us, who have the blood of Ruric the Varangian in our veins; and from her—this woman of Anhalt-Zerbst!"

Balgonie laughed; for the Ruric blood is to Russians what Captain John Smith's is to the Virginians, and the Norman element to the English.

"Yes," she continued, "'tis something novel, an insult to us, from this Catharine, misnamed the Great, who has enslaved all the Ukraine, and given men and women away by thousands, like herds of cattle, to her courtiers and her lovers!"

"Oh, be wary; I pray you, be wary, or speak in French!" said Balgonie imploringly, while laying his hand impressively—rather too impressively, we fear—upon hers, which was so delicately smooth and white, and was placed very temptingly within his reach, as they sat near each other for the purpose of conversing in low and confidential tones.

"The people are mere slaves under her rule," continued Natalie, lowering her voice but without withdrawing that coveted hand; perhaps she forgot it in her energy; but the omission made poor Charlie Balgonie's honest heart beat very fast indeed, and his colour came and went painfully while her dark and glorious eyes were bent on his: " in her I behold only a usurper, who wields a knout in lieu of a sceptre, and who seats herself on a throne of human skulls; but the time is coming when all these things shall be altered!"

"And this time, Natalie Mierowna—what do you mean?" asked Balgonie, who had been long enough in Russia to feel a thrill of terror at words so wild and dangerous.

"When it comes you will learn; if the blow fails, woe unto those on whom it recoils! You may escape as a stranger; but I fear me, she will punish the whole Regiment of Smolensko—"

"My regiment—mine, say you?"

"Yes, yours, Hospodeen, even as Peter the Great did the Battalion of Strelitz, for adherence to his sister Sophia; and that we know to be one of the most sanguinary sacrifices on record, even in Russia."

"Heaven knows that is admitting a great deal; but you say either too much or too little to satisfy my curiosity: explain this coming peril—this mystery—to which you refer."

In her growing energy, Natalie's other hand was now clasped above his, and truly " the situation had its charm."

"Let us speak of it no more," said she, recollecting herself, and with a strange smile; " ere long you shall know all; but not now—not now. Alas! the best I can wish you, Ivanovitch

Balgonie, is, that your chance visit here may not also compromise you with Catharine."

They pressed each other's hands: it was done, perhaps, merely in the energy of conversation; but, to be brief, Balgonie found himself now hopelessly and helplessly in love with Natalie Mierowna.

Though both cousins were remarkable for their beauty—one blonde, the other dark—he had never for a moment wavered between them; for he had been, from the first moment he beheld her, irresistibly attracted by the brilliant and black-eyed Natalie. Besides, he knew well that Mariolizza was betrothed, or, as the Russians might justly phrase it, assigned away, to his friend and brother-officer, Basil Mierowitz.

CHAPTER VIII.

IN LOVE.

It was scarcely possible that the result of his visit could be otherwise than it had proved; for Natalie was no common-place beauty, but one who had subdued the hearts of many more men than Charlie Balgonie—men, who now at Moscow and St. Petersburg were counting the days of her exile from the Court of Catharine: and when Charlie thought of her in after years, the calm repose of his days of convalescence, the aspect and furniture of his chamber in the old Castle of Louga, the genial glow of the peitchka, the double window sashes with their bright false flowers between, the Byzantine picture of the Holy Virgin with its shining metal halo, and the varnished panels of the walls, were all associated, as in a pleasant dream, with the dark and beautiful eyes, the round taper arms, the white and delicate hands on which so many diamonds glittered, the jetty hair that was twisted in massive braids (yet fell in ringlets too) round the superb head, — the graceful, floating, and statuesque figure of Natalie Mierowna, always so richly, even coquettishly attired. Natalie, so soft, so tender, and so true, in all the relations of life and the amenities of society; and yet who could be so keen in her hate, so fiery in her political rancour, when thinking of her own injuries, and the terrible wrongs of the captive Ivan, whose adherent she had become.

Charlie Balgonie blessed the exile and choice of circumstances, all so sudden and unforeseen, which had cast him in her path. He loved her with all the passionate adoration so beautiful and winning a woman could inspire in a young and ardent heart; nor was it long before Natalie became aware of this, and was affected by the same emotion. There was one glance given, by which "each read and understood each other's soul." Lovers soon find means to comprehend each other, and Mariolizza, who speedily guessed their secret, which she certainly thought a dangerous one, found many excuses to leave them often together.

The long, long dream of his youth and early manhood,—the waking dream of many a lonely hour of reverie in the summer woods, by the seashore, or in the still hours of military duty, in camp and bivouac—a fair face that would smile on him,—a girl to love, and worship, and trust,—one who would trust and love him in return, was embodied at last; and in Natalie he saw this hitherto imaginary sphinx of whom he had been thinking, and for whom he had been waiting so long.

Her voice, her smile, her presence, seemed to fill the air he breathed with a new charm, that made every nerve thrill, investing the most simple and common wants of every-day life with sudden delights and joys; in short, and in common phraseology, the poor young man was "over head and ears in love."

The declaration of his passion, and Natalie's acceptance of it, came about just as others have done; and for three days after,—without looking the future confidently or inquiringly in the face, —Balgonie abandoned himself to the delight of his new and successful passion, and forgot all about the troublesome Empress, her pressing dispatch, and the terrors of Lieutenant-General Weymarn.

How could he think of such, when seated in the half-curtained alcove which opened off the drawing-room, on those calm April evenings; when the soft breeze that floated over the vast forests came laden with the odour of the spruce and fir boughs? Seated, with Natalie—in all the glory of her youth, her beauty, and the flush of her first love—by his side, often deftly and with rapid fingers weaving up the coils of her heavy black hair (which would come down, somehow, on these occasions); as she did so, displaying to greater advantage than ever the magnificent contour of her bust, her white shoulders, and taper arms, and adding even to the coquettish side glance of the half-veiled eye, the most splendid of all her natural ornaments were those great, heavy loose braids on which the sunlight shone.

What was to be the future of all this?

On the strong friendship of Basil Mierowitz he could fully rely; but then Natalie was on bad terms with the vindictive Empress, and he, Balgonie, was a soldier, and, according to the rules of the Russian service, could not marry without permission from his colonel, who, at present, would not dare to accord it, circumstanced as the bride would be.

Marry? What would the proud old Russian boyar say, or do, or think, when he heard that the penniless Scot—the mere adventurer—the soldier of fortune, was the accepted lover of his daughter, and that he had dared to lift his eyes to her otherwise than in the way of solemn and awful respect?

If his High Excellency could have but peeped into the aforesaid alcove on some of the occasions referred to! The mere fact of being a Scot would not have conveyed much to the mind of the Count. If to any unlettered Englishman of the present day, the names of Moldavia, Croatia, Bulgaria, Servia, Pomerania, Grodno, Mingrelia, and so forth, give but a vague idea of their whereabouts or history, it was perhaps worse in the Count's instance; for so far as he, worthy man, was concerned, or for all he knew to the contrary, the Land of Cakes might have been in the flying island of Laputa.

"He would be furious, no doubt," thought Balgonie; "but he might soothe his troubled mind by flogging a few serfs, shooting a few brown bears, and draining sundry horns of quass."

Charlie had been present at more than one Russian marriage and betrothal, and the coolness of the ceremony had excited his astonishment and repugnance; for, in that country, those life-enduring arrangements are concluded by a mere match-maker, who makes the proposal, not to the girl, but to her father. He remembered particularly the case of Lieutenant Tschekin's espousal with the daughter of General Weymarn, who, having stated her dower to the go-between, —a thousand peasants or so,—the gallant subaltern was satisfied, and thus, as usual, the whole affair was settled without the taste or inclination of the young lady being consulted or considered. In Russia, the papa consents, and, according to some old custom, mamma pretends to object and weep.

"My daughter," said the General, "I have given you away in presence of my aide-de-camp."

"To one I know, father?" she asked.

"No."

"To whom, then?" she continued, perfectly undisturbed.

"One you shall soon know—here he comes; and this is thy bridegroom, daughter : art satisfied?"

The young lady, of course, declared she was satisfied. She and the Lieutenant placed their hands behind them, stretched out their necks, pouting their lips for a very frigid kiss, and the matter was soon concluded by a priest.

When Balgonie thought of the delicacy and gentleness of Natalie, and remembered the marriage of the Lieutenant Tschekin, he shrunk alike from the idea of seeing her subjected to the mummery of a Greek espousal and the vulgar horrors of a wedding feast and drinking bout à la Russe.

At last he began to wake from his dream, to find the stern necessity of departing; and, indeed, the snub-nosed Podatchkine, who was always hovering about, seemed as a perpetual reminder of the duty he was neglecting. The lovers were solemnly betrothed in secret,—Mariolizza was their only confidant,—and at present they could but arrange to wait until they could mutually confide in Basil Mierowitz, whom Natalie, ere long, expected to see. To write to each other, save by special messenger, was deemed at present unwise; but Balgonie would visit her as he returned again to Novgorod.

So the last evening they were to spend together came; and they were seated, wreathed in each other's arms, with Natalie's cheek resting on Balgonie's shoulder, in an embowered rustic seat, not far from the very place where he had so boldly crossed the swollen river on that eventful night.

Charlie's heart was full of sadness and bewilderment; he could but mutter and whisper of his love and their hopes, and again and again kiss Natalie on the cheek, on the lips and snowy neck, her hands and arms, while her tears flowed fast; for she had all the cooing tenderness of a ringdove now, and could only murmur from time to time :—

"Oh, Carl, Carl—my own Carl!" and so forth; and, like other young ladies similarly circumstanced on the eve of separation, believed herself to be the most miserable being in the world. But amid all this, she suddenly started and grew pale, on seeing a figure approach.

"See, Carl, see!" she exclaimed: "that horrible woman must be ominous of evil at such a time. Why has she been permitted to approach?"

Balgonie saw, at a little distance, only a Russian gipsy girl, possessed evidently of considerable personal attractions. She stood timidly, and irresolute whether to advance or retire; and bowed her head with great humility, while crossing her fine but dusky hands and arms upon her breast. In old age the Russian female gipsies are as remarkable for their extreme hideousness, as in youth they are famous for personal beauty; so this young girl was full of picturesque loveliness, and instead of being clothed in rags, as the wanderers of her race are elsewhere, her costume was brilliant in colours and rich in material. She had large glittering ear-rings; a gaudy kerchief bound her black tresses; and her rounded cheeks being freely rouged, added to the wonderful lustre of her dark and dusky eyes, and to the generally theatrical character of her singular beauty and bearing.

"Oh!" resumed Natalie, with something of a shudder, "'tis Olga Paulowna: don't let her speak to us in our parting hour, Carl, lest we be compelled to hear her sing, and that may perhaps bode evil. The dvornick, I understand, has thrice by dog and whip driven away this gipsy girl, who has come to the house again and again, ostensibly to seek alms, but doubtless only to steal or work mischief by her cunning; for though our Russian gipsies are not allowed to pitch their tents on any land without the express consent of the owner, this girl's brother, Nicholas Paulovitch (as he calls himself), a half-blood, has permanently settled on our estate, somewhere in the forests, though he is despised and loathed by the peasantry, whom, doubtless, he loathes and hates most cordially in turn. I do wish she would go away without being ordered to do so."

Little did Natalie know that those ill-requited visits of the poor gipsy girl had direct reference to the life and safety of him whose hand clasped hers so tenderly and confidingly.

"Faugh!" said Natalie, with increasing annoyance; "she is about to sing,—something naughty no doubt,—but her voice will soon summon the dvornick."

Many of those female wanderers in Russia can

sing divinely; and it is on record that even the great Catalani was so enchanted by the melodious voice of a gipsy girl at Moscow, that she took from her own shoulders a superb shawl, which had been given to her by the Empress, and placed it on those of the nomadic singer, "as a tribute from art to nature."

And Olga now began to sing with great sweetness one of those Russian songs, by which the gipsies, to flatter the people, sought to foretell the downfall of the Crescent; and many such prophetic strains were current even during the war in the Crimea, as foreshadowing the fate of the "sick man" at Constantinople.

> "Years after years shall roll,
>   Ages o'er ages glide,
> Before the world's control
>   Shall check the Crescent's pride.
> Banished from place to place,
>   Where'er the ocean's roar,
> The mighty gipsy race,
>   Shall visit every shore.
>
> "But when the hundredth year
>   Shall three times doubled be,
> Then shall the end appear
>   Of all their slavery.
> Then shall the warlike powers
>   From distant climes return,
> Egypt again be ours,
>   While the Turkish domes shall burn!
>
> "Again the Christian's cross
>   Shall over Stamboul wave,
> And ruin, weeds, and moss,
>   Mark the last Sooltan's grave!
> Again shall Christian bells
>   Ring where the Muezzins cry,
> When across the Dardanelles
>   The Moslem hordes shall fly!

"So Egypt shall be freed,
  Her tribes return once more,
Their flocks and herds to feed
  Where their fathers dwelt of yore:
When all our warlike powers
  From distant climes return,
Then Egypt shall be ours,
  While the Turkish turrets burn!"

The last line ended in a shriek, with which a cry from Natalie mingled; for the cruel dvornick had been stealing through the thicket unperceived, and now bestowed a heavy lash across the tender shoulders of the cowering and shrinking girl; but ere he could repeat it, Balgonie sprang forward, arrested the descending whip, and then placing in the hand of the singer a few Livonian groschen, bade her hasten away, on which she departed, with tears of pain and gratitude, after pressing his fingers to her lips; and, in her terror and confusion, leaving her task undone—her warning of coming treachery untold.

"Oh, Carl!" said Natalie, laying her head again on Balgonie's breast, "dearest Carl, I am so glad she has gone without anathematizing us—or, or weaving some mischievous spell; for, smile as you may, I can't help fearing those people! I am a true Russian, and dread the evil eye!"

Richer by a lock of dark and silky hair and a diamond ring (both the objects of many a secret kiss), but leaving his heart behind him, in one swift hour after this little episode, Balgonie had departed to meet, and, for greater security, to travel in consort with, a caravan of a hundred and fifty boors, who were conveying sugar from Moscow to St. Petersburg.

He was guided again by the sly Podatchkine, who had resolved to take especial good care that the said caravan should be avoided.

"God be with you, Hospodeen—God be with you—adieu," said the old Count, lifting his square velvet cap courteously, as he bade farewell to his guest at the porte-cochère.

Balgonie so respectfully kissed the hands of Natalie and Mariolizza, that none could have detected a difference in his manner to either; and certainly none could have suspected that the tears of the former were yet wet upon his cheek—her kisses lingering on his lip, that he seemed to leave his soul upon her hand, and that the wrung hearts of both were swollen with concealed emotion.

"Uich!" thought Corporal Michail Podatch-kine as he rode after the officer into the deep forest, "I'd as soon think of kissing the foot as the hand; who knows among what carrion either may have been stuck? By St. Nicholas, I would rather eat a sheep's tail or a rump steak from an old troop mare than kiss either."

Some hours after Balgonie's departure, and when Natalie in the solitude of her own room was abandoned to tears and unavailing regrets, a trusted messenger from her brother arrived with a brief note, written so enigmatically that none save herself could have understood or deciphered it; but the spirit of it was briefly this :—

"All is arranged for freeing the prisoner of S. (chlusselburg) by a stratagem. A dispatch that may counteract, if not baffle our plans, and fatally compromise us all, has been sent by old Weymarn to St. Petersburg. I know not who the bearer is; but be assured of this, *he will never reach it alive.* We have set Podatchkine on his track, and he, worthy Livonian, for two hundred roubles, would skin his own father alive."

After reading this pleasant epistle, little wonder is it that Natalie was found by Mariolizza, as the twilight deepened, half senseless upon her bed, cold, in tears, and utterly miserable.

CHAPTER IX.

DELUDED.

A LOVER has occasionally been likened to a fool, as being a man possessed by one idea, his mistress. This was certainly somewhat of poor Charlie Balgonie's state of mind. He saw only the dark eyes, the half drooped lids, and the farewell glance of Natalie; so full of hidden and tender meaning; and while thinking of her and of her last words and promises, their mutual hopes of the future, based almost entirely on Basil, he fell an easy prey to the plans and schemes of the wily Corporal Podatchkine, who saw only his antici-pated two hundred silver roubles; and who, knowing the country as well as if it had been every acre, rood, and verst his own property, led him on and on he knew not where; but, at all events, two hours after they should have met the caravan, they found themselves, to all appearance, lost in a dense forest of dark pine trees.

Failing the caravan, having now proceeded, as he believed, some twenty miles or so, Balgonie had thoughts of passing the night at the house of a friend of Count Mierowitz, a *duornin*, of whom he had been told by Mariolizza, who

laughingly assured him, that this personage was
"a fine Russian gentleman of the old school, who
beat his wife regularly every Thursday and
Saturday with a whip of thongs," and was
seldom sober.

Those duornins were country gentlemen, who
held their lands by knights' service, and were
bound to attend the Czar on horseback in time
of war. Formerly it was sufficient to send a man
well armed and mounted; but Peter the Great
first compelled them or their sons to serve in
person, if they could not pay for a substitute.

In short, though he knew it not, Balgonie had
been for the last two hours riding merely in a
wide circle, and, by the careful guidance of
Podatchkine, was now not many miles from the
hut of the gipsy woodman, Nicholas Paulovitch;
and, consequently, he was much nearer the Castle
of Louga than he had the least idea of.

On this night there was a glorious Aurora in
the north, and full of his love, his own tender
thoughts, and inspired by the beauty of the scene,
it seemed to the somewhat provoked Podatchkine,
that the dreaming Captain was quite disposed to
pass the night where he was.

When the dense wood of stupendous pines
opened into long vistas, the whole northern
quarter of the sky could be seen, illuminated from
the horizon to the zenith. Gloriously bright as
the most brilliant phosphorus, masses of fire arose
in the form of columns that waved, towered, and

shot into the air, with streaks of fainter light between. Anon they all blended and merged into each other with renewed grandeur, aslant, or radiating from a centre, like the sticks of a mighty fan. All that portion of the heavens seemed a mass of shining gold, rubies, and sapphires, with a wondrous light streaming over them, broadening, brightening, and deepening, then fading away, to flash forth again in greater beauty and glory, while, as if to enhance the magnificence of this illumination, many falling stars shot across it, leaving in their train sparkles of light, more brilliant even than the glory that blazed beyond. In black outline between, and in the immediate foreground, towered the dark and solemn pines, in solitude and silence.

Not a sound was heard but the occasional snort of their horses, or the cry of a distant wolf.

Balgonie was surmising whether Natalie would be surveying the beautiful natural illumination from her window, or from the terrace: he forgot that it was nothing new to her. Certainly it proved of little interest to Michail Podatchkine, who, under his thick beard, growled at the officer for loitering.

The Scottish islesmen call the streamers of the Aurora "the merry dancers;" but the Siberians name them "the raging host:" and Balgonie was reflecting what a relief their brilliance must prove to the lonely hunters, who at that very time were pursuing the white bear and the blue fox, far

beyond the Lena, and along the shores of the Icy
Sea, when his attendant disturbed his reverie.

"Well, Michail," said he, in reply to some
remark in which the Corporal, who saw nothing
wonderful in the matter, urged that they should
proceed, "we have missed the sugar caravan, and
cannot discover the residence of the duornin I
spoke of, so I am rather provoked with you."

"Oh, Excellency, who can withstand God
or the Great Novgorod?" whined the fellow,
using an old Russian proverb.

Jean Paul Richter says, "the more weakness,
the more lying; force goes straight, but any
cannon-ball with cavities in it goes crooked."
Some such thought as this occurred to Balgonie,
as he checked his horse, and half turning round,
with a stern expression in his face, which the
light in the north made sufficiently plain, he
said :—

"Rascal! I fear you are deceiving me again!"

Hustled up on his saddle, rather than in it,
with his knees on his holsters and his lance slung
behind him, Podatchkine made many signs of
the cross, and called on St. Sergius and all the
other *moshtschi*, or saints of Russia, to bear
witness that he was as innocent as a young bear
of any such foul idea; but only begged that his
Excellency would proceed, and assured him that
the track they were on must assuredly bring
them, ere long, to some woodman's dwelling.

At this time, such is the slavish influence of

superstition, that Podatchkine, for mere fellowship,
kept close to the very man against whom he had
formed the most fiendish schemes; for stories of
the Wood Fairies,—of the *Leechie*, or Forest-
demon, whose fangs tore the benighted asunder,—
of the *Domovoi*, or mischievous Russian Brownie,
—of the *Vodianoi*, or smiling River-spirit, who
lured travellers to a watery doom,—of wolves and
bears in ravening herds, came fast upon his
memory; for the forest was growing denser,
and the darkness deepened painfully after the
Aurora faded away, and a few solitary stars alone
glinted through the openings between the broad,
flat, pendant branches of the intertwisted pines.

The silence of the night was now broken only
by the whistling croak of the *valdchnep*, or great
woodcock, as he darted from amid the black
gloom of a pine tree, or the lighter shadow of the
graceful, but, as yet, leafless birch; and the
craven and clamorous anxiety that had been
giving real pangs, and even qualms of conscience,
to the superstitious Podatchkine began to sub-
side, when the wood opened a little, a red light
appeared, and they approached the cottage of
Nicholas Paulovitch, the half-bred.

It was, as already stated, built of logs, squared
by the hatchet outside and inside, and whitened
by chalk: before it yawned a deep draw-well,
with a bucket, handle, and winch.

" 'Tis the cottage of a man I know. Here,
Excellency, we can pass the night," said Podatch-

kine, leaping from his horse and dutifully taking
Balgonie's bridle, as if to anticipate any proposi-
tion of proceeding further. "There is a shed
behind where I shall stable our horses : Nicholas,
I know, will make us welcome to his lodge."

In a few minutes more, Balgonie found himself
seated in the cottage, the aspect of which struck
him as being peculiarly comfortless, dingy, and
squalid, as he viewed it by the light of a *loutchin*,
or species of pine torch, which stood in a rusty
iron holder on the rough deal table, whereon lay
a pack of frayed and dog-eared cards.

On the walls were some rude images, stuck
over with crumbs of black bread, which attracted
the flies in summer and the dirt at all times. In
a place of honour was a holy effigy, with some
train oil flaring before it in a tin sconce, as a
species of votive lamp; for the proprietor affected
religion quite as much as Mr. Gamaliel Balgonie
did in a more civilised part of the world.

The furniture consisted of a few plain stools,
and some very dirty bearskins spread on the floor
in the corners, as beds; and on the table was a
pitcher of foaming and seething quass, with
wooden bowls to drink it by.

Balgonie took in all these details at a glance.

How great would have been his surprise, if he
had known that after riding so many miles, he
was only a short distance from *her*, from Natalie,
who was now weeping bitterly and sleeplessly on
the bosom of her cousin for him, and for the fate

she dreaded, and yet had not the power to avert, or from which to save him.

In addition to Podatchkine and the host, Nicholas Paulovitch, who stood respectfully at a little distance from Balgonie, and was appraising the exact value of his costume, arms, and ornaments, even to Natalie's diamond ring, there was present another ill-visaged fellow, with a powerful figure, square shoulders, and giant beard, like every Russian of the lower order; eyes that were small and piercing, like those of a mouse; a long, fierce nose and jagged teeth, hair shorn off close above the eyebrows and brushed all down straight from the crown of his head, which in form resembled a cone or a pine-apple.

This barbarian, who was dressed chiefly in a shoubah of sheepskin, and had a small, but sharp, hatchet and dagger in his girdle, was a Stepniak, from a district where nothing like a town was ever seen or known, but whose aid and strength Paulovitch thought might be useful and necessary in the work he and Podatchkine had cut out for themselves in the night.

CHAPTER X.

BALGONIE was rather weary after his long and desultory ride by rough and unfrequented roads, chiefly devious forest paths; he felt thirsty, and looked at the pitcher of quass.

"Will his Excellency drink?" asked Nicholas Paulovitch, in his hoarse and husky voice.

Now as quass is simply a species of sour beer, made of rye and oatmeal, coloured by a red berry, and is generally the beverage by which the Russians wash down their coarse bread and salt, Balgonie declined: the Stepniak proposed to add thereto a dash of train oil; but the suggestion made the young officer shudder.

"I have fortunately one bottle of Rhine wine," said the woodman, with a rapid and furtive glance at his comrades; "his Excellency will doubtless honour us by taking it with his supper, at least with such fare as the forest produces, a stewed rabbit or so."

"I thank you, good fellow. Where is this cottage situated?"

"Situated," repeated Nicholas, with a quick

and uneasy glance at the Corporal, fearing there might be some discrepancy in their information.

"Yes, in what part of the country?" said Podatchkine ; "for we naturally wish to know."

"Near Velie."

"Then I am somewhere about forty versts from the Louga?"

"Yes, Excellency, precisely," replied the rascal.

"Hence, if my horse is fresh, I may reach Schlusselburg to-morrow?"

"Scarcely, as it lies fully a hundred versts beyond Velie," said Nicholas.

"Is the distance so great?" exclaimed Balgonie, little knowing that it was even more, and all unsuspicious of how these wretches were deluding him.*

"But, Excellency, we may prove more able guides than Michail Podatchkine," said the gipsy woodman; "for we—that is the Stepniak and I —must proceed to St. Petersburg to-morrow, on a little piece of business we shall have to perform together."

"Poor devils!" thought Podatchkine, "if you take his body to St. Petersburg, you will both be accused of murder and knouted, as sure as my name is Michail; so I shall save my fifty silver roubles."

---

* The cottage of those assassins is said to have been situated ten versts, or about eight miles distant from Louga on the road to Velie. *Vide* dispatch from General Weymarn to the Empress, dated 8th August, "concerning Carl Ivanovitch Balgonie, a Scottish Captain in the Regiment of Smolensko."—*Utrecht Gazette.*

Even at the present day in Russia, few will venture to receive or meddle with a dead body, or attempt to succour a dying or a drowning person, in dread of the dangerous accusations and extortions of the police.

A sound, as of footsteps, and of something like a drinking vessel falling on the floor of an upper apartment, made the woodman start up with an oath of astonishment and alarm. He hurriedly applied a ladder to the trap which gave admission to this place, and ascended into it; but returned almost immediately to say, " there was no one there." The evident surprise and alarm of the three men at this trivial occurrence, is said to have been the first cause of exciting Balgonie's suspicion.

He glanced at the Stepniak, who sat silently observant in a corner, drinking his quass, with his feet resting against the rude peitchka, or stone stove, which was built into the log wall of the cottage, and when surveying his vast bulk and colossal stature, together with his singularly ferocious aspect, the reflection occurred to him, that he should have placed his pistols in his girdle instead of leaving them in the holsters of the saddle.

He was the reverse of timid; he was "brave even to rashness, and had faced death many times" (to quote General Weymarn) since his career of wandering began; but the idea certainly did flash upon his mind, that his situation in that lonely forest had its perils, and that two men more repulsive in aspect and in bearing than the gipsy and Stepniak, he had never seen, even in Russia.

Was it some mysterious and intuitive sense of danger drawing near that made such thoughts pass through the steady mind of Balgonie?

He and Podatchkine were both armed, and even were these men outlaws, they would scarcely, he believed, dare to assault an officer on military duty; besides, the very name of Schlusselburg, whither he was proceeding, carried a wholesome terror with it; so dismissing his casual suspicions, Charlie unbuckled his sword, and seated himself at the table, on which a cold supper of stewed rabbits and coarse rye bread was laid for the four who were present.

A platter was placed for a fifth person whom Nicholas remarked to Podatchkine in a growling tone was still abroad in the forest, or had not returned from some place which was named in a whisper.

With an affectation of extreme respect and courtesy, none of the three worthies would seat themselves at the table, until Balgonie specially invited and urged them in succession to do so.

The bottle of Rhine wine was produced from the apartment above and opened. The length of the cork and the dust on the bottle (wherever it came from originally) argued well of the contents, and two horns, one of which had a hand-

some silver rim, were placed for the Captain and
the Corporal.

The former was rather surprised to find such a
drinking vessel as this silver mounted cup in a
place so squalid, and he was about to lift and
examine it, when Nicholas Paulovitch, with
almost nervous haste, filled it, and also that of
the Corporal, to the brim.

To the surprise of Balgonie, the latter exhibited
some undisguised alarm on seeing wine placed
before *him;* it was an attention under all the
circumstances he neither wished nor expected;
and so he declined to drink of it, saying that he
was "a true Russ, and would adhere to the
quass."

"Nay, fear not, friend Michail," said the woodman, "'tis the best of Rhine wine. The cup with
the silver mounting is of course for his Excellency
the Hospodeen," he added with a quiet but grim
significance, which the wily Cossack quite understood, so he drained the wine horn without further
objection.

Soon after having supped, and imbibed his full
share of the wine bottle, Balgonie expressed a
desire for repose, as he wished to depart by day-
break; but he had other reasons for retiring so
early. He did not much relish the society of the
gipsy, the Stepniak, and the Corporal of Cossacks;
and he wished to indulge in reverie, to commune
with himself, and let the current of his thoughts
run undisturbed on Natalie and their adieux.

" This way, Excellency," said Nicholas, with alacrity, lifting the pine torch in its iron loutchin, and ushering him up the stair, a mere common ladder, and through the trap-door into the little apartment above, where his couch, composed merely of skins of the bear and sheep awaited him, and where he could see the dark forest and the occasional stars through a small window that gave light and air to the place, which was so limited in size, that it somewhat resembled a little cabin in a ship.

Left in this miserable den to his own reflections and to darkness—when Nicholas descended with the pine torch, carefully closed the trap-door and secured it on the lower side by a wooden bolt, moreover, softly removing the ladder—Charlie Balgonie placed his sword conveniently at hand, and cast himself upon the pile of skins that were to form his bed, and thought he had often fared worse in the bivouacs of Silesia and Bavaria.

"So—he is safe," said Nicholas Paulovitch, looking upward with a grin of savage satisfaction at the closed trap, as he replaced the loutchin on the table, and then closely scrutinised the Corporal, whose eyes had already become red and inflamed.

"Hush!" said Podatchkine, "take care."

"Why?" asked Nicholas, in a hoarse whisper.

"Because all may not be yet as you wish it, and in Russia sometimes the tongue flays the shoulders and cuts off the head."

"True," said the hitherto taciturn Stepniak, who was carefully feeling the keen edge of his hatchet ; " as the Tartars have it, 'when you have spoken the word, it rules over you; while it is yet unspoken, you rule over it.'   But it seems to me, Michail Podatchkine, that you have taken a great deal of trouble, and wasted much time in the matter of this dispatch.   As you passed through the forest together, why the devil did you not give him a good *tzchick*"—(which we can only render "prod ")—"in the back with your lance ? "

"Because, if a wound is found on him, folks might say he had been murdered ; and he must bear not a scar."

" And neither shall you, friend Podatchkine," said Paulovitch with a cruel grin.

"Come—don't make unpleasant jests," growled the Corporal, with a yawn and a shudder ; " wounds have not been fashionable since Orloff and Bernikoff supped with Peter III."

"You grow wary as you grow older, Corporal."

"I have no desire to travel with the next caravan to Siberia, with one side of my head and face shaved, and an iron rosary, some five pound weight, at my wrists."

" Fear not—you will never see Siberia."

"Then you have made all sure about this Ivanovitch Balgonie ? " said Podatchkine, whose utterance was becoming somewhat inarticulate.

"Ay, sure enough ; the cups were——"

" The cups ! "

" The cup, I mean, was drugged with those black berries which grow in the forest hereabout ; the same stuff used by fine ladies to whiten their hands."

"But why the cup and not the wine ? "

" For this reason : I might have been constrained to drink with him ; and I had no desire to fall, like some one else, into a trap of my own baiting."

Podatchkine, on whom the powerful soporific with which his cup had been drugged—the sleepy nightshade—had been rapidly taking effect, and whose small cunning eyes had been opening and shutting alternately, while a numbness stole with a weariness over all his faculties, seemed suddenly to grasp at the terrible meaning of the speaker. He gave a start—he essayed to rouse himself and shout, but in doing so, toppled off his stool, and sank on the clay floor in a profound slumber.

" At last ! " said the half-breed, administering a kick to the prostrate figure; " at last he has gone to sleep; now to make sure that he shall never waken more. Ah ! the Asiatic ! he was just getting suspicious at the end."

" There are two kopecs in his pocket," said the Stepniak, after investigating the garments of the snorting Podatchkine, who was now breathing heavily through his red snub nose, which between his scrubby beard and his shock of hair, was almost the only feature of his face that was visible.

"Leave the kopecs where you found them!" said Nicholas, with a gipsy oath.

"Wherefore?" asked the Stepniak with surprise.

"It will seem all the more honest in thee, my good Stepniak, when you take the body—bodies, I should say—to the nearest military post. You have but to say you found them dead in the forest."

"And the wet clothing?"

"Dew or rain—what a head you have!"

"True—true; ah! what a man you are, Nicholas Paulovitch, so full of bright thoughts! That idea would never have occurred to me."

"Nor the other either. Quick, now; we have not a moment to lose!"

They extinguished the pine torch, and tying the Corporal's hands securely with a cord, carried him forth to the draw-well before the cottage. Then they substituted that worthy warrior's heels for the bucket which was usually appended to the rope, and permitting the winch to revolve softly and gently, lowered him down, snorting and gasping in his unnatural slumber, head foremost, into the deep dark water below!

The Stepniak turned the iron handle of the winch or windlass, while the gipsy guided the rope with its heavy burden. He was deliberately lowered down until only his heels remained above

H

water, as the two wretches could see by the star-light when stooping and peering into the darkness below.

The snorting had ceased now!

The dying Corporal was heard to struggle with his hands, as if he sought to free them from the cords; a few bubbles filled with air rose to the surface and burst. This continued for a minute, during which all was silent elsewhere, save the half-suppressed breathing of the two assassins, and the dreary sound of the night wind, as it shook the dark branches of the giant pines that towered in solemn gloom around them.

Nicholas Paulovitch listened intently, and kept his eyes fixed on the cottage where their other victim lay, as he doubted not, sunk in what was intended to be his last sleep.

Anon, all became still—deathly still—in the depths of the dark well; the rope ceased to vibrate, and the bubbles came no more.

"Let us leave him here for a few minutes, and now for the Captain and his dispatch! By the time that we return, the Corporal will be as stiff as if he stood for sale in the frozen market on the fête of St. Nicholas!" said the gipsy, with one of his diabolical grins; while the Stepniak, with a smile of satisfaction that showed all his huge yellow teeth, smoothed down to his eyebrows the thick coarse black hair that grew from the apex of his conical caput.

They now re-entered the cottage, and again

lighted the torch in its iron loutchin. All remained just as they had left it; the quass pitcher, the wooden bowls, the two cups, and the empty wine bottle were on the table, and the platters, with the débris of their rustic supper; but the superstitious gipsy felt a species of shudder come over him, for when the torch flared up in the night wind and cast strange shadows on the dingy and discoloured walls of the log-hut, it seemed to his diseased imagination, for a moment, as if the outline of the drowned Corporal still occupied the stool on which he had been seated.

"Come," said he huskily, "the dispatch!—and then for the other!"

They listened intently, and placed the ladder against the trap-door. All was still—not even the breathing of Balgonie was heard. Ascending first, with a knife in his teeth, in case of unexpected resistance, the gipsy knocked thrice on the trap without receiving any response. He then withdrew the wooden bolt, pushed it up, and introducing his head and shoulders, held aloft the pine torch, and turned towards the bed of skins.

It was unoccupied; and in a moment he saw that the bare and desolate chamber was without a tenant!

"Malediction!" he shouted; "he has escaped us—but how? Search—search! He cannot be far off, after the dose I have given him; search —and we must use our hatchets now!"

CHAPTER XI.

BALGONIE had scarcely thrown himself at length on the soft, but not very odorous, pile of skins which formed his couch, when a face appeared at the little window, which was pulled open, and a voice called to him in a low and earnest whisper:

"Hospodeen—Carl Ivanovitch! Hospodeen, attend to me; but oh, be silent, as you value your life!"

He started up, softly approached the window, and saw, by the dim starlight, a fair female face with very dark eyes, white and regular teeth, and long, glittering ear-rings.

"I have seen this face before," thought he; "but when, and where?"

Balgonie, in truth, was too much of a lover to have more than one female face ever before his eyes—that of Natalie Mierowna.

"I am Olga, the gipsy," said the girl, humbly.

"Olga! Olga! whom I saw at the house of Count Mierowitz this evening?"

"The same, Hospodeen!" (Balgonie expressed an exclamation of astonishment to find her, as he thought, so far from that place.) "You gave me a silver kopec once upon a time, at Krejko, when passing through that town with Michail Podatchkine; and, this evening you saved me from the whip of the dvornick, when for the third time I had ventured near the Count's mansion, in a vain search for you, or the Hospoza Mierowna."

"In search of us—and for what purpose, girl ?"

"To warn you, that for nearly a month past, a plot has been formed to deprive you of a valuable paper, and even of your life."

"My life—when ?"

"On the first opportunity."

"By whom—and where, girl—where ?"

"Here in this solitary hut—even now your assassins are in consultation—listen."

He placed his ear to the trap-door, and heard the murmur of hoarse whispers below.

"Hush," said Podatchkine, as already related, "take care !" Then followed the question of the subtle and ferocious Stepniak, as to why he had not given Balgonie a "prod" with his lance in the forest ; and the whole conversation in all its horrible details, up to the moment when the wretched Corporal with death and terror mingling in his soul, fell from his seat in a stupor.

"Father in heaven !" exclaimed Balgonie, full of despair and horror, as he mechanically felt for his fatal dispatch, to ascertain that it was yet safe, "I have drunk of this drugged stuff, and am also lost!"

"Nay," said the gipsy, hurriedly, "nay——"

"I drank the accursed wine from a cup——"

"True; but not from the cup which was intended for you."

"How?—speak!—speak!"

"The wine and the cups too were all stolen by Podatchkine, with many other things, at different times, from the household of Count Mierowitz. This night you were duly expected here, and thus a plan was laid to destroy both you and your treacherous guide. Two cups were fully and deeply drugged by my brother Nicholas: one was richly mounted with silver; and knowing well that it was to be set before you, I abstracted it barely an hour ago, substituting another of the same kind, and now I have it here. Oh, Hospodeen, a narrow escape you have had!"

Balgonie began to breathe more freely; but, assured that never had he run so narrow a risk of death, he felt, though enraged and furious, his blood run cold, when contemplating the fate intended for him. Peeping through a chink of the hatch or trap-door, he saw that the ladder of access had been removed, and that the door of the squalid cottage was open now, for the loutchin flared more than ever in the night wind. It was then extinguished; but still he could see, and hear them dragging forth the passive form of Corporal Podatchkine, whom he supposed to be dead.

Personally, Balgonie felt that he was no match for either of the powerful giants below—men whose bodily strength was quite equal to their ferocity, and whose daggers and hatchets might make mince-meat of him. Moreover, they had now deprived Podatchkine of his sabre and loaded pistols, and were thus more completely armed. Charlie had his hand on his sword—a handsome Turkish sabre; but relinquishing the ideas either of attack or defence, while the glow of rage rose in his breast and cheek, he thought only of immediate flight.

"If you would save your life and the dispatch of the Empress, follow me this instant, and get your horse before they return: you have not a moment to lose."

It was the gipsy girl who spoke again, in her low earnest whisper, and with perfect decision.

"Then I owe my escape—my safety——"

"To my gratitude. Pass through the window and descend by the wall."

"Women," says a certain philosopher, "are not at all inferior to men in coolness and courage, and perhaps much less in resolution than is commonly imagined; the reason they appear so is, because women affect to be more afraid than they really are, and men pretend to be less."

Balgonie found that the courageous girl to whose guidance he now trusted himself, had been enabled to reach the window by standing on the roof of the outhouse, or shed, in which Podatchkine had stabled their horses. The whole edifice being built of squared logs, was not very high, and it afforded easy means of ascent and descent, by the interstices consequent to its rude construction by the hatchet. He soon leaped to the ground, and softly assisted her to descend.

"Here is your horse: you see, Hospodeen, that your kindness to the poor gipsy girl was not thrown away."

Balgonie looked rapidly to his bit and girth, adjusted himself in his saddle, hooked up the hilt of his sabre, and shortened his rein, almost unaware of the black tragedy being so coolly and deliberately acted on the other side of the cottage.

"Ten versts farther from this will bring you to the monastery of the Troitza, which you will know by its three domes. You have but to ride straight westward by the forest path; God keep you, and may you and the beautiful Hospoza be happy in your loves!"

"Tell me, gipsy girl——"

"Ah, I can foretell nothing, save that in love mere merit is of little matter."

"What is of most importance—beauty?"

"No."

"What then?"

"Success, Hospodeen."

He almost laughed, as he slipped into her hand two xervonitz (the largest coins he had), and in a moment more was galloping over the soft grass of the forest path she had indicated.

"By Jove," thought he, as he spurred on, "I shall not be sorry when this infernal dispatch is safe in the hands of old Bernikoff; and to think of that wretch of a Podatchkine! I always expected the fellow to be a rogue, but not of so deep a dye!"

The unfortunate Corporal, now, as he deserved, hanging head foremost downward in the draw-well, stark and stiff and cold, had been to all appearance a good Russian, Balgonie reflected: he neither confessed, fasted, nor did penance (too much bother all that would have been for the Corporal of Cossacks); but he kept Lent regularly to all appearance; made a sign of the cross fussily before and after every meal; always went to church when in camp or quarters; and never omitted his prayers and genuflexions at night, if in haunted places or when passing a wayside cross, especially if any one was by. All this was no doubt studiously hypocritical; and Charlie remembered that his worthy Uncle Gam kept Fast-days and "Sabbaths" with stern and gloomy rigour; that he said a long and sonorous prayer before meals—a longer prayer after them; that he went thrice daily to kirk at the ordained periods, and had nightly a noisy expounding and out-pouring of the spirit that would have put the great John of Geneva himself to the blush.

"Ah," thought poor Charlie, as he trotted on his lonely way through the darkened forest, "decidedly there are Podatchkines in Scotland as well as elsewhere, and in Russia."

The light was beginning to dawn, for it was
the morning of one of the first days of May, so
long had he been detained by illness—shall we say
by love ?—at the castle by the Louga, that Muscovite Eden, as now it seemed to him. The birds
were chirping merrily in the woods ; and in some
places he saw the brown rocks shaded by a species
of graceful silver birch and dark rowan tree,
similar to those that grew in his native strath at
home.

By midsummer he knew that the birchen glades
he traversed would be in full foliage, and that the
rowan berries would hang in ripe red clusters among
the thick green leaves ; and that there, too, would
be grey lichens on the granite cliffs, and in their
clefts soft emerald moss, the wild strawberries, and
the drooping bells of the purple foxglove, just as
he had seen them where the Earn " gurgling
kissed her pebbled shore " as it flowed towards
the Tay.

They seemed like old friends in that strange
place, and with a sigh of gratitude for his escape
from a perilous and deadly snare was mingled
one of hope—a wish—a bootless wish, that one
day he might sit by the banks of the lovely Earn
with Natalie by his side, amid all the security his
native land afforded, and under the white blooming hawthorns that cast their sweet fragrance to
the soft winds of the Perthshire valley.

Beloved Natalie—so fair and delicate, so dark
haired and so bright-eyed ! Her diamond ring,

and still more her lock of soft and silky hair,
brought all the charm and sense of her presence
vividly before him.   He counted the brief hours
since they had parted, and sighed to think how
many hours and days and weeks must inevitably
elapse before they met again.

In memory and imagination, he conned over
and over again each tender speech and glance,
each mute caress and passionate kiss, with every
circumstance and minutiæ of their occurrence and
bestowal; and what lover has not done so since
time began, and apples grew, and roses bloomed
in Eden!   Even his recent narrow escape and
the gipsy's gratitude were forgotten in the ardour
of his thoughts.

And he sighed again, when thinking how wild
and insane were the dreams in which he was
indulging, as he touched his horse with the spurs,
on seeing the three shining domes of the Troitza,
or monastery of the Holy Trinity, rise before him
amid the green woodlands.

CHAPTER XII.

AFTER traversing a green valley some five or six miles in length, bordered on each side by forests of fir trees, dark, solemn and acutely conical, where the sunlight could scarcely ever penetrate to the thick rank grass and herbage that grew below, and where a merry gurgling brook rushed noisily along by the side of the narrow horseway, Charlie Balgonie drew his bridle at the gates of the Troitza monastery, when its white walls, its three great cupolas, shaped each like a gigantic onion inverted, covered with plates of burnished copper, and all painted and bestarred, were shining gaily in the morning sun.

There he was made welcome by the monks—quaint-looking men, in long black caftans, with high black caps, fashioned like our modern hats, but without brims, and having black veils floating behind over their long, straight hair. He deposited some money with the treasurer, declined the invitation of the sacristan to see the uncorrupted body of some saint with an unpronounceable name, reposing in its shrine like a silver bedstead, and its head begirt by a diadem with pearls as large as pistol bullets; for the saint had been a martyr, who, in the days of Ivan Basilovitch, the Tartars had rewarded for his attempts to convert them by knocking out his brains; and now he was a miserable mummified relic of humanity, before which, for many ages, thousands of devotees had knelt and wept and smote their breasts in paroxysms of prayer. Charlie waived the invitation; and after having a good breakfast in the refectory, and there telling his story to the monks, he was somewhat bewildered when informed by them, that after all his (certainly circuitous) journey with Podatchkine on the preceding evening and night, and after his riding since he had left the cottage of the gipsy, he was still barely twenty miles from the Louga!

Was a spell cast upon him? was his horse bewitched, that he was to continue travelling thus, and yet never make progress? It almost seemed so; but one of the monks, a more shrewd man than his brothers, explained the whole affair as being consequent to the cunning of Podatchkine, and his scheme for destroying the dispatch-bearer.

A large party of pilgrims on horse and foot were returning to St. Petersburg that afternoon. With them Balgonie travelled for the remainder of his journey; and, after traversing a wild and desert tract of country, on the evening of the next day he had the pleasure of beholding, in the distance before him, that new but vast and splendid capital,—

> "Proud city ! Sovereign mother thou
> Of all Sclavonian cities now,"—

covering the once wild waste whereon, before the time of Peter the Great, the father of his country, a few wretched fishermen were wont to contend with the wolves and bears for a spot to erect their huts—where, as Count Segur says, winter reigned for eight months of the year, rye was an article of garden culture, and a bee-hive a curiosity.

Its bulbous-shaped Byzantine domes, and tall needle-like spires, and all its countless roofs, that rose beyond each other in ridgy succession like the waves of the sea, and are generally like the sea in colour, being of a brilliant green or an ashy hue, were now all tinted redly by the rays of the setting sun, which cast the shadows of its many bridges on the waters of the Neva and of the canals that glided silently and darkly beneath them.

As the sun sank beyond the Gulf of Finland, and the shadows deepened on every plated dome and granite rampart, the great gilt crosses of our Lady of Kazan (a fane which was ten years in building) and of many other noble churches glittered, or rather seemed to burn like stars, amid the deep blue of the cloudless sky beyond.

Balgonie's satisfaction, on finding himself so near the end of his journey, was somewhat clouded by a trivial circumstance.

After entering the city by a palisaded barrier, where stood a guard of the Regiment of Valiko-lutz, he checked his horse's pace, while the caravan of pilgrims, whom he now wished to quit, traversed a long street of small wooden houses that lay beyond. Here, close by the margin of the Neva, lay a man with his loose caftan wet and dripping, and a piece of sack or old canvas spread over his face. On his breast lay his fur cap, as if to receive alms for his burial; for none doubted that he was a poor drowned fellow just fished up from the Neva, and that money was required of the religious and charitable alike for his obsequies and masses for the repose of his soul. So all the pilgrims from the Troitza threw something into the fur cap, where denuscas, kopecs, even roubles and Polish ducats, jingled fast together, while the passers muttered prayers and made signs of the cross.

All the caravan had passed, so the clatter of Balgonie's charger, steel-scabbard, and accoutrements, seemed to create a different effect on the attentive ear of the seemingly drowned man; for the knave, who had only been acting, started up, and, with his spoil, fled like a hare down one of the little alleys that opened off the wooden street. He vanished in the twilight, yet not so quickly but that Balgonie was able to recognise in his face and form, the bulky and muscular half-bred, the gipsy, Nicholas Paulovitch.

What had brought him to St. Petersburg?

Was he still dogging the luckless dispatch-bearer, or had he only fled thither that, among its thousands, he might elude the punishment with which Count Mierowitz would be sure to visit him, if the murder of the Corporal was discovered?

This episode made Balgonie feel uncomfortable, and suspicious that other and hidden dangers yet menaced him, as he rode steadily but watchfully through the densely crowded, but monotonously regular streets of houses, which are stuccoed, white-washed, and decorated with different colours, roofed with wood and iron, painted in most instances green, and nearly all pillared and piazzaed —each long vista, with its oil lamps, being terminated by domes and spires; and erelong he saw the lights shining in the lofty windows of that magnificent crescent, which, for a time, was the palace of Catharine's most cherished favourite, " the fair-faced Lanskoi," as Byron has it—

> "A lover who had cost her many a tear,
> And yet but made a middling Grenadier."

And now the melodious bells were ringing for vespers in the towers of our Lady of Kazan—a Greek cruciform fane, which was founded as a rival to St. Peter's at Rome, and named after the Tartar kingdom of Kazan. It is the greatest church in the city, and one of high sanctity.

Along the northern margin of the Neva, a river broad as the Thames at London Bridge, but (unlike the Thames) deep, blue, and transparent as crystal, lined with solid granite quays, and bordered by many stately palatial edifices, Balgonie pursued his way; but the stars were shining at midnight on the vast sheet of water called the Lake of Ladoga, before he, weary and worn with fatigue, dismounted beneath the formidable gates of the castellated prison of Schlusselburg, which had been strengthened and fortified anew by General Count Todleben, whose arrest and quarrel with the Empress had made so much noise three years before the time our story opens.

CHAPTER XIII.

TWENTY-FOUR miles eastward of the city, the small town and fortress of Schlusselburg stand, at a point where the Neva issues from the Lake of Ladoga, and on the left bank of the river. The little town had then somewhere about three thousand inhabitants, who chiefly lived by the manufacture of cotton and porcelain.

On an island, where the river joins the lake and moats it round, is built the fort, which is about four hundred yards square : its walls are of stone, massive, and fifty feet in height, terminating in battlements and turrets of antique form.

The passage to this island is by a long drawbridge.

The guard which kept this formidable state prison, where many a hopeless sigh was wafted through the rusty bars of its prison grilles across the waters of Ladoga, was composed entirely of a body of dismounted Cossacks, selected for the purpose, as the task of keeping or secluding the dethroned Emperor Ivan was one of no small responsibility and importance ; so these men were all Cossacks of a high class, and were rather richly dressed.

Their short blue jackets were elaborately embroidered with yellow lace, and a multitude of gilt buttons, but were hooked across the chest; their trowsers of scarlet cloth were loose, long, and gathered into their boots, which were of brown Russian leather, and reached to six inches above the ankle. Their busbies of black shining fur had bright scarlet bags, tall white feathers, a cockade, and tasselled cord. They were all clean and soldier-like men, well moustached, and sternly resolute in bearing; and all were armed with musketoons, short sabres, and brass pistols.

A guard of these men received Balgonie at the gate and drawbridge with a profound military salute; and a picturesque aspect they presented, as their arms flashed in the murky light of the great oil lantern that swung in the dark, weird, and deep-mouthed archway, where a massive portcullis showed its iron teeth, all red and rusted by the mists of the Neva and the stormy blasts that swept across the Lake of Ladoga.

The great masses of the fortress, ghostly and shrouded, with faint red lights gleaming out here and there; the enormous strength of the gates, their planking, bolts, and bars; the thickness of the walls; the number of embrasures and loopholes for cannon and musketry, all converging to one point, the approach or river entrance; the number of sentinels, and, more than all, the vast

strength of the portcullis and double gates, together with the difficulties he experienced in procuring admission, though in uniform, and though
a staff officer bearing a dispatch of the Empress,
all served to impress unpleasantly on the mind of
Charlie Balgonie a state of extreme watchfulness,
of suspicion, and mistrust; and also a sense of
the vast responsibility of the charge confided by
Catharine to Colonel Bernikoff.

That gallant officer and estimable personage
had retired long since, after a deep drinking bout,
and would be—as Lieutenant Tschekin (the son-
in-law of General Weymarn), who was third in
command of the fortress, informed Balgonie—
quite invisible till breakfast time to-morrow, when
the dispatch would be delivered to him : and a
sigh of real annoyance escaped Charlie, when he
found that this odious paper was to be yet some
eight hours or more in his secret pocket.

He repaired to the officers' guard-room at the
barrier gate, and there, wrapped in his cloak,
without undressing (as he hoped next day to ex-
change the atmosphere of Schlusselburg for that
of some hotel in the Vasili-Ostrov), lay down to
sleep, and if possible to dream of Natalie; but
he had undergone too much toil for such gentle
phantasms, so he slept like a dormouse, till the
sun was high in heaven, unawakened even by the
deep boom of the morning gun, a 36-pounder, as
it pealed across the Lake of Ladoga; but ultimately he was roused by Tschekin and Captain

Vlasfief, a very handsome young man, but a cruel and heartless *roué*, whom ultimately he detested. These, after shaking him heartily, announced that Colonel Bernikoff awaited him at breakfast, and was not in a mood to brook much delay.

His hasty toilette was soon complete, and he was speedily ushered into a plain, almost naked whitewashed apartment arched with stone. Through its grated windows the morning sun shone cheerily, and the blue waters of the lake could be seen with the white sails of many a tiny coasting vessel.

Here, at a table of plain Memel timber, destitute of cloth, but on which massive silver vessels with rudely formed wooden bowls and platters were oddly intermingled, was seated the Governor, who, like the czars and boyars of old, still took quass for breakfast with roasted beef or bear's ham, bread with caviare, greens with vinegar, salted plums and other abominations. But Balgonie saw that coffee and even tea, with ham, eggs, and kippered salmon, were prepared, with other condiments, for those who, like himself, had nothing of the Tartar in their blood.

"Hail to you—I wish you health," said Bernikoff, courteously enough, in the old Russian fashion, and presenting his hand to Charlie, who took it, shuddering as he remembered the fate of Peter III.; "welcome to Schlusselburg, Captain Ivanovitch Balgonie."

Bernikoff, who wore a dark-green undress uniform faced with scarlet, was a man well up in years; he had fierce and shining black eyes that made soldier and serf alike quail beneath their gaze; yet they were small, cunning, and twinkling eyes, the lashes of which were half closed—the eyes of one who could act the cruel tyrant on one hand, and the cringing slave on the other. He had a massive, square, and brutal jaw, thin wicked lips, a nose as round as a grape-shot, close short grizzled hair, and long snaky mustachioes.

He was of Tartar blood, and came of those " warlike and merciless tribes who studied nothing but the use of arms; who passed their lives on horseback; who even lived on their horses in this sense, that their chief food was horseflesh and the milk of mares; who, at the same time, could go for days without food; and who, when they took a city by storm, put all the inhabitants to the sword except the working men."

" Seat yourself, Captain, and proceed to breakfast, while I read your dispatch," said the Governor. " Holy Sergius! it is from Catharine Christianowna herself! The Czarina is great, but Heaven is higher!" he added, placing the paper on his forehead, as he bowed over it; and then taking an enormous pinch of Beresovski snuff, a most pungent compound, from a gold box said to have been found in the pocket of Peter III., he proceeded to peruse that document which had proved of such trouble to the bearer.

The eyes of Balgonie, Tschekin, and Vlasfief,

who alone were present, were fixed inquiringly upon him, and they could see that the contents disturbed him greatly; he grew pale and flushed by turns; his brows contracted to a terrible frown; a red spark of devilish light glittered in his eyes, and his lips were compressed.

" Ah, the Asiatics! the accursed Asiatics!" he muttered. This is a most opprobrious epithet in Russia, and excited some surprise in his hearers.

He carefully folded the dispatch, and turning sternly to Charlie, who was keeping his eyes on him and drinking his coffee the while, he said :—

" Ivanovitch Balgonie, there is a feather in the seal—the usual sign of *haste* among us here in Russia ; yet you have not troubled yourself much with speed, for this dispatch is dated at Novgorod more than a month back !"

" Permit me to explain, Excellency," said Balgonie eagerly, and anxiously too.

" I shall be glad if you *can* explain it," replied Bernikoff, with increasing sternness. " I have known a general, a leader in ten battles, degraded, knouted, and sent to hunt the ermine with a cannon ball at his heels for a smaller dereliction of duty than this."

Balgonie's heart beat very fast while he related his story—of his being misled by a traitor twice ; of the passage of the Louga at such terrible hazard ; of his subsequent illness ; and the episode at that log hut.

" That you were in the guidance of a traitor,

I knew before your arrival; and I am extremely glad that he fell into his own snare," replied Bernikoff, a little more calmly; "but this matter is extremely awkward for you, and becomes more complicated every hour."

After glancing again at the dispatch, and bending his keen, rat-like eyes on Balgonie, he asked:

" Were Basil Mierowitz or Usakoff, the grandson of Mazeppa, at the Castle of Louga any time during your sojourn there?"

" No, Excellency, neither of them were."

" Spies say differently—but you can swear it?"

"On my honour do I swear it!   But why?"

"I have had bad news from the head-quarters of your regiment, and from Lieutenant-General Weymarn, since you left Novgorod."

"And these tidings, Excellency?"

" Are to the effect that your friends, the two subalterns, have both deserted, with several soldiers, all of whom are natives of the Ukraine."

" Deserted!"

" And are nowhere to be found, though pursued by a whole sotnia of Cossacks."

"Deserted!" reiterated Balgonie with real concern.

" Yes—the cursed Asiatics!" replied Bernikoff, expectorating with great vehemence, and thoroughly believing that each time he did so, he cast out a devil.

For some moments intense anxiety and alarm bewildered Balgonie, and he felt himself grow pale at a time when six searching eyes were bent with a doubtful expression upon him. He remembered the hostility, the threatening and mysterious words of Natalie, and grew almost sick with apprehension of he knew not what, as he muttered inaudibly—

"Basil deserted—and his cousin too! The whole family will be inculpated and degraded. Oh, Natalie, my hapless love! Did General Weymarn state this in *his* dispatch?" he asked aloud.

"He did, and at its end referred to you."

"To me, Excellency?"

"Yes; here is the document, and it concludes thus: 'as I and the Regiment of Smolensko will shortly march into St. Petersburg, Captain Carl Ivanovitch Balgonie need not return to Novgorod; but until then, shall attach himself to your staff, and remain in Schlusselburg, where, erelong, you may require all the good service he can render you.—WEYMARN.'"

Great were the mortification and disgust of Balgonie on learning that he was to remain for an indefinite period in a place so revolting and uncomfortable, and with no other society than that of three military jailers,—cruel, hard-hearted, and avaricious Muscovites of the worst kind; and with these orders died his hopes of revisiting, as he intended, Louga, on his return, and of seeing Natalie again.

Under ban as all the household of Mierowitz

would be now, should he ever see **her more ?**
Every way fate and the tide of events seemed to
be against him and her, already in the very dawn
of their love.

"And now, gentlemen," said the Governor,
lowering his voice, " the Empress's dispatch contains only two lines, thus: 'A scheme is formed
to free Prince Ivan. *Let him not fall alive into the
hands of those who come to seek for him!'* Nor
shall he!" exclaimed Bernikoff with ferocious
enthusiasm, as he dashed a cup of vodka among
his quass, and drained the goblet, after shouting,
"The health of Her Imperial Majesty Catharine
Christianowna—hurrah!"

"Hurrah, hurrah!" added Vlasfief and the
Lieutenant.

Balgonie also, as in duty bound, essayed to
"hurrah," but the sound died away on his lips.

CHAPTER XIV.

FULL of anxious thoughts, he passed more than half of the succeeding day on the ramparts of the castled-prison, alone, avoiding Colonel Bernikoff, Captain Vlasfief, and their subaltern, Tschekin, none of whom were consonant to his taste, for all were deep gamblers and heavy drinkers.

His mind was full of care for Natalie and all her family. Some desperate and revengeful plot, of which the desertion of her brother and of his cousin Usakoff was but the beginning, the means to an end, was certainly hatching—a plot that might too surely end in bloodshed, in the savage punishment and the ruin of all.

He sorrowed keenly for his two friends Basil Mierowitz and Apollo Usakoff, for both were polished and educated gentlemen, men of a class and style more common in some corps of the Russian army now, than in those days. And there was poor Mariolizza, too—so brightly beautiful, so happy, and so merry! Her love, her hopes and schemes, would all be crushed and blighted, as well as his own.

Balgonie was not without fears for himself, and

of being compromised in the affair ; or, perhaps, lured into subtle state intrigues and deep plots, in the failure or success of which he could have no interest politically or personally, save in his love for Natalie—a love that had changed the whole current of his ideas and opened up a new realm of thought and incentive to action.

Already he was beginning to revolt at the Russian service, and yet he had been happy in the Regiment of Smolensko, and had found in the land of his adoption, like every Scottish adventurer that has trod the Russian soil, honours scarcely to be won at home.

How long was he to be on the staff of this ferocious Commandant, and in this horrible prison, where many an innocent victim was pining hopelessly in chains and misery? "The mutual distrust in which people live in Russia," says the Abbé Chappe D'Auteroche in his scarce travels about this time, " and the total silence of the nation upon everything which may have the least relation either to the government or the sovereign, arise chiefly from the privilege every Russian has, without distinction, of crying out in public, *slowo dielo* ; that is to say, ' I declare you are guilty of high treason, both in words and actions.' All the bystanders are then obliged to assist in arresting the person so accused ; a father his son, and the son his father, while nature suffers in silence. The accuser and accused are at once conveyed to prison, and afterwards to

St. Petersburg, where they are tried by the Secret Court of Chancery."

Thanks to this pleasant state of society, the chambers and chains of Schlusselburg were seldom unoccupied.

Vlasfief was hollow-hearted, avaricious, and sensual; Tschekin, the Lieutenant, a slimy, cruel, reckless, and ignorant Muscovite; but old Bernikoff was really a character whom Balgonie equally dreaded and despised.

His subtlety and oppression had been the means of reducing, at different times, some thirty officers to the ranks, with permission to serve and work their way up again; and many more were now cursing him and their fate, at Irkutsk and remoter Siberia, for their inability to purchase his mercy or good-will. When commanding at Cronstadt, he had been detected once in the act of transmitting whole sledge loads of government shot, shell, lead, and ropes, across the frozen gulf for sale in Sweden; and also in buying at a cheap rate base denuscas to pay the troops: but so trusted was the old rascal by the Empress, that he always escaped the degradation, the hanging or shooting, which, on those discoveries, were so freely meted out to his subalterns.

On the estate of Bernikoff a serf once amassed ten thousand roubles, and offered them for the freedom of his daughter, who was about to be married.

"Let me see the girl!" was the reply.

As a serf can possess nothing, the father trembled in his soul at this demand, as his daughter, unfortunately for herself, was beautiful.

"Holy Sergius!" exclaimed Bernikoff, "what business has a serf with ten thousand roubles; the girl and the money are alike mine!"

And so he literally and lawfully seized them both.

Though a savage soldier, like every old Muscovite, he was the slave of mechanical devotion. No statue or picture of the Holy Virgin, of St. Sergius, or St. Alexander Newski, was ever passed by him without a profound reverence and a sign of the cross. To such effigies he would address himself before he knelt even to the Empress: and before them he had been known to kneel and kiss the ground five minutes before or after he had knouted a miserable boor (whose pockets were empty), or nearly slain a soldier by making him run the gauntlet, for merely having the seams of his gloves sewn outward instead of in; for wearing his hat on the left side of his head instead of the right; or for some other offence equally heinous.

And it was on the staff of this distinguished officer (temporarily, however) that Charlie now, to his great disgust, found himself.

On three sides, far around this island prison, stretched the waters of Ladoga—the largest lake in Europe, being one hundred and thirty miles long, by nearly ninety broad; full of rocky isles and dangerous quicksands, over which, from its flat shores, sweep frequent and perilous storms.

From the somewhat dreary view of this small inland sea, whose northern and eastern coast could not be discerned, he turned to survey the fortress, with all its strength of gloomy walls, grated windows, and frowning cannon, till suddenly his eye was arrested by a very remarkable face, which was observing him from the sombre depth of a strongly barred and arched window of the great tower.

It was a pale face, but singularly handsome—grave, and even sad in expression—a young man's face with the slightest indication of a moustache, but for which, in its paleness and extreme delicacy of feature and tint, it might have passed for that of a twin brother of Natalie Mierowna!

Suddenly it was detected by a Cossack sentinel, who shouted shrilly, and slapped the but-end of his loaded musketoon: on this, the face instantly disappeared.

This was he concerning whom Balgonie had brought that terrible dispatch—Ivan, the deposed Emperor—the prisoner of Schlusselburg!

"Twenty-three years!" thought Balgonie with a shudder; "twenty-three years in that tower—since his very babyhood—oh, it is terrible!"

Other ears had heard the shout of the sentinel; for now a man, who in a boat had been fishing near the fortress, suddenly shipped a pair of sculls, and pulled away towards the town with an air of alarm that seemed equalled only by his dexterity. This fisher had been hovering about the fortress all day. "Can he be the gipsy—the half-breed?" thought Charlie: "ah! the dispatch is out of my hands now."

Lieutenant Tschekin now approached with an invitation from Bernikoff to join him at dinner, adding, "remember that with the Colonel, eating is indeed a science, and temperance he views as mere want of spirit."

As they proceeded together through various archways and gates, the shrieks and entreaties of a man apparently in mortal agony rang through the echoing prisons with a horrible cadence, that chilled the free blood in Balgonie's veins.

A court through which they had to pass was crowded by soldiers, formed in hollow square, and Balgonie was compelled to linger and look on with Tschekin, who seemed rather to enjoy the spectacle.

"Hah," said he, "the punishment is nearly ended—let us wait and see the *batogg!*"

It was a soldier being knouted, which is simply the Russian word for "whipped."

Stripped to the loins, he was strapped to an erect board, formed like an inverted cone, and having three notches at the upper end, one to receive his chin, and the other two his wrists, while the torturer wielded a knout, the handle of which is usually eighteen inches long with a thong of thirty-six inches. This is always boiled in milk, by which process it swells and the edges become sharp, hard, and more destructive.

The whipper was skilful : he laid on his lashes from the neck to the loins, so as to deal them at intervals of one inch artistically apart, leaving a stripe of flesh between each ; but these regulated and omitted stripes, after receiving a fresh knout, he proceeded to take off in succession, with wonderful and terrible precision, till the man's entire back was a mass of blood, and he hung, fainting and well-nigh speechless, by the wrists.

"Oh, Excellency," he said, in an imploring voice, "remember that my brother, Alexis Jagouski, aided you in escaping from the battle of Zorndorff ! "

This was most true, but the story was a terrible one. At Zorndorff, where the Russians were defeated with such slaughter and driven towards the frontiers of Poland, the horse of Bernikoff was shot under him, and he was in danger of being cut down by the Prussian Hussars. In this sore extremity a Cossack named Alexis Jagouski took his leader behind him on his crupper ; but that personage, finding that the double weight impeded the horse's speed, and that the Hussars were close behind, shortened his sabre in his hand, and plunging the blade into the body of his preserver, flung the corpse from the saddle, and escaped alone.

At this reminiscence Bernikoff only scowled more deeply ; and now the lacerated back of the sufferer was strewed with coarse gunpowder, to which a match was applied. This is technically known as the *batogg*, and the agony it produced is indescribable.

The culprit was now cast loose, but was still able, according to the slavish usage of the country, to crawl on his hands and knees towards Bernikoff, and he gasped out :—

"Hospodeen—Excellency, I thank you humbly for this most merciful punishment."

"Begone, dog of an Asiatic!" replied the governor, kicking him in the face; "when next you seek to fill your pipe, this will teach you to keep your filthy fingers out of my tobacco pouch."

These were the defenders of their country, the Holy Russia, among whom a wayward fate had cast the Scottish palatine: the blood of the latter boiled within him; but he knew too well that to expostulate would be but to excite suspicion, and to court degradation and the musket. Something, however, in the expression of his face did not escape Bernikoff's keen and angry eyes.

"Ivanovitch Balgonie, a superior can never act unjustly to his inferior," said he sternly; and these words terribly embodied the genuine spirit of the true Russian *Tchinnovnik*, or noble class. "I am in the service of the state," he added; "and the state is the Czarina!"

Yet this upright Governor, who knouted the poor Cossack for pilfering a pipeful of tobacco, had always a garrison double its actual strength on paper, the pay and rations of the men of straw forming a pleasant addition to his many secret perquisites, while his soldiers starved and frequently begged food from the very prisoners they guarded.

It was neither hospitality nor love of society which had procured the honour of an invitation for Balgonie; but Bernikoff shrewdly suspecting that he might have some loose cash, resolved to possess himself thereof at cards; so barely was a dinner of *shee* (which is identically Scotch broth), croquettes, with *purée* of beet-root, beef in the Hussar style, with salad of baked beet-root and biscuits, dismissed, than champagne-cup, and vodka (or corn-brandy) punch became the order of the evening; and Bernikoff, who was a great gourmand, with his face flushed and his uniform open, after signing the cross and bowing thrice to a picture of St. Sergius, sat down to cards with Vlasfief and Tschekin, who were quite as sharp as himself, and with poor simple-hearted Charlie Balgonie, who dreaded to decline, circumstanced as he was on all hands; and who was glad when allowed to quit the table with the loss, he never could understand how, of twenty xervonitz, or pieces worth nine shillings sterling each.

"Now, Vlasfief—'tis you and I; rouge-et-noir!" exclaimed Bernikoff, draining a goblet of vodka punch at a draught.

"I am too weary to play, most excellent

Colonel; pray excuse me," urged the Captain, who had lost considerably to his senior also.

"You, then, Tschekin?" said Bernikoff savagely.

"I hav'n't a kopec to spare, Excellency!"

"Well—I saw a pretty housemaid at your mansion in the town yesterday—the daughter of a serf apparently."

"Feodorowna?"

"Very likely—with red hair and brown eyes."

"Ah! the same; she came with Madame Tschekin from the household of her father, General Weymarn."

"By all the devils, she is very like old Weymarn!"

"She is the daughter of my old nurse, Colonel," said Tschekin gravely, with an air of annoyance.

"I don't care whose daughter she is!"

"Well?"

"I'll put a hundred silver roubles on her."

"Done! I put her on the ace."

"The ace hath lost!" exclaimed Bernikoff, with a shout of laughter. "Holy Sergius! the girl is mine. To-morrow," he added, "I'll send a corporal and a file of men for her, with a covered kabitka. See that all her things are packed and ready, friend Tschekin, or write to your wife about it, and say you have lost her at cards."

"The devil!—Excellency—this can't be."

"Why? I won her fairly."

"But the girl is about to be married to her cousin."

" *Was*, you mean ; the cards have changed her destiny, like that of the serfs whom Vlasfief drank away in champagne last night."

So passed Charlie's first day at Schlusselburg.

CHAPTER XV.

FORTUNATELY for Balgonie, there was a chaplain, or priest, of the Russian Greek Church, attached to the fortress; and his society, at times, tended to alleviate what he endured from having to associate with such a human bear as Colonel Bernikoff,—an annoyance from which he would only be relieved by the longed-for return of General Weymarn and the Regiment of Smolensko to St. Petersburg.

The ceremonies of religion retain in Russia all their pristine influence, and afford the miserable and unlettered serf a short season of relaxation from labour and severity during festivals, when he may enjoy his can of fiery vodka and revel in intoxication. Unlike many of the Russian clergy, who adopt the cowl merely as the means of evading slavery in civil life, or slavery added to peril in the army, and also as a chance of attaining to power and nobility, Father Chrysostom, the Chaplain of Schlusselburg, was a humane, gentle, and learned old priest, whom the Commandant had been depraved enough to strike with his clenched hand on more than one occasion; but prior to doing so, he had always contrived, oddly and superstitiously enough, to have the chief badge of the father's sacred office, his baretta, abstracted and hidden.

Through the good offices of the Chaplain, with the permission of the Governor, which was yielded very unwillingly, Balgonie (whose curiosity and commiseration were greatly excited) was presented one evening to the deposed Emperor Ivan, and the particulars and incidents of that inter-

made a deep and sad impression upon him. small, arc nce-door of the central tower was were carved of great strength. Above it by Ivan Basilovitch an arms, first adopted spread-eagle, having on its teenth century: a bearing St Michael and a dra n escutcheon crowns in chief for Muscovy and the three kingdoms of Kazan and Astracan.

On passing through a little paved court, grated over with iron, where the royal recluse was permitted to breathe the external air, while a sentinel trod to and fro above his head; another door-way, secured by a portcullis grooved into the wall, gave access to the narrow stair which led to his apartments. These were two in number: their windows and doors were all grated with iron; and sentinels, with loaded arms, watched every avenue by day and night.

His sitting-room was plainly, even neatly furnished: its chief ornaments being a pretty

Madonna and some gaudy pictures of Muscovite saints; and it had one window, which opened towards the vast expanse of the Lake of Ladoga.

Pale, handsome, and resigned, gentle in eye and manner, the poor young Prince had grown to manhood in total ignorance of the outer world and of all he had lost. He knew only the four walls of the prison, the changing hues of the waves and clouds, the wild swans and the waters of Ladoga.

As related in our fifth chapter, the Prisoness Schlusselburg was the eldest son of t^ niece of of Mecklenburg, Elizabeth-Ca' was Anthony the Empress Anne. H^ Wolfenbuttel, whose Ulric, Duke of B--oned Russia by the usurp- whole famil^ --abeth. ing E^ --unt Ivan had been dethroned, after g a king for exactly one year.

During the reign of the Empress Catharine, he was detained in Schlusselburg "under the denomination of a *Person Unknown*, and it was given out that his senses were impaired, though it is pretty well understood that this is without foundation." "His fate has been particularly lamentable," continues a newspaper of the period; "torn from the bosom of his family, he has now passed twenty-three years in close captivity The late Empress Elizabeth, towards the latter end of her life, seemed disposed to treat this noble captive with clemency and favour, either from sentiments of justice and compassion, or to render two great personages more circumspect and submissive."

These personages were her successors, the unfortunate Peter III. and Catharine II.

Ivan's mother is said to have died of grief; but Duke Anthony Ulric and his four other children were all confined for life in a house at Horsens, a town of Jutland, at the extremity of the Baltic, where they had a precinct of a mile English; but it was surrounded by high palisades, beyond which they dared not venture under pain of death; and there the Duke, old and blind, passed the last years of his melancholy life.

His youngest daughter, Elizabeth, "was a woman of high spirit and elegant manners," according to Coxe, the traveller, who visited her; "she possessed portraits of her father and mother, and even contrived to procure a rouble of her brother Ivan, struck during his short reign. It is difficult to conjecture how she could obtain a coin, the possession of which was more than once punished by the Empress Elizabeth as high-treason, and it is still more difficult to imagine how she could secret it from the knowledge of her guards during her long imprisonment."

Confinement had rendered Ivan's features unnaturally pale and delicate; and, by years of systematic constraint and oppression, his fine, clear, and very beautiful dark eyes had a soft, subdued, and chastened expression, that was singularly touching and winning.

The tone of his voice was also gentle and alluring.

"Hospodeen," said he, presenting his hand to Balgonie, "I rejoice to meet you, if one who leads a life so strange as mine can be said to rejoice; but you are one to whom I may talk a little without danger—eh, Father Chrysostom? And he has told me, Hospodeen, that you are not a Russian, but a native of some island that is far away in the sea. What are you? A Tartar—a Tcherkesse? Oh no, you cannot be either. I know them; for they guard me," he added, with a little shudder.

"I am your friend, believe me, Ivan Antonovitch," replied Balgonie, who was touched by the childlike simplicity of the poor recluse, who was plainly attired in a caftan of fine green cloth, edged with a narrow trimming of yellow fur; the square crowned cap, which he only wore when in the grated court, was of the same materials. A small gold cross was at his neck, a rosary of amber hung at his right wrist, and a little pipe, the only luxury allowed him, was dangling from one of his breast buttons.

When in his presence, Balgonie always thought with horror of the cruel tenor of the dispatch he had brought, and trembled for the result of his friends' conspiracy.

To teach Ivan anything, even to read or to write, was treason; yet he had gleaned a little of his own history, and that of his family, from

the casual remarks of his guards and from the
Chaplain, during the long, long years of his
captivity, the reason for which he failed to understand, but the system of which had become
as a second nature to him; and the little he
learned, made a deep, rather than a bitter impression upon him.

The whole energies of each successive Chaplain had been given to preparing him for another
and a brighter state of existence, and to turning
his hopes and wishes towards it, rather than to
this world, of which he was well-nigh weary if
not utterly ignorant; and so much was he impressed by the uncertainty of human life in
general, and of his own in particular, that daily,
for years, he had seen the sun rise from the
waters of Ladoga in doubt whether he would see
it set; and nightly had he laid down his head
without the assurance of being a live man in the
morning.

Life had no charm—death no terror for
Ivan.

In his visits, which were frequent, as the young
Prince had conceived a great regard for him,
Charlie Balgonie knew not upon what topics to
converse; for he experienced great difficulty in
fashioning his sentences and observations to suit
a listener whose knowledge of the external world
and of all the machinery of life was so limited.
In those visits, Balgonie was always accompanied
by the Chaplain, or Captain Vlasfief, as the

watchful and suspicious Bernikoff would by no
means permit them to have an interview alone.

"I am so glad to have you for a friend, Ivanovitch Balgonie," the Prince would say sometimes; "though Father Chrysostom assures me
that kings may have peers and soldiers, serfs and
slaves, but, alas! they can never have a *friend!* I
have heard my guards say that I was once a King
—an Emperor; but I cannot remember when.
It must have been long, long ago, as Russia has
had four monarchs since. I have not even a dream
of it—an Emperor? Yet I shall too probably
die even as Demetrius did. I cannot remember
even my mother; for they tell me that she died
of sorrow, when I was brought here from a place
called Moscow Do you, Hospodeen, remember
yours?"

"When I was but a child she died, to my
sorrow Had she lived, I might not have been
here in Russia to-day," replied Balgonie.

"Well—but you may remember," persisted
the young Prince.

"True, your Highness; memories I have of
a soft fair face that bent over my little bed at
night; of one who kissed and hushed me to sleep;
but those memories are faint or vivid, broken and
uncertain, according to my mood of mind; and
strange it is that they come to me more in dreams
by night than thoughts by day, especially as I
grow older."

"I should like to have some such dreams, but

then I have nothing to remember; I know not even my own age or when I came here," said Ivan thoughtfully. "If I do dream by night, I seem to hear only what I hear by day—the voices of the Cossack sentinels, the screams of the sea-birds, the dashing of the waves when the wind crosses the lake, or the clanging of the castle bell. Then there are times when I dream that I see Demetrius, and then I awake in a cold perspiration. Tell me of the things that are being acted in the great world that lies beyond the Lake of Ladoga, for Father Chrysostom speaks to me only of Heaven."

"It is said that the King of Prussia has agreed to the proposal of—of—the Empress, about the county of Wirtemberg, in Silesia."

"How, agreed?"

"Count Biron is to have the estate as Duke of Courland, on paying eight thousand guineas to Field-Marshal Count Munich," said Balgonie.

The Prince sighed with a bewildered air, for all those names were quite new to him.

"And who is Count Biron?" he asked.

"A friend of the Empress," said Father Chrysostom rather hastily, to anticipate the reply of Balgonie.

"Tell me something more. Nay, Father Chrysostom, don't chide us, pray," said he, seeing that the white bearded chaplain looked uneasy and rose to retire.

"Conversation of this kind is strictly forbidden," said he ; " and if Captain Vlasfief was here——"

" Oh ! " exclaimed the Prince, with a shudder, but not of anger (he seemed too gentle for that emotion), " don't talk of Vlasficf I implore you. Pray tell me more news, Hospodeen; I shall learn all the names in time, and try to remember them."

"There arc strange tidings from Warsaw," replied Balgonie, who began to get bewildered and knew not on what to converse, if the most simple topics of the day were forbidden; " a battle has been fought at Slonim, between Prince Radzivil and the Russians, who defeated him after a five hours' engagement, and the Princess Radzivil, who is newly married and remarkably beautiful, fought on horseback among the Polish troops."

" Ah, Demetrius fought on horseback too," said the Prince, as if speaking to himself, and a gesture of undisguised impatience escaped the chaplain ; "pray tell me something morc, for no one ever speaks of such things to me."

" A new theatre has been opened at St. Petersburg," replied Balgonic (who thought to himself, " the devil is in it, if I cannot speak of *that !* "), " and there was represented an opera, entitled *Charles the Great.*"

"Ah, I don't quite understand all that ; say it again."

Indeed, Balgonie might as well have spokcn of carbonic gas or the Atlantic cable, had he ever heard of such things; for the mind of the young Prince could not comprehend the most simple matters of every day-life. This was merely the result of his entire seclusion; but the adherents of the Empress, her favourites and lovers, industriously circulated through Russia the report that he was in a state of idiotcy.

" And this place that you spoke of ?" he resumed enquiringly.

" The theatre ? "

" Yes, Hospodeen; who lives in it ? "

" One of the actresses performed a magnificent cantata, in honour of the Empress."

" Ah ! 'tis she, I understand, who keeps me here," said the Prince, with a sad smile; and now in real terror, and quite repenting the introduction he had brought about, Father Chrysostom rose to hurry Balgonie away.

As they were retiring, the Prince said :—

" Hospodeen, you have dropped something."

It was the locket with Natalie's hair.

" What is in this ? " asked Ivan, with childlike interest.

" A lock of hair, your Highness."

" How odd ! and you wear it, just as I wear my cross ? "

" It is the gift, the souvenir of a lady I love, and who loves me: a countrywoman of your own."

" A woman ? " said Ivan, ponderingly.

" Yes, Excellency."

" I have never looked upon a woman's face,

and know not what it is like, though the Empress
(whom God long preserve!) visited me when a
child, as I have been told. I have heard that
they are not bearded like men. I shall never see
one, it is forbidden; yet—yet—as I often tell
Father Chrysostom, I have dreams by day—
dreams of something else than wild swans and
bearded Cossacks—of something to cling to, some
one to love and be loved by. It must be this kind
of love you speak of—oh yes, it must!" said Ivan,
as he gazed with stupid, but reverent wonder at
the lock of hair, ere he returned it to Balgonie.

"Poor young Prince!" exclaimed the latter, as
the chaplain hurried him away, and the portcullis
clanged behind them in its grooves of stone.

The priest now urged upon Balgonie, that if his
visits were to be continued, the affairs of the outer
world must in no way be referred to, or the result
might be most disastrous for all concerned.

"The seclusion in which the prisoner is kept,
has, I fear, impaired his understanding," said
Balgonie.

"Hah! do you think so?" grunted Colonel
Bernikoff, who overheard the remark, as they
issued from the tower of Ivan. "You must know,
that your genuine Russian is like a tiger, as some
writer has it—a tiger who licks the hand of his
keeper, so long as he is chained; but who tears
him asunder when loose. The Empress quite
understands this!"

"How is it that you intrust me so freely to

visit your prisoner?" asked Charlie, who began to fear that Bernikoff might be laying some snare for him, by according this hitherto unwonted permission.

" Do you really wish to know?"

" Yes, Colonel—why I in particular—I only?"

" Because you are the safest man in Russia to have this liberty."

" How?"

" As a soldier of fortune,—a stranger among us,—you can have no sympathy with anything but the strict and steady execution of your duty ; and the line of that," added Bernikoff, darting a keen glance at the Scot, " as with us all, lies in fidelity to the Empress."

" True," replied Balgonie, with something of sadness in his tone, and very little of enthusiasm.

" Thus, were I to order you to blow Ivan Antonovitch from the mouth of a cannon, I should expect you to obey ! "

" I trust that no such test of my obedience will ever be necessary," replied Balgonie, with a hauteur which Bernikoff was somewhat unused to see among his subordinates.

" We shall have some other and more troublesome prisoners in Schlusselburg ere long," said the Governor, with knitted brows.

" Whom do you mean?"

" Old Count Mierowitz and his family. Warrants have been issued by the Chancellor to arrest them all."

"All!" said Balgonie, in a faint voice.

"Yes, women as well as men : an escort of the Regiment of Smolensko arrived at St. Petersburg yesterday with the Count and the Hospoza Mariolizza. His daughter, who seems to be deeply involved in some plot, has for the time effected her escape. But they will soon be all before the Secret Chancery, and then the knout and the wheel will be at work with a vengeance!"

The reader may judge how these and similar remarks affected poor Charlie, while the Governor, as if pleased that he could thus inflict pain, walked away with a malicious smile on his sombre visage, cramming tobacco into the bowl of his pipe.

There were times, however, when the captive Prince, after his acquaintance with Balgonie, was a little less resigned, and had strange longings to see something of the great world that lay beyond his prison walls, and the waves that lashed them ; to see other faces than those of the fierce and bearded Tchernemoski and Volga Cossacks who guarded him ; a longing even to do something great and daring, to be remembered in after years with love and reverence ; to be remembered, as he said, "in tradition, like Demetrius." Then, feeling all the utter hopelessness of such new aspirations, he would strive to be contented, to repeat with fresh energy the daily prayers set for him by Father Chrysostom, and to be grateful for life, lest he should die even as Demetrius died.

"Who is this Demetrius, of whom he constantly speaks, and whose fate he fears so much may be his own?" asked Balgonie one day.

"It is an old, but a strange and terrible story," replied the chaplain. "When Ivan Basilovitch died about the end of the sixteenth century, his widow was banished to Northern Russia by the new Czar Feodor, whose Prime Minister urged that he could never reign in peace or security unless he imitated the Turks by sacrificing all who were nearly allied to the throne; so he exiled his mother, as I have said, and ordered an officer to assassinate his younger brother Demetrius.

"The officer, being a humane man, was filled with horror on receiving an order so barbarous; but fearing alike to disobey, or to leave the terrible task to be fulfilled by one less scrupulous, he took the child with him to a remote district, travelling many days' journey from Moscow. Then he wrote some words indelibly on the skin of the little Prince, tied a cross of brilliants about his neck, laid him at the door of a peasant's hut, and galloped away.

"To the tyrant Feodor he gave a circumstantial detail of how and where he had killed the infant Prince, and sought the promised reward.

"'Receive it *thus!*' replied Feodor, who plunged a sword into his heart, the further to suppress all proof of guilt.

"The young tyrant died of a poison administered by his Chancellor, and others inherited his crown; but all to perish miserably in succession. And no less than four pretenders all appeared, each calling himself Demetrius, to contest for the throne; and all the land was deluged with blood.

"Some twenty years after the alleged death of the brother of Ivan, a young Cossack of the Volga was bathing in that river with some of his companions, who saw with surprise that he had chained round his neck a cross of brilliants, and that certain words in the old Muscovite character were pricked upon his back. They were examined by a neighbouring priest and found to be—

' This is Demetrius, son of the Czar.'

"Then all exclaimed that the true Demetrius had been found at last, and that a miracle from Heaven had saved him. His life was soon in peril, so he fled to Holstein, the Duke of which, after keeping him long in prison, sold him to the Emperor Michael, by whom he was savagely quartered alive. And it is the fate of this hapless heir of Russia, whose story he thinks in some points resembles his own (although he really knows but little of his own annals), that haunts the unfortunate Ivan in his gloomiest hours."

CHAPTER XVI.

THE TRATKIR.

WITH evident suspicion and mistrust, Bernikoff viewed the growing intimacy between his prisoner Ivan and the Scottish Captain; and though he neither recommended that it should cease or interdicted it, as he might and perhaps ought to have done, he made many mental notes thereof.

Though Balgonie sympathised with Ivan to the fullest extent, he knew too well the danger of doing more; and he felt that he had his own share of secret sorrow and anxiety, and might yet have greater to endure. The girl he loved with all the strength of a first and romantic passion was already a political fugitive; her father and cousin were prisoners, and perhaps in chains; her brother and his kinsman, Usakoff, already viewed as criminals; and with the terrors of despotism hanging over them all.

Natalie a fugitive—and where? In the wild forests, perhaps, where wolves and outlaws lurked: what perils and privations might she not be suffering! Natalie so delicate, so pure, so gently nurtured, and so highly bred.

Balgonie was aware, also, that intimacy with

the family of Count Mierowitz, and the deep interest he had in their fate, was fraught with personal peril to himself in such a land of tyranny as
Russia.   Full of such thoughts as these one fore-
noon, he was leaning on a cannon in one of those
deep embrasures of the fortress which faced the
drawbridge communicating with the land.   The
guard was in the act of lowering the bridge to
permit a man to pass out.   This person was just
parting from Bernikoff, with whom he had been
for some time in close and earnest conversation,
and from whom he was evidently receiving money
—an unusual circumstance, as that distinguished
field-officer generally lavished more kicks and
cuffs than thanks or kopecs.

On beholding this man, as he bowed humbly,
cap in hand, cross the bridge and disappear
among the houses of the town beyond, Balgonie
experienced a species of nervous shock.   He could
not doubt that this fellow, so gigantic in stature
and powerful in muscular development, in the
coarse caftan and leathern girdle, with the long
lock of grizzled hair dangling behind his right
ear, was Nicholas Paulovitch, the murderer of
Podatchkine, the gipsy woodman, and the swind-
ling mendicant of the barrier at the Neva.

"This man here in Schlusselburg," thought
Balgonie, with indignation and alarm; "here in
earnest conversation with Bernikoff!   The spirit
of mischief seems to pervade the air again!"

A few minutes afterwards the Cossack Jagouski

who, as related, had been so severely knouted by
Bernikoff for pilfering a pipeful of tobacco, came
forward with tottering steps, and looking painfully thin and feeble from recent suffering; and
with the crouching bearing of the Muscovite towards a superior, said that his Excellency the
Governor wished to speak with him in his quarters, whither Balgonie at once repaired, after
having, as military etiquette required, buckled on
his sword.

" Carl Ivanovitch," said Bernikoff, who certainly had rather a perturbed air, "some suspicious characters are in our vicinity, and have
actually been hovering in boats about the fortress.
What think you of that?"

" Suspicious characters, Excellency—how?"

" In a Tratkir of the town, one dropped this
coin—a silver rouble of the prisoner Ivan—Ivan
the Unknown Person. To possess one, unless as
I do *this*, for proof of treason, is to court death
or Siberia."

" And from whom had you this?"

" A spy," replied the Colonel curtly.

"The man who has just left you?"

" The same."

" Nicholas Paulovitch," continued Balgonie,
with increasing astonishment at the other's coolness; " the assassin of the Corporal—the wretch
of whom I told you when I first arrived here!"

" All that may, or may not be," replied
Bernikoff, with a stern air, almost amounting to

rudeness : "when I require this devil of a fellow no more, you may impale him, if you please ; but molest him not at present."

"I do not see, Excellency, that all this in any way concerns me," said Balgonie haughtily, as he lifted his hat, and put his sabre under his arm, as if about to retire.

"It does concern you thus far. I shall anticipate any attempt that be made by those lurkers, whoever they may be. You must remember," he added, lowering his voice, "the tenor of the dispatch you brought me ? "

"Perfectly," replied Charlie, in a somewhat faint voice, as he knew not how terrible or repugnant might be the duty assigned him by this military despot.

"Well, you shall pass forth into the town to-night, with a patrol of twenty men, armed with sabres and carbines. Surround and search the Tratkir in the main street, and compel all therein, who seem suspicious, to produce their papers ; and if they are without such, bring them to *me*, and I shall question them in a fashion of my own."

By the laws of Russia, at that time, persons could not travel from St. Petersburg, or even from place to place, without a passport, describing their occupation, appearance, and route, which they were not at liberty to alter ; and in the rural districts, travellers required a pass from the lord whose estate they may have been upon, before they were at liberty to quit it. Without such a

document, no one would dare to furnish them with
food or shelter, nor could a postmaster give them
horses, however high their rank, or great their
offer of reward. Such complete subjection had
accepted despotism reduced the the ....

" And I am to take twenty men with me ? " said
Balgonie, after an unpleasant pause.

" Yes! the bridge will be lowered for you after
sunset. Whoever these lurkers are, they have
been seen and overheard ; and this coin is proof
sufficient to warrant the transportation of a whole
province. Be they who they may, by every dome
in sacred Mother Moscow, they shall find *me* ready
for them ! "

And Bernikoff grimly touched his small dagger,
a species of weapon which a Russian officer is
seldom or never without, even in the present day;
and when Charlie Balgonie remembered how that
same dagger had been thrust into the throat of
the half-strangled Peter III., a flush of indignant
hate and aversion crossed his honest face. To him
it was evident that the spirit of mischief or male-
volence made Bernikoff select him, as one whom
he suspected of a friendly interest in the family
of Count Mierowitz, for this unpleasant duty,
instead of Captain Vlasfief, the Lieutenant of
Schlusselburg, or any other officer, who must have
been better acquainted with the adjacent town
and all its places of entertainment, than he, a
total stranger, could ever be.

THE SECRET DISPATCH.

But he was a soldier; he had no resource but to obey in silence; and an angry sigh escaped him, as he stuck his loaded pistols in his girdle, when the sun sank behind the wooden town, and the even painted roofs of from the ramparts across the Lake of Ilm. boomed

Defiling in the twilight through the streets of Schlusselburg, he marched straight to where he knew that the principal Tratkir, or tea-house, was situated; and while his heart sank within him in fear of *whom* he might arrest,—perhaps Natalie herself,—he at once surrounded the building, to prevent all egress, and to the evident alarm and perturbation of all who were within.

These tea-houses are no longer to be found in the capital of Russia now, for there all the *restaurants* are constituted and arranged upon the French and German models; but they still exist in Moscow and elsewhere; and under their roofs, the genuine Muscovite consumes what would seem a fabulous amount of the Chinese plant. They are chiefly the resort of soldiers, porters, and droski drivers, all of whom must behave in a polite and orderly manner while there. All must enter the great room where the tea is served, cap in hand, alike out of respect for the company, and to the holy pictures, Souzdal daubs of SS. Sergius, Alexander Newski, and so forth, which decorate the walls; and all must salute the bar-keeper, after first saluting the Holy Image, which is to be found in every Russian apartment, and before which, a lamp of train oil is frequently burning.

When the crooked sabres of the dismounted Cossacks were seen flashing in the porch, and when Balgonie entered with his sword drawn, passing along the narrow way between the numerous tables, at which the groups were seated, amid an oppressive odour of strong tea, coarse tobacco, and Russian leather from boots, caps, and girdles ; many a peasant in his canvas caftan, and many a stout moujik in his fur shoubah, felt his heart quail with apprehension, he knew not of what ; and every saucer—the tea is not drunk from cups—was set down untasted, while one or two men nearly choked themselves with their lumps of sugar ; for usually it is not put into the tea, but is retained in the mouth of the drinker, so that, in a spirit of economy, the poor Muscovite may indulge in two, perhaps three cups of his favourite beverage, and use thereto but one piece of sugar.

For his intrusion Balgonie apologised ; this, though a very unusual proceeding in a country so despotic, failed to reassure the tea drinkers, who were all hushed in silence and expectation; and a girl who had been singing for their amusement, crouched down in a corner for concealment.

Balgonie counted the number of persons in the Tratkir, and noted the exact hour by his watch ; he then proceeded, with a heart full of anxiety and dread, to examine each person in succession, in reality looking for those he had no wish to find.

All who possessed the requisite papers, showed them; others proved, all in succession, to be soldiers in uniform, moujiks, and droski drivers, with their brass badges, sailors, and serfs; thus, after a time, a load seemed to be lifted from the mind of the young officer. As he turned to leave the apartment without a prisoner, the Cossack Jagouski rather roughly dragged the singing girl from the nook where she had sought concealment, and then Balgonie recognised the fine dark face, the black eyes, and the large glittering ear-rings of Olga Paulowna, the gipsy girl whom he had befriended at Louga—she who saved him from a terrible fate in the forest.

" Let the girl go free, Jagouski," said Balgonie; " I shall answer for her if required."

Olga drew a paper from her bosom and showed that it was her passport from the Commandant of Krejko, permitting her to travel to and from Schlusselburg.

Jagouski saluted and withdrew a few paces; and now, as if the cloud of doubt and dread Balgonie's arrival had cast over all was dispersed, again the noisy hum of voices pervaded the long room of the tea-house, and laughter even broke forth at intervals.

" Olga," said Balgonie, " you here—so far from home ?"

" Yes, Hospodeen, for my home is anywhere,

or wherever night finds me ; but I have news for you."

" News—and for me ?"

" Yes," said she, sinking her voice to a whisper; " I have news of Natalie Mierowna——"

" Hush, for heaven's sake, girl!—hush !" said Balgonie with a nervous start.

" She is here——"

" Here in this house ?"

" No, Hospodeen."

" Where then ?—oh, speak quickly !"

" In the neighbourhood of Schlusselburg."

Charlie felt his heart die within him at this intelligence, for such a vicinity was full of peril.

" Be to-morrow at noon on the road that leads to Tosna, and you shall learn more; but do you know it, Hospodeen ?"

" I shall soon discover it—and the place ?"

" The skirts of the wood four versts from this."

" Good—till then, adieu ; and God be with you."

Balgonie retired all unaware or heedless that his Cossacks were secretly jesting at his whispering with the pretty gipsy; and through the dark streets he marched them towards the great and sombre masses of the fort which loomed between him and the star-lighted sky, his heart the while being literally sick with alarm and dismay, in the conviction that the long-dreaded crisis was coming —that Natalie was near, and the place of her concealment was known to a vagrant gipsy girl, the sister of Nicholas Paulovitch, who, if he knew it not already, might wrest the secret from her with the point of his knife, for the information of him whose spy he was—the hateful Bernikoff!

Ruin and sorrow were close at hand, indeed.

On receiving the official but verbal report of Balgonie, and learning that the visit to the identical tea-house where the dangerous rouble was found had proved abortive, and that there was no one to be knouted or hanged in the morning, Colonel Bernikoff became transported with rage, and lifted his cane somewhat threateningly. On this, Balgonie's hand was instantly laid on the hilt of his sword.

"Beware, Excellency," said he firmly : "a blow to an equal is a foul insult; to an inferior it is mean tyranny; and, in either instance, blood alone should wash it out."

On this the Colonel's rage assumed a new phase; he trod on his cocked hat, and ordered the wax candles which he had always burning before the image of his patron, St. Sergius, to be extinguished. He loaded the effigy with the bitterest reproaches, and for that night left the poor saint in total darkness, despite the intercession of Father Chrysostom.

CHAPTER XVII.

THE WOOD OF THE HONEY TREE.

THE noon of the following day saw Charlie Balgonie—after an anxious and almost sleepless night—proceeding on foot along the road that leads southward to Tosna, a little town which stands on a stream of the same name, a tributary of the Neva, but some thirty versts distant from Schlusselburg.

His military ardour was already fading, so far as the Russian service was concerned, amid his pressing anxiety for the dangers that menaced Natalie ; and he felt himself only a species of serf in an imperial uniform. Unlike the Admirals Douglas, Mackenzie, Count Balmaine, and hundreds of other Scotsmen who served the Empress by sea and land, he had thoughtlessly omitted to stipulate, as they had more warily done, that he was to be at perfect liberty, as a British subject, to return to his native land whenever he felt disposed to do so. The poor friendless boy—the kidnapped palatine, who had been rescued from the burning wreck of the *Piscatona*, while floating adrift in the North Sea—could know little how necessary such stipulations were when he joined

the Regiment of Smolensko as a cadet; and now
he felt himself literally a military slave of the
ambitious and lascivious Catharine II.

Before him rose the tall fir trees of the forest
where he was to meet Olga—the Wood of the
Honey Tree, as it was named from an episode (related by Demetrius, the ambassador, in his History of Muscovy) which occurred to a serf of Bernikoff's, Alexis Jagouski, father of the same man
whom he slew so wickedly and ungratefully in the
flight from Zorndorf; and the whole anecdote reads
so very like one of the adventures of Baron Mun-
chausen, or Sir Jonah Barrington's " bounces,"
that we may be pardoned translating it here.

" This man," says Demetrius, " when seeking
honey, got into a hollow tree, where the bees had
concealed such a quantity thereof, that it sucked
him up to the breast, and being unable to extri-
cate himself, he subsisted for two day upon honey
alone, and finding that his shouts were answered
only by the echoes of the vast forest, he began to
despair of being freed from his sweet captivity.
At last, to his terror, there came a large brown
bear from the Neva, to eat of the honey which the
old tree contained, and of which these animals are
greedily fond.   As the bear was descending with
hinder part foremost, the poor serf caught hold of
his loins.   This sudden grasp among his fur so
terrified the bear, that he started and fled, and in
doing so, drew the peasant from that sweet prison,
which otherwise had proved his grave: hence

was the forest named, the Wood of the Honey Tree."

There, as Balgonie approached, all was still save the voice of the valdchnep, or woodcock, and the hum of insects ; he lingered for a few minutes on the outskirts, just where the highway to Tosna dipped down into a deep and gloomy dingle of intertwisted branches, which formed a species of leafy tunnel overhead.

Three miles distant to the northward, he could see the place he had left, the gloomy Castle of Schlusselburg, moated round by the Neva and Lake of Ladoga, jutting into the latter on its rock, its towers wearing a sombre brown tint even in the noonday sunshine, as if no light could brighten them ; and the white flag of Russia was fluttering on the summit of the keep, where Ivan was pining away the years of youth in silence and seclusion.

Balgonie heard a voice waking the echoes of the dingle ; three notes were struck on a tambourine, as a signal to him, and Olga approached singing a verse of that prophetic song, which is so soothing to Russian military and religious vanity :—

> " But when the hundredth year
>   Shall three times doubled be ;
> Then shall the end appear
>   Of all our slavery.
> Then shall the warlike powers
>   From distant climes return,
> Egypt again be ours,
>   While the Turkish domes shall burn !"

" I have kept my appointment, Olga,"

M

"And I mine," she replied gaily, while tripping towards him in a playful manner; "now follow me, Hospodeen, and I shall take you to those who will be right glad to see you."

"First let us be sure that we are unwatched."

"Right," said she; and stooping in her earnestness, her keen, dark, and glittering eyes swept the whole landscape that lay between the wood and Schlusselburg, and glanced keenly beyond the stems of the trees into the dingles and vistas; but, save the birds on the branches and the gnats revolving in the sunshine, no living thing was visible.

"Follow me, Hospodeen," said the gipsy; "we have not far to go."

They descended into the dark dingle, or hollow, and then quitted the highway; Olga gathering up her skirts that she might tread with greater facility among the thick gorse and long rank grass, displaying, as she did so, two very handsome and taper ankles cased in scarlet stockings with elaborate clocks of yellow braid.

She explained to Balgonie that, as there was no path to guide them, her chief clues were a set of notches, cut to all appearance carelessly, as if with a woodman's axe, on the bark of the great pine trees.

"These marks seem fresh, and recently cut—who made them?" asked Balgonie.

"The Hospodeen, Basil Mierowitz," she whispered.

"Poor Basil!" responded Charlie, in a low tone.

After toiling through the dense forest for more than half an hour, pausing ever and anon to listen and watch whether they were observed, they arrived at the foot of a grey granite cliff, the face of which was screened, or nearly covered, by masses of depending ivy, creepers, and green lichens, forming a background which, at a little distance, blended with the greenery of the woods.

"We have arrived," said she, turning, with a flush on her dark face which made it radiantly beautiful. She struck three strokes on her tambourine, and shook its bells.

Charlie thought of her kinsman, Nicholas Paulovitch, and instinctively grasped one of the pistols at his girdle, on seeing the dark and bearded face of a man appear among the ivy leaves some twenty feet above him. A rope ladder was lowered, and whatever doubts or misgivings were in his mind, he felt himself constrained now to go through the adventure to its end.

He clambered up, and on the great screen of ivy being lifted aside, found himself face to face with his old friend Basil Mierowitz, the subaltern of his company, who, grasping both his hands with kindly warmth of manner, led him into a cavern or grotto, one of a series of many, into which the granite rocks had there been hollowed by some long past convulsion of nature.

Another hand was instantly laid on his,—a smaller and softer one,—and two beautiful dark eyes were bending tenderly on his face.

"Natalie!" he exclaimed, in a tremulous voice, and would have pressed her to his breast, but for the presence of Basil and several other men.

Amid the twilight of the cavern, he could perceive its rough natural walls and arch, with hazy but sunny rays that streamed faintly in the background, athwart the obscurity, as if the vault communicated with other galleries in the rock, through which the upper light of day stole in by the crannies and chasms. He was also enabled to see, that with Natalie, her brother Basil, and her cousin Usakoff, who had been a Lieutenant of the Valikolutz Grenadiers, there were about twenty men in the place, all clad in sheepskin shoubahs, canvas doublets, or the caftan, the invariable dress of the Russian peasant, and nearly all had red serge breeches, rough boots, and girdles of rope or untanned leather.

Though attired like woodmen or labouring serfs, all these men had unmistakably the bearing of well-trained soldiers: all were strong, active, and resolute in aspect; and Balgonie had no doubt that they were those natives of the Ukraine, the deserters from the Livonian frontier, of whom Bernikoff had spoken; for against the walls of the cavern were ranged a number of muskets and bayonets, with sets of accoutrements, sabres, and pistols. There, too, stood a regimental drum, decorated with the imperial arms, and the forbidden name of the Emperor *Ivan* !

Every moment seemed to increase the perils that surrounded the luckless Balgonie, for now he was in the very den of the conspirators.

All carried in their girdles a dagger or knife and double brace of pistols. They seemed to be chiefly soldiers of the Regiment of Valikolutz : and his sudden appearance among them, in the full uniform of the Smolensko Infantry, evidently excited, if it did not alarm them ; for discipline becomes so completely a habit—a second nature ; and, as if the presence of an epaulette rendered them uneasy, they all withdrew into the back or more obscure portion of the cavern, leaving him and their two leaders together.

" Oh ! Basil—Usakoff—my friends, if indeed I may yet dare to call you so, and live," said Balgonie, in a voice that was broken by emotion, "for what rash and dreadful purpose do I find you and these unfortunate fellows here ? "

" You, and all Russia too, shall learn ere long," replied Mierowitz calmly and sternly, yet with a grave and noble air, with which his coarse canvas caftan assorted oddly.

" And poor Natalie ! " exclaimed Balgonie, in a tone of grief and reproach ; " have you no pity for her ? "

" Until Natalie informed me, I knew not, my friend, Carl Ivanovitch, that *you* were the bearer of that secret dispatch, which might have cost you limb or life, when it was too late to arrest those I had set upon your track."

"Well, certainly, I was not much indebted to the good offices of your rogue, Podatchkine."

"The Corporal's orders were simply to abstract the document, and bring it to me; not to slay its bearer, unless such a catastrophe became unavoidable."

"He fell into his own snare—a dark and deadly one."

"Happily you escaped it; and I have saved two hundred silver roubles, for the service of the Emperor."

"Who do you mean?" asked Balgonie, in a whisper.

"Ivan—the Prisoner of Schlusselburg!" exclaimed Usakoff, with enthusiasm.

"Alas!" added Balgonie, "you court but your own destruction."

"Think not so; but join us, and share our perils and our glory," replied the other.

"I am bound by allegiance to the Empress."

"You are but a tool in her hands, Carl Balgonie."

"Perhaps so; but one with a devilish sharp edge, I hope," replied Balgonie, who felt only genuine sorrow; and a silence of nearly a minute ensued.

The manner and voice of Basil Mierowitz were singularly soft and winning, yet he was bold and resolute; and though a young man, he had all the free and easy bearing of a courtly soldier, blended with something of the calm severity of a priest—a manner that was very impressive.

The Polish and Cossack blood that mingled in the veins of Apollo Usakoff gave a freer and bolder, perhaps a wilder, bearing and style of language; his nose was aquiline, and expressed fierceness of disposition; yet his features otherwise were essentially delicate and noble, and his eyes were strangely beautiful in colour and variety of expression. They were dark grey, encircled by a ring of light, clear brown; and when he spoke, or became excited, the iris contracted and expanded, as the blood flowed and ebbed in his fiery and enthusiastic heart, for he was a grandson of the Hetman Mazeppa—that Pole, whose story is so well known, and who, after being bound naked on a wild and maddened horse, to punish him for having an intrigue with a noble lady of his own country, was carried by his steed through woods and wastes, and herds of wolves and bears, into the heart of the Ukraine, where he lived to become the prince and leader of those wild Cossacks who dwell upon the banks of the Dnieper.

Sleeping in a cavern, among rough soldiers, on a bed of dried leaves and moss, had not improved either the costume or the appearance of Natalie Mierowna. With pain and sorrow,—almost with agony,—Charlie Balgonie could perceive how her once rich dress of yellow silk, with its trimmings of narrow ermine, was faded and soiled—even tattered and worn; her laces and her soft hair alike dishevelled and uncared for; and that already had a hunted and haggard expression been imparted to her beautiful eyes, and soft, pale, delicate face. Anger and pride alone remained; but both were for a time subdued by the sudden presence of Balgonie, and the love she was compelled to repress outwardly, at least, when before so many eyes.

Katinka, the sturdy Polish attendant, who loved Natalie dearly, alone seemed unimpaired by the hardships of a forest life.

"Concerning the secret dispatch of the woman, Catharine Christianowna, to the Governor of Schlusselburg," said Usakoff, resuming the subject of conversation, "you, Carl, are perhaps aware of its contents?"

"Yes," replied Balgonie, and then paused.

"Say on, my friend," said Usakoff; "we can hear anything now."

"They were to the effect, that a scheme had been formed to free the Unknown Person in Schlusselburg, and that he was not to be permitted to fall *alive into the hands of any one who came to seek him.*"

"Savage orders, which there can be no mistaking."

"Orders which Bernikoff is quite capable of fulfilling," added Mierowitz in a sad and stern voice, while their listening followers burst into low and whispered, but fierce imprecations against the Empress.

"Bernikoff is a man without one human sympathy," said Basil.

"And no marvel is it?" exclaimed Usakoff, while the strange light already described gleamed in his dark grey eyes; "his mother, like a true Tartar woman, is said to have anointed her breasts daily with blood, as she suckled him, even as Dion tells us the mother of Caligula did, that her child might, in manhood, be merciless."

Vlasfief they stigmatised as "the son of a goat," being originally a boy of the great foundling Hospital at Moscow, where, when the increase of children became so great that nurses could not be found, the lacteal food of animals was introduced, and a herd of goats adopted as wet-nurses for the establishment.

"Carl," said Basil, taking the hand of Balgonie, "Natalie has told me all."

"All!"

"Yes—all that passed in Louga. Dear Natalie has never had a secret from me."

"And you forgive me?" said Balgonie earnestly.

"I do—but on this condition."

"Oh name it, Basil!"

"That if you do not join us, you will, at least, not actively oppose our scheme."

"I scarcely know what it is."

"Know this then," replied the other emphatically, yet softly, "that on its success depends the success of your love; for if it fails, then all our lives are lost!"

" You say that you love my cousin Natalie ?"
said young Usakoff, in a somewhat loftier tone.

" With all my heart—with all my soul, I do !"
replied Balgonie, pressing a hand of Natalie
between his own.

" Yet, Carl, if you valued generosity and loved
pity—if you loved glory and honour, as a soldier
should, you would risk the loss even of *her*,—yea,
give her up, if necessary,—and join us !"

" What would either life or glory be after such
a sacrifice ? Ah, my friend, you never loved
as I do !" replied Charlie, with some irritation of
manner.

" Perhaps; but I have always thought how
grandly terrible a figure was made by Mohammed
the Great, when, on a stage, before his discontented army, he struck off the head of a favourite
Sultana to convince his soldiers that he preferred
glory to love."

" Cousin, cousin," said Natalie, who felt all
the peril and delicacy of her lover's position,
" you talk thus to-day, when last night you shed
tears—yes, bitter tears for the loss of your sister.
We were all taken prisoners together, Carl—
my poor father, Mariolizza, and I. Bound with
cords,—see, the marks are on me still," she
added, showing her white wrists, while her dark
eyes filled with a dusky fire,—" we were conveyed in a covered kabitka towards St. Petersburg, on the way to which it broke down, in a
wood near Paulovsk, not far from the outer walls

of the imperial gardens. There, in the confusion, I was enabled to escape, by the aid of the gipsy girl Olga, who, hoping some such chance might occur, had followed us afoot from Louga; and through her further knowledge and assistance, I was enabled to join my brother Basil here."

"My dear old father—and my soft and tender Mariolizza—a blow must be rapidly struck, if we would save them from greater horrors than those they now endure!" exclaimed Basil: "the die has been cast now; and if I cannot save them and our legitimate Emperor, we can at least all perish together."

"Dangers menace you closely; the roads around the fortress are patrolled, and gun-boats watch the shores of the lake. A coin of Ivan found in a tea-house——"

"Malediction—yes! 'twas I, Carl, who dropped it there," exclaimed Basil: "well, and this coin?"

"Has roused all the suspicions of Bernikoff; and he knows that you and your cousin have deserted from your posts in Livonia."

"Already, does he know of this?"

"Yes, with many other details."

"Then," replied Basil Mierowitz, with growing sternness, "we have not an hour to lose. Who informed him?"

"Lieutenant-General Weymarn, by a special messenger, while I was loitering at Louga."

"So, so! By our Lady of Kazan, we must be

prompt in action. I have cruised thrice round
Schlusselburg disguised as a fisherman, and know
well all the approaches."

"Basil, Usakoff, I implore you by all you hold
dear on earth and sacred in Heaven to pause while
there is yet time—to abandon your wild scheme,
and make your peace, if possible, with the Empress."

"You were right to add 'if possible,' my
friend," replied the other calmly but bitterly.
"Already compromised by desertion, my father
and betrothed wife chained in a fortress by the
Neva, what terms would Catharine offer us?
Carl Ivanovitch," he added, with a lofty smile,
"I do not press you to join us, or seek to
lure you into the dangers of an enterprise the
enthusiasm of which you cannot share. I do not
seek even to turn your presence as a trusted staff
officer in Schlusselburg to account, though it
might further our objects, and be the means, perhaps, by strategy, of saving many a valuable life.
Still less do I desire to turn to account your intimacy with the young Emperor Ivan, though I
envy you that great privilege. Even in the love
I bear my sister (though it might tempt you to
cast your lot with us—*with her* shall I say?), I
leave you unquestioned and free."

"I thank you, Basil," said Balgonie sadly, and
with a heightened colour, caused by irrepressible
annoyance at the last remark of Mierowitz.

"But we have all sworn before the altar of our

Lady of Kazan, and the image of St. Sergius, to devote our lives to the matter in hand; so retreat is impossible—advice and entreaty alike unavailing."

Balgonie felt an acute pang on hearing this; for he knew that in Russia no place was esteemed as more holy than the church of our Lady of Kazan in St. Petersburg. Around its shrine—the *sanctum sanctorum* of which no woman has ever entered—are the keys of conquered cities, the banners of a thousand slaughtered armies, and the bâtons and sabres of their leaders, the Frenchman, the Turk, the Pole, the Persian, and the Dane, the Swede and the German; and he knew, too, that no image, to the Muscovite mind, is more sacred than that of St. Sergius—the same absurd idol which the Kazan column bore with them at the battle of the Alma, and displayed in vain to the advancing bayonets of old Sir Colin's Highland Brigade.

"The blow once struck," resumed Basil, "we shall be joined by the Cossacks of the Ukraine and the Don, among whom we have many impatient adherents, and by all who hold of the Houses of Brunswick-Wolfenbuttel, of Holstein Gottorp, and of all who *hate* Anhalt Zerbst; all Russia will soon follow, from the shores of the Black Sea to those of the White—from Revel to the Ural Mountains. We have not forgotten the reign of Elizabeth: how many noses were slit, how many foreheads were branded, how many ears cropped,

and tongues shortened, and how many eyes were
darkened for ever during that time of tyranny;
how many backs flayed by the knout; how many
nobles banished to Siberia, or drowned in prison
vaults by the swollen waters of the Neva.   Pure
nationality is dying now; but we must revive
Russia—not as it is ruled by a lascivious woman
and her jealous lovers, but Holy Russia of Peter
the Great—strong, invincible, and the terror
alike of the Eastern and Western world.   Let us
save our country from those who oppress it, and
replace upon its throne the Grand Duke, the Czar
—the Emperor Ivan; for the right given by God
and by inheritance can never be destroyed!"

A murmur of applause from his followers
succeeded this outburst (which we can render
but feebly in English), and they clashed their
weapons in approval, while, fired by her
brother's energy, Natalie sung a verse of a
well known Russian song :—

> " Now, as of old, the sabre's ready,
>   And its might they'll feel afar,
> When but three short words are utter'd,
>   *God*, our *Country*, and the *Czar !* "

" Without cannon, you cannot mean to assault
a place so strong as Schlusselburg, fortified as it
has been by all the skill of Todleben ?" said Balgonie, after a pause.

" Ask me not what we mean to do, Carl: for
your own sake, my dear friend, the less you know
of us, and of our plans, the better.   We shall

come upon you all when you least expect us, and in that hour take no heed of what you see or hear. Mix yourself up with it as little as you can: if we fail, we perish in our failure; if we triumph, and Ivan is replaced upon his throne, be assured that Basil Mierowitz will not forget the lover of his sister—the comrade of many a brave and happy day with the Regiment of Smolensko. Now adieu —and come hither no more, lest your steps be watched."

Balgonie pressed the hands of his two friends, whom he viewed as fated and foredoomed men; he kissed Natalie with a tenderness that was alike sorrowful and despairing, for he trembled in his heart lest he should never see her more; and, in another moment or so, like one in a bewildering dream, he had descended the rope ladder, and was traversing the forest—the Wood of the Honey Tree—forgetful or oblivious of whether he was watched or not.

He foresaw but woe and ruin now; and proceeded slowly back to Schlusselburg, with his mind a prey to doubt, anxiety, and dread of what might be the sequel to the impending catastrophe. He felt assured of one thing only—that a deed, bold, reckless, and desperate, would be the result of his friend's desertion from Livonia, their political rancour, and personal desire for vengeance on the Empress and her favourites.

In that deed, and its too probable failure, he foresaw the destruction of his love; and he felt

bitterly that rather than have known and lost
Natalie, it would have been better had fate
drowned him when the Palatine ship was burned,
or shot him when warring in Silesia!

CHAPTER XVIII.

DOUBT AND DREAD.

NEARLY all the events which followed the secret visit of Balgonie to the conspirators will be found in the more recent histories of Russia, and in the manifestoes published by the Empress Catharine at the time—especially her *oukaz* subsequent to the revolt of Basil Mierowitz.

On returning to Schlusselburg, Balgonie found the Governor, Colonel Bernikoff, in a very bad humour indeed. The Grand Chancellor had recently sent him a prisoner, with a note to the effect that he wrote verses, and was otherwise a dangerous fellow—to keep him for a week or two, and then get rid of him. He had thrice sent to the Chancellor, to learn under what name the man was to be *buried*, for the fellow was dead now —so much had the damp atmosphere of the lower vaults disagreed with his poetical temperament; but no answer had been returned, which was very annoying. So Bernikoff, whose patience was never very extensive, was furious; but he strove to soothe his ruffled feelings by several enormous pinches of the sharp snuff of Beresovski, from the box which—as we have before hinted—had been

N

found in the fob of the late Peter III. ; and by
batooning, or beating with his cane, the Cossack
Jagouski, whom he had suddenly detected in the
act of praying secretly before the little image of
St. Sergius, which was his—Colonel Bernikoff's—
own peculiar and particular property.

By the old laws of Muscovy, to be found wor-
shipping at an image, erected by, or the property
of another, designing thereby to have a share in
the favour of the saint it represented, without
being at any expense, was punishable by a fine, to
refund "the owner some part of the money laid
out for the said image;" but as the poor Cossack
had not a copper denusca wherewith to bless himself, the Governor took it out of his back and
shoulders (scarcely healed after his recent knout-
ing), with the aid of a knotted walking cane.

"'To steal and to lie,' according to Bulharyn,
a famous Russian writer, 'are the two auxiliary
verbs of our language,'" said the Colonel, panting
with exertion, as the Cossack crept away with a
glance of subdued ferocity in his stealthy eyes;
"we take all that for granted; but this slave
has been stealing the interest of my saint for
himself!"

He ordered an extra supply of wax candles to
be lighted before the image, and then he knelt,
bowed, and muttered :—

"Holy St. Sergius, heed not the prayers of that
rascal, he is only a vile serf, a slave, a Cossack from
the Ukraine. Thou hast been very good to me, and

shalt be treated handsomely. Candles of the finest wax shall burn before thee all night. I will love and pray for thee, so do thou protect and intercede for me, most holy Sergius!"

And so he prayed till the dinner drum beat; and then, muttering an oath as he tripped over his sabre, the old savage hobbled away, to commit at least two of the seven deadly sins at table.

"No tidings yet, Carl Ivanovitch, of those traitors!" said Bernikoff, when he had somewhat recovered his breath, after a deep draught of quass, the froth of which adhered to his grisly mustachio: "the Captain Vlasfief, and my faithful friend Tschekin, with forty picked Cossacks, and a clever guide——"

"Nicholas Paulovitch, I presume."

"The same," continued Bernikoff, with a fierce grimace on his lips and a cruel leer in his eyes, as he masticated a huge mouthful of green *borsch* with beef and eggs; "the same, sir,—and what then?"

"Nothing, Excellency: but this *oukha* of sterlet is excellent. Well, these and the forty Cossacks——"

"Are scouring all the roads between this and St. Petersburg on one flank, and between this and North Ladoga on the other; so the cursed Asiatics cannot escape me."

"Who will betray them to you?" asked Balgonie, making a terrible effort to appear calm and unconcerned, as he played with his sword knot and the tassels of his sash, and forgot to eat.

"Who?" exclaimed Bernikoff, grinding his teeth, and eating very fast. "Their own friends —their own dear comrades—adherents, which you will. Russia is full of people, yea of many nations. The Empress can reckon her faithful slaves by millions; yet, when a Russian hath his hat on his head, its rim contains the only friend on whom he can rely."

"This is a severe libel on your country surely, Excellency."

"'Tis truth though; so Basil Mierowitz, Usakoff, and the rest, are all doomed men. No one was ever lost on a straight road; thus the soldier who diverges from the straight line of duty must speedily find himself face to face with degradation and death. Punishment to those traitors will be swift and sure! So, I only fear that the Grand Chancellor will never give me the pleasure of having them under my judicious care in Schlusselburg. We have certain old vaults, built below the tide mark by Ivan the Terrible, for some of those people of Novgorod who leagued with the King of Poland. They are always full of fog; and I am curious to know how long an able-bodied prisoner might live there, or rather how long he would be in dying. But excuse me, Hospodeen, I confess me to-morrow, and there rings the bell for vespers already;" and making many Greek signs of the cross and other genu-flexions, Bernikoff, after having gorged himself at table, hurried away to the chapel, where Father Chrysostom officiated.

Charlie gladly sought the solitude afforded by the stockades and outworks of the fortress on the side towards the Lake of Ladoga. There, as elsewhere, was of course, a chain of sentinels; but they did not interrupt his lonely communing with himself.

By his interest in Natalie, by his deep love for her, and more than all, perhaps, by his recent visit and interview, he already felt himself "art and part" (to use a Scottish legal phrase), or *particeps criminis*, with the rash adherents of Ivan. If one of these deserted the cause in which they had embarked, then would their lurking place be at once discovered, and the story of his recent visit be revealed.

He dreaded lest Bernikoff and others suspected his friendly interest in the family of Count Mierowitz, and that more might yet be learned of it; thus he would have experienced neither shock nor surprise, had he, at any hour, in that land of treachery and espionage, seen either Captain Vlasfief, Lieutenant Tschekin, or any other officer of the fortress, advancing towards him sabre in hand, with an armed party, to demand his sword, to make him a prisoner, and march him off to the same prison which already held the old Count and Mariolizza, the innocent betrothed of Basil, and might soon hold another, who was dearer still —Natalie!

"If I love her," he would say to himself at
times, "why should I shrink from sharing all that
she suffers now—all she may yet endure ?   Yet
it would be wiser to watch well for her sake, and
seek to save, or bear her away; but how—and
where to ?" was the next bewildering thought.

And the generous Basil, the fiery and chivalrous Usakoff, oh that he might save them too!
He mourned for Usakoff, who was the very soul
of honour and heroism, the worthy grandson of
that Mazeppa who, when Charles the XII. was
retreating from Pultowa, swam the Borysthenes
by the side of the fugitive king, and of whom
the latter said in the words of the bard :—

> "Of all our band,
> Though firm of heart and strong of hand,
> In skirmish, march, or forage, none
> Can less have said or more have done
> Than thee, Mazeppa! on the earth
> So fit a pair had never birth,
> Since Alexander's day till now,
> As thy Bucephalus and thou ;
> All Scythia's fame to thine should yield,
> For pricking on o'er flood and field."

So worthy of such an ancestor, was he, too, to
perish ?

This was, indeed, a miserable mood of mind in
which to pass the nights and days of inactivity—
of suspense and anxiety in which none could
share, in that strong, guarded, and somewhat
lonely fortress, which was washed, as we have
said, on one side by the Neva, and on the
other by the Lake of Ladoga, the very ripples of

whose waves sounded hatefully in the ears of Balgonie.

" Oh," thought he, " to be with Natalie on the side of a green and breezy Scottish mountain—on any part of the shore of free and happy Britain ! to be with her there in peace and security, far, far from this land of suspicion and ferocious despotism, of state intrigues and savage punishments, where every second man is the spy upon, and the betrayer of, his fellow."

Britain he might never see more : and now he found himself vaguely speculating on the probable comforts and public amusements afforded by Siberia, and those growing cities of the sorrowing and the banished, Tobolsk and Irkutsk, on the banks of the Lower Angara.

He feared to look much, or often, towards the distant Wood of the Honey Tree, lest watchful eyes might be upon him to gather hints therefrom ; still more did he fear to visit Natalie again, lest, by doing so, he might lead to the discovery and arrest of all : so the days and nights of dread, of longing, and suspense, passed slowly after each other now.

The barriers of rank and wealth—the wealth afforded by the Count's estates and mines, his populous villages of serfs, and vast forests of timber—had all been removed now, and Natalie was reduced to a level lower even than her lover's ; yet he cursed the mad schemes that had brought about such a revolution, and tossed feverishly and sleeplessly on his bed, when he thought of Natalie Mierowna,—his own loving and beloved Natalie, —so delicate and so tender, with her white soft skin and silky hair, her earnest and beautiful eyes, lurking among stern and outlawed soldiers in yonder damp cavern of the rocks, upon her bed of leaves and moss, at the mercy, perhaps, of any adherent of Basil's, who, to save his own head, might prove a traitor to them all! This dread was ever before him.

The whole affair reminded him of some of the old Scottish raids or Jacobite plots, of years long passed away; and it was fated to resemble the former more strongly in some of its features, as the dark sequel will show.

The guards and sentinels at Schlusselburg were doubled; the patrols were incessant by land, while on the lake the gun-boats of Admiral Mackenzie cruised near the walls; the cannons were loaded; the watch-words changed some-times twice within four-and-twenty hours; and the general state of preparation for a sudden attack was unremitting: but time passed on quietly until the night of the fifteenth of September, when the crowning catastrophe came.

CHAPTER XIX.

THE past day had been unusually gloomy for the season. The sun had set in fiery clouds beyond the spires of St. Petersburg. The night was without a moon, and a strong east wind rolled the waters of Ladoga in billows of inky hue against the massive walls of the fortress in foam and fury on one side, while on the other, the waters of the Neva, swollen by recent rains, gurgled and chafed round the mouldy and mossgrown piers of the drawbridge.

The wind moaned with a sullen sound past the mouths of the cannon, and whistled drearily through the deep embrasures and the loopholes for musketry in the casemates. Thunder had been heard at times, but afar; Elias, as the Russians poetically phrase it, was driving his chariot among the stars. Lightning had reddened all the lake, and cast the weird shadow of the castle athwart it for an instant; and, that a complete and melodramatic omen of impending evil might not be wanting, a huge sea-bird had perched upon the castle clock, and forcing round the hands,

struck midnight four hours before the proper
time.

Since morning roll-call, Jagouski, the knouted,
beaten, and ill-used Cossack, had been missing;
he had quitted the fortress on some trivial pretence and had not since returned; patrols had
seen nothing of him. Then Colonel Bernikoff
was more than ever on the alert; but Balgonie,
who now deemed anything better than the torture
of suspense, had gone weary and feverishly to
bed, to court for a time the happiness of oblivion,
after having spent nearly the entire day upon the
lake with an armed boat's crew, patrolling by
water.

From sleep, however, a sudden sound aroused
him : he looked at his watch, and saw that the
hands indicated twelve o'clock, midnight.

What had he heard ?

In another moment the sound came again—
the drums were beating to arms! He heard the
clamour of hoarse Muscovite voices in court and
corridor; the clanging of the castle bell; and
he saw the gleam of torches reddening the old
black walls and towers, and flaring on the grated
windows as they were borne to and fro.

His heart was beating with wild anxiety as he
threw on his staff uniform, belted his sabre about
him, placed his pistols in his girdle, and hurried
forth to meet—it might be to cross blades—with
the only friends he had in Russia !

As he crossed the castle-yard by torchlight, he

could perceive that the Cossacks, clad in their short blue jackets, red loose breeches, short boots, and tall, black, woollen busbies, were falling into their ranks with musketoon and sabre; and that the gunners were standing by their cannon with port-fires lighted: the latter casting a pale, ghastly, and unearthly glare upon the yawning embrasures, the walls of the fortress, and on their own stolid visages, which were pale and cadaverous as those of people usually who are hastily summoned from sleep in the night.

As a staff officer who had no particular post, Charlie Balgonie knew that his duty attached him chiefly to Bernikoff, whom he now met hurrying forth in uniform, with a great cocked hat thrust angrily over his cunning and twinkling eyes, which were sparkling with anger, while every hair of his grizzled mustachioes, though these were long and snaky, bristled with excitement. There was a dangerous pallor in his visage; his square jaw looked still more tiger-like in contour, as his teeth were clenched; and he had his sabre drawn.

By his side were his two favourite brother officers, who in face, form, and bearing, bore indications of being each, originally, a serf of the lowest, basest, and most unthinking kind—Captain Vlasfief, cruel and hollow-hearted, with his unfathomable smile; and Lieutenant Tschekin, the slimy, savage, and unscrupulous Muscovite. With these came several officers of the Cossack

guard, with their elevated eyebrows, black mustachioes, their keen features, the plumes and cock-
ades in their black fur caps, and their glittering
costumes, forming altogether a striking and picturesque group, when seen by the light of several
torches, which streamed through the deep and
small arch, or doorway, of the keep in which Ivan
was confined.

The portcullis of this tower was up; and Balgonie could perceive its row of lower bars, like a
line of black fangs in an open jaw, between him
and the outline of the lighted archway.

"What is the matter, Colonel Bernikoff,"
asked Balgonie; "what is the cause of all this
alarm?"

"Matter enough! We have had an *alerte*—the
place seems to be invested by troops—Infantry of
the Line, by all the devils—the head of a column
—look for yourself, Balgonie!" exclaimed Bernikoff, with an oath.

To omit the christian name of a person addressed, and that of his father also, is a direct
insult in Russia; but Balgonie heeded it not then.
He hurried to the curtain wall which faced the
landside, the outer gate, and drawbridge, and then,
by the light of a torch, he could see that which
certainly seemed to be the head of a column—a
front rank of nearly fifty men, clad in the hideous
uniform then worn by the Russian army, before it
was altered, a few years after, by the superior taste
of the notorious Major Semple Lisle, a Scottish

adventurer,* who was well known as a lounger about St. James's Park, London, in 1804. Their coats were green, lined and faced with red, very tight in the body, with preposterously long skirts, tight breeches, and boots to the knee, with small cocked hats, having long flannel flaps to cover the ears in winter.

By the light of the same torch, Balgonie could see the bayonets fixed, and that two officers, with their sabres drawn, and a drummer, were in front of their little line. Having possession of the parole and countersign, which, no doubt, had been betrayed to them by the absent Jagouski, the whole party had contrived to delude the *Putparooschick* (sub-lieutenant) in charge of the outer guard, and were now past the first barrier, and had actually taken possession of the drawbridge, which they had lowered across the Neva. The gate and guns of the second barrier were yet to be forced or passed; and thus these midnight visitors were in a species of trap.

Too well could Balgonie recognise in the two officers—Basil Mierowitz, wearing the familiar uniform of the Regiment of Smolensko; and Usakoff, in the gay trappings of the Grenadiers of Valikolutz; and now, for the second time, their drummer beat a *chamade*, or summons for a parley, but as yet there was no response.

Balgonie hastened after Bernikoff and the other

* *Vide* "Life of Major J. G. Semple Lisle, written by himself. London, 1800. Printed for W Stewart, 194, Piccadilly."

officers. They had now ascended to the chamber of the unfortunate Ivan, from whose presence they had somewhat roughly expelled the chaplain, Father Chrysostom. On entering, he found that the royal recluse had sprung from bed, inspired by natural alarm, on finding his chamber suddenly entered at midnight, and full of armed men ; but Ivan manifested no indignation—he was too gentle, too subdued, and completely broken in spirit for that.

His singularly beautiful face was very pale ; there was a strange calmness in his manner ; and whatever he thought or anticipated, there was more of calm inquiry than of fear in his tone and in the expression of his fine soft eyes. Over his night-dress he had thrown a *robe-de-chambre* of fine scarlet cloth edged with white ermine; and in this attire, with his long hair and delicate features, so chastened in expression by long solitude and complete seclusion from the outer world, he seemed more like a tall handsome woman, than a young man of three and twenty years.

"What is this you tell me, Colonel Bernikoff," he was asking, as Balgonie entered; "my unhappy life threatened say you ?"

"Even so," said Bernikoff hoarsely, while averting his stealthy eyes from the young man's open and earnest face; "even so, Ivan Antonovitch; but your death will not be of our seeking."

"Whose then, whose then ?"

" Your friends."

" Oh, what dreadful paradox is this ?" asked the Prince calmly; "must I die, even as Demetrius died ?"

" Yes," replied the other hoarsely.

" And wherefore ?"

" There are those without the gates who seek you, and you must not fall alive into their hands," said Captain Vlasfief sternly, as he felt the point of his sabre with a finger.

" Alas ! I do not understand who can come to seek me !" replied the poor Prince, shuddering now, while an expression of horror began to spread over his fine face,— a horror gathered from the fierce and relentless aspect he read in the visages of those around him,—and he withdrew a pace or so towards his bed, saying, in a touching voice :—

" Ah, do not leave me, good Colonel Bernikoff, or at least give me a sword—a sword——"

" Fool—child—dolt ! thou with a sword, and for what purpose ?" thundered Bernikoff, as he sought to lash himself into the requisite pitch of fury; "for what purpose, I say ?"

" That I may defend myself."

" 'Tis needless," said Tschekin, with a cold smile; " we shall take every care of you."

" Oh, Carl Ivanovitch Balgonie, my friend, my good friend ! you I can trust—you I can command—come hither, and remain by my side," said the Prince, in an imploring accent, as a

solemn foreboding came upon him when he saw
the sabres stealthily drawn from their scabbards
on every side, and even the terrible Nicholas
Paulovitch drawing near, dagger in hand, with
his long lock of hair, his scowling front, and a
cruel expression, the very lust of blood, in his
deep-set stony eyes. "Carl, Carl," cried Ivan;
"your hand!"

"Captain Balgonie—*he* here!" roared Bernikoff, with one of his terrible maledictions.

"Oh Excellency!" implored Balgonie, scarcely
knowing what he should ask or urge.

"Begone, sir, to the barrier gate, and keep the
guard there to their duty—begone, sir, I command you, on your allegiance to the Empress!"

To refuse or linger were alike impossible,
though a wild cry of entreaty escaped the lips
of the young Prince, who sprang forward, but
was thrust roughly back towards his couch by
many hands and many levelled weapons.

The sword of Damocles, which had hung over
his unhappy head so long, was about to descend
at last!

Balgonie, his heart swollen almost to bursting
with shame, rage, and grief, rushed down the
stair of the keep; but at the foot, and just as he
passed where the old Chaplain Chrysostom was
saying devoutly on his knees the prayers for the
dying, he heard a shrill and protracted cry of
agony ring through the vaulted tower—a cry
that made his blood run cold!

Humanity, generosity, and all his own good impulses would have drawn him back to the side, and, if possible, to the aid, of Ivan; but the force of discipline, and a knowledge of his own utter powerlessness, made him pause : for he was but one man—a young officer—a foreigner, too, opposed to a whole garrison of ferocious and unscrupulous soldiers.

When, from the inner barrier gate, he looked up to the window of Ivan's room, he saw that the lights had been extinguished and all was darkness now.

CHAPTER XX.

WHEN Bernikoff appeared with his group of officers, Charlie Balgonie perceived that there were spots of blood upon his long, white leather gauntlets, that his sabre blade was broken off within six inches of the hilt, and that a terrible expression of ferocity clouded his features and those of all around him, the glare of the uplifted torches now paling as the light of day stole in, adding to the sinister significance of their faces.

At that moment the drummer of the summoners beat a *chamade* for the third time, and Bernikoff, advancing to the klinket, or wicket, in the palisades of the second inner gate, opened it, and, with a great sternness of manner, demanded what they required.

"The release of His Imperial Majesty Ivan IV.," replied Basil Mierowitz, in a firm voice, while courteously saluting Bernikoff, in recognition of his superior rank.

" If I refuse——"

" You do so at your own peril," replied Basil, as sternly and as proudly as if, instead of a few discontented deserters and enthusiasts, the whole armies of Russia were at his back.

"You cannot be mad enough, Basil Mierowitz, to think of assaulting us ?"

"That may or may not be, Excellency, according to circumstances," was the reply.

"What troops are these under your orders ?"

"A guard of honour for the Emperor, if you peacefully comply—the first portion of an investing force, if you refuse," replied Mierowitz ; but a sinister gleam of triumph flashed in the malicious eyes of Bernikoff, who gathered more of his real weakness from this evasive reply, than the rash young noble intended.

"Listen, Colonel Bernikoff," he continued, while drawing from his breast a long paper of official aspect, to which several green and scarlet seals were attached : "Her Majesty Catharine II. —for a time of all the Russias—having come to the conclusion of resigning the imperial crown (convinced at last that she has no claim thereto), and of replacing it on the head of the Emperor Ivan (son of Anthony Ulric, Duke of Wolfenbuttel), whom she now feels herself compelled to acknowledge as her lawful sovereign, though basely deposed in infancy by her predecessors, the Empress Elizabeth, and the Emperor Peter III. ; therefore she hereby commands you, Colonel Bernikoff, Governor of her Castle of Schlusselburg, to set the Prince at liberty, with all speed and honour."

For a document and summons of this artful and remarkable nature, Bernikoff was altogether unprepared. For a moment he grew deadly pale, but for a moment only, and glanced at the startled faces of those around him. Had he been too precipitate in bloodshed?

"Where is Her Majesty just now?" he asked.

"In the palace of the Czars, at Novgorod."

"Was Novgorod so empty of all the great nobles and officers of Russia, that a document of such a nature was entrusted to a mere Lieutenant of Infantry—a deserter from Livonia?" said Bernikoff, with sudden rage. "'Tis an imposture—a forgery; there is but one God in Heaven—one monarch on earth, the Empress Catharine; and you, Mierowitz, and all who league with you, are but base dogs and traitors!"

"Forward!" cried Basil, brandishing his sabre; "storm the gate—bayonet all who oppose us!"

"Long live Ivan Antonovitch—long live the Emperor!" exclaimed his soldiers, rushing forward. But the klinket in the palisades was at once closed, and secured against them by an enormous transverse beam of wood; and though a confused volley of musketry was exchanged between them and the main guard, no one was struck, save Bernikoff, who staggered back into the arms of Vlasfief, having been bayoneted in the breast by the deserter Jagouski, who drove his weapon between the palisades, nearly finishing what Basil had begun by the blow of a musket but, which crushed the Colonel's hat, and nearly fractured his skull.

"Ah! dogs and Asiatics, you have struck me!" shouted Bernikoff, whose voice was hoarse with rage and pain. "Dost know the penalty of wounding an officer—of striking a soldier who wears a decoration?"

"Accursed Tartar, I neither know nor care. I revenge my brother's death at Zorndorf, my own wrongs, and the murder of Peter III.!" replied the exulting Cossack, with a bitter laugh.

"May my right hand wither, and my tongue cleave to the roof of my mouth, when most I need them both, if I have not a terrible vengeance for all this work!" cried Bernikoff. "Vlasfief, Tschekin, show them their Prince!"

While the undaunted Basil and his friend Usakoff, with their soldiers, proceeded to wheel round a cannon of the outworks, a 32-pounder, for the purpose of blowing open the klinket of the inner barrier; and while Balgonie, a silent but excited and sick-hearted spectator of the whole affair, lingered close by, heedless whether the round-shot and grape, with which they were charging the gun, came his way, or not,—a window in the first story of the keep was dashed open, and while every torch and every eye were uplifted to the place, a terrible spectacle, which hushed all into momentary silence, was exhibited.

It was the dead body of the young and hand-

some Ivan, suspended by the neck, at the end of
a rope, stripped even of his night-dress, cold and
white as the marble of Paros, and gashed with
ten gaping wounds ; for, as we are told in the
newspapers of the period, " the unfortunate prince
had struggled some time for his life, and even
broke the Governor's sword in the conflict ; but
assistance was called for, and another bloody
assassin (Vlasfief) appeared, who finished the
horrid work."

An exclamation of dismay and grief escaped
Balgonie, on beholding this appalling spectacle ;
the weird and ghastly horror of which was en-
hanced by the uncertain light in which it was
exhibited, and which imparted a wavering and
almost life-like action to the corpse, as with its
long hair floating, head and arms pendent, it
swayed to and fro in the morning wind against
the castle wall.

" *Hospodi pomilui ! Hospodi pomilui !*"* cried
Basil Mierowitz, covering his face with his hands,
and permitting the musket with which he had
armed himself to fall to the ground with a clash,
which, together with his most mournful exclamation, alone broke the silence.

" 'Behold,' said Bernikoff, in cruel triumph,
while blasphemously using the words of Ezekiel—
" 'behold, I take away from thee the desire of
thine eyes with a stroke!' Glory to God and to the

---

* Lord have mercy upon us!

Empress!   This is your Emperor—now let him head your troops.   Doubtless he will make a fine figure on the Imperial throne."

"Oh! Bernikoff," exclaimed Basil, "you are like Judas, as we may see him at the Kazan church—one hand on the mouth denoting trea- chery, and the other on a bag of money."

"Thou liest, Lieutenant! my fingers know more of the grip of steel than of gold," said the other furiously, as he hurled the hilt of his broken sabre at the speaker.

"So—so—this has been your work and decision?"

"Yes—how do you like it?" was the mocking reply.

"Thou art a cruel judge; but remember the law of Peter the Great——"

"Which makes the judge answerable for his decision?"

"Yes."

"Then shall I content me, traitor, and be answerable for my decision as well as for its exe- cution.   I have done my duty to the Czarina."

"You have done a deed for which hell must blush and angels weep," was the forcible reply of Mierowitz, who seemed so overcome by grief and horror as to lose all self-possession; for he now ordered his men to disperse to the woods—to seek safety in flight; and then calmly taking off his sword-belt and sash, he threw them on the ground saying—

"Since my Imperial master is dead, further resistance would be vain in me."

He was almost immediately afterwards struck to the earth, and made prisoner by Lieutenant Tschekin, who, with a party of dismounted Cossacks, had stolen through the casemates and galleries to a postern opening on the rear of the drawbridge, and these, after firing a confused volley with their pistols and musketoons, fell with their sharp crooked sabres upon the now thoroughly disheartened adherents of Mierowitz. Lieutenant Usakoff and Jagouski alone made any vigorous resistance, resolving not to be taken alive.

Fighting desperately, almost back to back, the former armed with the sabre of Mazeppa, and the latter with a musket, and both bleeding from many wounds, they were driven through the outer barrier towards the town. On the pathway Jagouski stumbled over a comrade, and was taken; but Apollo Usakoff, with a shout in which triumph and despair were mingled, leaped into the Neva, the waters of which swept him away, and he was seen no more by his pursuers.

When Tschekin's Cossacks joined in the *mêlée* with the fugitives, Balgonie sprang through the klinket, sword in hand, resolved to succour his friend at all hazards, and fortunately arrived just in time to save him (when struck down and trod under foot) from the bulky giant Nicholas Paulovitch, who, with a clubbed musket, was about to give him a blow that must inevitably have proved fatal.

Paulovitch he ran through the heart—or at least the place where his heart might be supposed to have been—and spurning him off the blade with his foot, hurled the snorting ruffian to the ground, and raised his friend, with the assistance of a soldier and Lieutenant Tschekin.

"Made prisoner, and by *you* too, Carl!" said Basil, reproachfully and in a low voice, for he was faint with wounds and bruises.

"By me, but to save you."

"Seek rather to save Natalie, if you can," he whispered; "she is, she is—"

"Where, *where?*" said Balgonie, impetuously and imploringly.

But there was no reply. Basil had fainted, and was borne into the Castle of Schlusselburg, a prisoner of State.

Balgonie never saw the face of his friend again!

So ended, for a time, a scheme, the importance of which was only equalled by its bold reckless-ness—the scheme of two subaltern officers to revolutionise the vast empire of Russia, and to subvert the firm dominion of Catharine II., one of the most powerful and popular, though licentious, monarchs that ever sat on the bar-barous throne of the Czars ; and such was the ter-rible sequel to the *Secret Dispatch* of Balgonie.

Day had completely broken when he was sum-

moned by Bernikoff. Shuddering as he passed
through the court of the Castle and under the
very window where the corpse was yet swaying
mournfully to and fro in the morning breeze that
swept from the broad waters of the vast lake,
whose ripples were shining like gold in the first
beams of the autumnal sun, Charlie sought the
presence of this detestable personage, the thunder
of whose wrath he feared was about to descend
upon himself.

He found the Colonel in his shirt sleeves, and
almost covered with blood, which was flowing
from a wound in his breast and another on the
head, from whence it was trickling to the ends of
his long and snaky grey mustaches. To both of
these cuts the barber was about to apply dressings,
while the patient solaced himself by scheming out
some dreadful punishment for Jagouski, who, with
several others, had fallen into his gentle hands,
and by uttering deep oaths, and imbibing deep
draughts from a great wooden bowl of quass,
dashed with fiery vodka.

Balgonie, whose thoughts ran chiefly upon how
to discover and succour Natalie, was roused to
attention by Bernikoff saying grimly—

" Carl Ivanovitch Balgonie, for aiding in the
capture of the rebel Mierowitz, I thank you; suspicions I had, but they are gone. You are now,
perhaps, to rejoin the Regiment of Smolensko,
and shall bear a dispatch from me to Lieutenant-
General Weymarn and Lieutenant-Colonel Casch-

kin (who are both in St. Petersburg), relating the
affair of the last twelve hours. Vlasfief shall prepare it, and I will sign it. Place a feather in the
seal, lest the Captain lingers as he did at Louga!
Here, Carl Ivanovitch, taste the quass; 'tis the
trisna of Ivan the Unknown Person!"

There was something so horrible in this levity
and impiety to the Cossacks, that even they exchanged uneasy glances, for the trisna at funeral
feasts is a mixture of rum, beer, and wine, and is
an ancient Sclavonian beverage. When it is
handed round, all stand up uncovered, the clergy
recite a solemn prayer, and at its close the trisna
is drunk to the health of the departed Christian
soul; so Balgonie shuddered, as he thought of the
gashed and dishonoured corpse that swung by the
neck without the castle wall.

This emotion did not escape the fierce eyes of
Bernikoff, though his wounds were most severe,
and his mind was wandering.

"Nay, look not at me thus, Scot," said the
genuine old Russian fatalist; "God willed it that
Prince Ivan should be put in my charge; and the
devil, together with my duty to the Empress, inspired me to destroy him. What is done, is done,
and is the will of God; and you know, or ought
to know, our Muscovite proverb—the Czar is
high, and God is everywhere!"

"Three times has this old reprobate mentioned
that terrible Name, and each time bowing his sinful
head!" thought Charlie, with disgust and wonder.

" Hah!" resumed Bernikoff, pursuing his own thoughts, and clenching his teeth in rage and pain, " did that suckling of a Lieutenant think to deceive me—I, who have been forty years in the Russian army, and have to deal with the most cunning scoundrels between the Black Sea and the Baltic! Jagouski, too, I'll fill his mouth with gunpowder, put a fuse between his teeth, and blow his head off. By St. Sergius, I will! But, holy Saint, alleviate these pangs, by ever so little, and this night six pounds of the finest white wax shall burn before thee." He gnashed his teeth with pain, and added, " Be ready to ride in an hour, Captain; till then, leave me."

CHAPTER XXI.

UNDERGROUND.

THE Empress's court of Secret Chancery soon decided on the fate of Basil Mierowitz; the Count, his father, and his cousin Mariolizza, who had been passive, though suspected in the matter, had their cases taken into future consideration, so they were kept close prisoners while their properties and possessions were given up to pillage and military execution. Basil was condemned to be broken alive upon the wheel; but the Empress, who had a particular tenderness for handsome men, "mitigated his punishment to the less severe one of being beheaded."

A brief paragraph in the *London Gazette* of the 23rd October records this brave fellow's death, just fourteen days after his rash affair at Schlusselburg :

"M. Mierowitz, in pursuance of his sentence, was publicly beheaded on Wednesday last; he behaved at his execution, as he had done throughout the whole transaction, with the greatest resignation. Six of the soldiers and under-officers who were engaged with him ran the gantelope the same day; they were so severely whipped that it is said three of them are since dead. Many more are to be punished. One, Usakoff, a Lieutenant in the Regiment of Welikolutz (*sic*) who was privy to the design, was accidentally drowned."

Notwithstanding his rank and years, old Count Mierowitz was retained in a dungeon among a number of miserable Russian rogues and Polish prisoners, clad in filthy sheepskin shoubahs, many of them being afflicted with the terrible disease known as *plica polonica*, or matted hair, which hung over their necks in clotted lumps, every tube being swollen and dilated with globules of blood.

The lower vaults of Schlusselburg were those built by Ivan the Terrible, for the reception of a few of the revolters of Novgorod, after he had put twenty-five thousand of her citizens to the sword. They were such prisons as—let us hope —are no longer in use, even in Russia, although the London press has asserted that, until lately, exactly such *oubliettes* or dungeons were in active operation, and never without tenants, under the royal rule of the deposed Francis II., and prior to the remodelling of Italy by Victor Emmanuel.

They were like the frightful cells of the Bastile, which Victor Hugo has described in "Notre Dame;" those of the Inquisition at Goa or Madrid, or of old castles of the middle ages; but apart from the happily departed horrors of such places, even English jails have been little better than

living graves within the memory of many now
alive ; for one of the greatest glories of modern
civilisation, in all countries, has been the amelio-
ration of prisons and their government, and the
substitution of mercy and protection in their
general economy for that irresponsible despotism
and wanton cruelty which have formed such
ample materials for the romancer and novelist
to excite compassion and even dismay.

Yet it is exactly such a place—a prison of the
middle ages—a rival to that Chillon to which
Byron's genius has given a greater name than
ever its terrors won it—we are now about to
describe : one of the lower vaults of Schlusselburg, a den, the floor of which was below the rocks
whereon the seals of Ladoga basked in the sunshine, and which was consequently liable to be
flooded during those inundations that at certain
seasons, overflow all the country for a great way
north, so that no crops will grow save upon the
eminences.

Vaulted with stone, it was nearly square, and
measured twelve feet each way, with a floor
that sloped down at one end, having been un-
evenly hewn out when the rock was pierced ;
and from a portion of this rock sprang the solid
arch of granite blocks which formed the roof.
A narrow slit, six inches broad by twelve high,
and having even in that small space a thick iron
bar, admitted to the interior a feeble ray of light.
This slit was partly built of stone, but its sill was

the living rock of Schlusselburg. It opened towards the lake, but gave no prospect save the clouds, for it was high up in the wall ; yet the melancholy cries of the waterfowl and of the seabirds, which often came up the Neva from the Baltic, were heard through it at times.

The prisoner, when seated on the stone bench which formed a bed or seat alternately, could only see the changing hues of the sky and patches of cloud, and know by the darkness which gradually obscured this mere shot-hole that day was passing away, and that another night, chill, dark, dreary, and hopeless, was at hand.

As the floor sloped down some twelve inches or more, the lower end was always full of water, into which the slime that gathered on the vault of the arch fell at intervals with a regular plash that, to the silent and apparently forgotten prisoner, became maddening in its monotony of sound, by day and night, by morning and evening, by dawn and sunset. Then, as the tides rose and fell, or as the waters of the vast inland lake of Ladoga are affected by the Baltic stopping the downward flow of the Neva, or by rains flooding the many tributaries that join them, so did this dark pool in the dungeon rise and fall, when the current oozed through secret and unknown channels or crannies in the granite rocks.

It was in this vault, or one of those adjoining —such a den as that in which Dante placed his

Demon—that the betrayed wife of Count Orloff, the beautiful daughter of the Empress Elizabeth, was drowned, ten years after the date of this history, when the waters of the Neva rose ten feet ; and, as they subsided, bore her body to the Gulf of Finland.

No one could live very long in such a place —low, damp, cold, and horrible. And well did Bernikoff know this, when, in the blind transports of rage and agony resulting from his double wounds, he barbarously consigned Natalie Mierowna to such a place—ay, even Natalie, the soft and delicate, the highly-bred and tenderly-nurtured daughter of Count Mierowitz ; and she had now been in the underground vault for three days and nights,—seventy-two hours, —which to her had resembled a horrible and protracted nightmare.

She was ignorant as yet of her brother's execution, a week before. Betrayed by one of their most trusted adherents as the price of his own liberty, she and Katirka had been taken. Of the fate of the latter she knew nothing : a mere Polish waiting-maid, a pretty soubrette, she had too probably become the lawful prey of the Cossacks, whom Natalie had last seen in the forest, with terrible significance rattling their dice on a kettle-drum head.

For herself, the poor girl only knew that she was placed there to await the pleasure of the Empress and the Grand Chancellor.

P

Hope was dead completely in her heart; and though the desire to live was strong, her former life seemed all a dream, or something that had happened long, long ago!

Crouching on a damp pallet that lay on the couch of stone, her hair dishevelled, her dress more than ever torn, discoloured, and disordered, her snowy arms and hands stripped of every ornament and ring, her tender feet well-nigh shoeless, her eyes half closed and surrounded by dark inflamed circles, her cheeks sunk and haggard,— it would be difficult to recognise in her the once beautiful and brilliant Natalie, whose coquetry had excited the ready jealousy of Catharine in that fatal Mazurka; the Natalie of the imperial *salons* at Moscow, at Oranienbaum, or the palace of Tsarsky Selo; or the Natalie of that princely old château near the Louga—the proud, bright-eyed, and beautiful girl whom Charlie Balgonie had loved, and worshipped as a goddess.

As she crouched in a species of stupor beside a wooden bowl of stale water and a mouldy loaf of black bread, there seemed to be no breath in her tender nostrils, no sound in those little ears over which the black hair rolled in unheeded masses —no sound save the monotonous plash of the dropping slime. She was pale as white marble,— cold as death,—a prey to utter confusion rather than profound grief. There were times when she felt and thought and knew of nothing: but there were others when all the past—the memory of her ruined house, her shattered love, her slaughtered friends, their fatal project, and her lost position in society—brought a cruel and keen pang to her heart, and made her writhe and start and wring her hands, but not weep; for she had not a tear left; and her hard dry eyeballs were the only warm part of her shuddering frame.

Seventy-two hours had she been there, yet the time seemed so long already, that she knew not whether it were seventy-two days or the same number of weeks.

When she did rouse herself to steady reflection and the realities of her position, thought well-nigh drove her mad.

Her old father—his sturdy figure, his venerable beard and white eyebrows, his silver hair queued by a simple ribbon, his quaint old-fashioned costume of the first Peter's time, rose vividly before her; and with a gush of memory came all his peculiarities of disposition, his warmth of heart and temper, his kindness and irritability, his pride of race and family. Where were all these now?

Her lover too—his voice, and eyes, and gentle manner came next, to add to her pangs; for him too must she relinquish for ever: no shelter was there now for her save the cold grave, which was perhaps to receive them all! Basil, Usakoff, and Mariolizza—alas! terrible though her own sufferings, she little knew those to which the fairer beauty and more unwary tongue of Mariolizza had subjected that unhappy girl.

The excellent taste, the polished education, and high accomplishments of Natalie, which were so far superior to those of most ladies of her own rank and country then, gave a greater poignancy to the horrors of reality and imagination; yet imagination could supply no horror but what was real and sternly so.

Their princely old dwelling amid the pine forests—never more would she see its dome of polished copper shining in the sun, or the wooded domain that stretched for uncounted versts around it; or her father's patrimonial village, nestling by the Louga, which bore his rafts of timber to the sea, and by night reflected the glare of those furnaces which were another source of his vast wealth, and the means of procuring a thousand luxuries.

Better would it have been, had she and they and all succumbed to Catharine's iron rule, than sought the freedom of Ivan IV ; but it was too late—too late, now !

Was it all a dream from which she must awaken ? Strange it was, that as weariness, sleep, or a stupor stole over her, scraps of songs, frivolous ones especially, airs from operas, and so forth, occurred to her drowsy ear, as if her brain was turning ; and to these the filtering plash and the sound of the rising waves and wind without seemed to mark a cadence.

Suddenly a scream escaped her : she was in total darkness. Amid her sleep or stupor, a fourth night had come on—a night of storm too; for she heard the roar of the autumn rain, as it descended like a vast sheet upon the lake without.

Cold and slimy things had often crossed her slender ankles, making her shrink and shudder: but now she became sensible that her feet were completely immersed in water; that the wind was bellowing without and rolling the waves against the rocks; and that the current of the lake was flooding the floor of her vault, and rising fast within it.

It rose with appalling rapidity: and now the terror of a dreadful death made Natalie utter a succession of piercing shrieks, mingled with prayers to heaven. But her cries were unheard; for the same cold, icy tide that flooded her cell, filled all the corridors by which it and others on the same floor were approached.

Rapidly it rose, this dark, silent, and terrible tide—rapidly and without a sound.

She sprang upon her stone couch, but already the pallet was floated away. Up yet rose the invading water, and it was soon nearly to her waist; and gasping and shuddering cries were mingled with her prayers. A little more, and the narrow slit through which she could hear the bellowing wind and see the black clouds careering past one red and fiery northern star—the last gleam of life and of the outer world—would vanish from her eyes, as she perished in that miserable tomb: even as the Princess Orloff and many others have done, helpless and unheeded in their dying agony

—drowned miserably, like the prison rats that swam around them.

In the last energies of her despair, she made her way to the enormously thick door which closed this trap of stone, and, applying her lips to the joints, shrieked loudly again and again for succour, and beat wildly and fruitlessly with her tender hands upon its massive planks and iron bolts.

Her brain seemed bursting, for she was suffocating as the air lessened. She thought she saw a red light shining through the crannies of the doorway; but whether this were fancy or reality, it was impossible to say, as a faintness came over her, and she sank down choking and drowning in the dark flood that rose within the walls and against the door of the prison.

CHAPTER XXII.

HEAVY and sad was the heart of Charlie Balgonie when, on the evening of the 16th September, that which was subsequent to the episode at Schlusselburg, he saw the domes and towers of St. Petersburg glittering in gold and bronze, in green and fiery or fantastic colours, amid the rich glow of a ruddy sunset; and where rising from the haze of the vast city, the polished cupola of St. Isaac's Cathedral, and the slender spire of the Admiralty, like a needle of flame, seemed to float in mid air.

As he entered the first guarded barrier, he met a party of Lancers riding at a trot, their tall fur caps having scarlet kalpecs and large plumes, their lances, each with a long bannerole of the same colour, waving in the wind. They escorted a covered kabitka, or waggon, and were led by the Count de Balmain, a Scottish officer, who, in after years, stormed Kaffa, in the Crimea.

" Whither go you, Count?" he asked.

" For Schlusselburg—the place of sorrow."

" With a prisoner, of course?"

" Yes, I regret to say, with the niece of Count

Mierowitz, with Mademoiselle Mariolizza. She is to be confined under a warrant from the Grand Chancellor—poor girl!"

Sadder and heavier grew the honest heart of Balgonie, as the escort and its hearse-like carriage passed on; and, as he looked after it, the fair merry face, the full and voluptuous figure, the gay manner, and remarkable *finesse d'esprit* of the betrothed of poor Basil, as he had last seen her at Louga, came back vividly to memory now.

Balgonie was at St. Petersburg when Mierowitz was executed, and when other horrors followed. Moreover, he was closely and repeatedly interrogated by the Grand Chancellor, the Privy Councillor, Count Panim, by Count Orloff (the present lover of the Empress), and by General Weymarn, as to all he knew and had seen of the conspirators —so closely, that nothing surprised him so much as to find that no suspicion was attached to himself. But being a soldier of fortune, who possessed nothing in the world but his sword and his epaulettes, he was not worth suspecting by the Imperial Government.

Ere long, the name of Natalie came before the Secret Chancery, as a prisoner in Schlusselburg; and, like the rest, she was tried and condemned in absence, undefended and unheard; and sentenced, too, amid the solitude of her prison.

To Balgonie the charm of life seemed to have passed away; and, during the week or two that followed his return to St. Petersburg, dreary,

weary, and unmeaning, indeed, seemed the rou-
tine of his duties as aide-de-camp at the vast
parades, the brilliant receptions, the courts-mar-
tial, and other public affairs to which he followed
his *chef*, General Weymarn, at the palaces of
Tsarsky Selo or Oranienbaum, and elsewhere,
while ignorant of the fate of Natalie—while the
very life of her he loved hung in the balance.

When compared with their fate, how happy
seemed those lovers, who, though separated for a
period, could look confidently forward through the
long succession of hours, of days and nights, of
weeks, and months, or even years, and reckon with
certainty on the time of reunion! With him and
Natalie, time stretched into a length that seemed
interminable: their future had no background;
their separation was one without hope.

Charlie, in his desperation, applied to the Mar-
quis de Bausset and to Sir George Macartney,
then the Ambassadors from France and Britain;
and both received his verbal prayers—he dared
not write on such a subject—for mercy to the
Count's family: but they were unheeded; and the
Ministers replied only by bows, grimaces, and
shrugs of their diplomatic shoulders. Their interference was impossible—quite; and, unfortunately, his old patron, Admiral Thomas Mackenzie, was with the fleet in the Black Sea.

The suspicions excited against his Regiment
and the Grenadiers of Valikolutz, might procure
the banishment of both; he feared it in the form

of service in Siberia, or at the Crimean lines of
Perecop.   In either case, unless Weymarn stood
his friend, how.could he hope to succour Natalie!

At every tea-house, hotel, and café, his uniform
of the Smolensko Infantry, and the knowledge
that he was the staff officer who had been in
Schlusselburg, and who brought the first tidings
of the late affair, made him an object of special
interest; but the subject was alike a perilous and
painful one.   Walls have many ears in Russia; so
he was compelled to be silent, or discreet, even to
rudeness, though the following declaration, which
was issued by the Empress, might have allayed
his fears :—

"We, Catharine the Second, by the Grace of
God, Empress and Sovereign of all the Russias,
&c., &c., make known to our Regiment of Smolensko Infantry that, according to the equity
which we exert towards our faithful subjects, we
cannot represent to ourselves, without profound
grief, how much that regiment must be afflicted,
for having among its officers a wretch in the
person of Mierowitz : nevertheless, as the crime
of one man cannot affect those who had no part
in it, and that, besides, we know the bravery with
which the regiment has distinguished itself upon
all occasions, its attachment to strict discipline,
and its exactness in the military duty of our empire; therefore we grant it, through our imperial
good-will, the same assurances of protection which

it has in all times deserved. In consequence, we forbid all and every one, to reproach or upbraid the said regiment concerning the treason of Mierowitz, under pain of incurring our indignation, and drawing on themselves the effects of our just resentment.

(*Signed*)   " CATHARINE."

Hope seemed to revive a little after the issue of this conciliatory *oukaz;* but it was speedily dashed, when Balgonie, on returning from Cronstadt, whither he had been sent by General Weymarn, suddenly met Captain Vlasfief face to face, near the palace of the favourite Lanskoi.

This personage he would have avoided like a toad or a leper; but from him only might he learn something of her he loved in Schlusselburg, that hateful place to which the Captain was returning; so, overcoming, or rather concealing, his repugnance, he adjourned with him to a café, and ordered wine.

"I dare say you have heard," said Vlasfief, with a strange leer in his eyes, as he tossed his hat and sabre on one sofa and deposited his jack-booted limbs on another, " how the estates of the Count and those of Usakoff have been sold or gifted away; pillaged and ravaged by Lanskoi with a party of Tchernemoski Cossacks; and that the plunder has been stored up in Schlusselburg?"

"Something of all this I have heard," replied

Balgonie, when the waiter had filled their glasses and withdrawn, "and—and—but you have there two ladies of the Count's family?"

"True—Mademoiselle Mariolizza, who was engaged to Mierowitz, and the Count's daughter: one beautifully fair, the other black-haired like a Pole. Poor girls!" he continued, while leisurely filling the large china bowl of a tasselled pipe, which suspiciously resembled one Charlie had often seen the old Count smoking, "I remember them both in happier and brighter times; but those who play with fire will, you know, be burned. The sentences on all have been found, recorded, and, in two instances, executed; and they are truly terrible!"

"Executed—the sentence!" repeated Balgonie, in a faint voice.

"Yes; you have been four days at Cronstadt: well, in those four days many things have been done—a light; thank you. The Count is now travelling towards Tobolsk under an escort of Balmain's Lancers. There he will have to hunt the ermine, cultivate asafœtida, or dig in the mines, with a collar at his neck, for the remainder of his days; but for the ladies of his family, a more severe punishment was reserved: ah! he is a stern fellow, old Panim!"

"How—what? Vlasfief, you jest?"

"'Tis no jest: we don't jest on such matters in Russia," replied Vlasfief, who was too thorough a *roué*—too "used up," in fact—to care for what any woman might suffer or undergo ; for every human emotion and sympathy were dead in this man now.

"What new horrors am I to hear ?" exclaimed Balgonie, with passionate vehemence, as he dashed his heavy Turkish sabre on the table.

Vlasfief smiled sourly, and his cunning eyes twinkled.

"You are a Scot, like Balmain," said he disdainfully ; "and as the Turks—those accursed unbelievers—say, but truly, 'Those who have never seen the world think it is all like their father's house.' Pass the bottle—'tis Cracow wine this, and not worth four ducats the flask. In short, the—the two ladies of the Count's family, in the wildness of their grief,—Mariolizza especially,—on hearing of the death of Mierowitz, permitted their tongues to run riot, and to say such things of Her Imperial Majesty and some of her favourites, such as Count Orloff, Lanskoi, the Grenadier, and so forth, as no woman would pardon, you understand ; so they are to be given in succession to *le maître d'entre les épaules*—the master of the shoulders," added Vlasfief, with a species of laugh at the strange expression which he saw gathering in Balgonie's face.

"Explain, I implore you, explain !" asked the latter, with quivering lips, as he set down a crystal goblet of Hungarian wine untasted on the table.

"Mademoiselle Mariolizza — but you don't

drink fairly, Ivanovitch—has received six blows of the knout.   The torturer is a new man, and mangled her cruelly.   She has had her tongue cut out, and her forehead branded with the executioner's mark;* and she goes to Siberia as soon as she recovers : but she will never reach it alive, even if she escapes the fever that has now seized her; for as the whole family has been degraded, —declared infamous and without protection,— being tongueless, she will become the prey of the Cossacks *en route*.   Once beyond the Volga, we never know what happens.   The Count's daughter will undergo exactly similar punishment; and, if she survives it, they will be mercifully permitted to travel together: and there ends the House of Mierowitz, which boasts of its descent from Ruric of Kiev—Ruric the Varagian of Old Ladoga !''

With wonderful coolness of manner, over his wine and pipe, almost with an occasional jest, the cruel and snakelike Vlasfief—who, as a *parvenu* of the foundling hospital (the son of a goat), hated the hereditary aristocracy—detailed these matters; and Balgonie felt as if a black cloud enveloped him.   He heard the Captain talking ; but his mind and thoughts were far, far away; and, after a time, he found himself alone.

Vlasfief had mounted and ridden off ; and mechanically, like an automaton, Balgonie had bidden him adieu at the portico of the café, and returned to finish his wine, as one in a waking

* The latter punishment is abolished *now*.

dream : nor was it until the bell of St. Isaac's tolled midnight, when the lights were burned low, the fire in the peitchka had died away, the decanters were empty, and he saw a drowsy waiter hovering near him, that he rose to depart ; for to him, now, all places seemed alike.

In the street a shower of tears revived him ; and he wept unseen, like a great boy, while grinding his teeth and twisting his mustaches like a furious and desperate man. Russia, her laws, her rulers, her very air, he loathed and detested. But what was he to do?—which way was he to turn ? —was he to permit these horrors, and live ?

He had been present when the Regiment of Smolensko guarded the punishment of Madame Lapouchin, one of the most beautiful women of the Imperial Court, where she shone like a planet, was loved, admired, and more than once was fought for. An alleged conspiracy brought her to the knout in all her nude loveliness, in the light of open day ; and Charlie remembered that sickening scene, before the eyes of assembled thousands, and how, as the Abbé d'Anterroche records, "in a few moments all the skin of her tender back was cut away in small slips, most of which remained hanging on her shift. Her tongue was cut out immediately after ; and she was banished into Siberia."

"Oh Natalie, Natalie !" he could but repeat, while he wrung his hands ; and thus the dawn of day found him.

After mature consideration of his position, his powerlessness, and the difficulties that beset him, with the horrors impending over Natalie, poor Charlie Balgonie felt maddened, crushed, and heart-broken. Could he see her perish without a struggle, an effort, however reckless, fruitless, and futile, on her behalf, even if he pistoled the executioner? Could he know that she too, probably, would die, in agony and mutilation, a horrible and ignominious death,—she, so gentle, delicate, and pure,—and would he survive it?

"Hearts will break in this life," says a recent writer; "it is the nature of them; but if God wills it, and it were possible, it is honester, braver, and nobler to live than to die." Most true; but to live is to hope. Balgonie vaguely, but sternly, resolved that he would do something, or—like the hero of a melodrama—"die in the attempt;" but being a poor, bewildered, loving young fellow, he could in no way practically see what that something might be.

Let not the reader flatter himself or herself that their own beloved country was entirely free from legal barbarism at this time; for in the very year of Ivan's murder,—the fourth year of the reign of His Majesty George III.,—a woman was *burned* at the stake in Ilchester for poisoning her husband. During the reign of his son, more than one head was chopped off for treason; and women were flogged by tap of drum, for petty theft, at the Market Cross of Edinburgh. Neither need the superstitions of the poor Muscovites excite surprise, when we find, in 1867, Highlanders in Scotland putting clay figures into running streams to bring consumption and wasting upon their enemies; burying a living cock (as the Pagan sacrificed to Hermes) to cure epilepsy; and a woman in Somersetshire* cooking toads in a pan, exactly as the "black and midnight hags" did in the days of Macbeth, for the amiable purpose of bewitching her neighbours. So truly does the world reproduce itself, in spite of its boasted civilisation.

The next day was not far advanced when Balgonie was summoned by General Weymarn, whose staff he had been resolving to quit; but for what purpose, or whither to go, he knew not. With something of a shudder, he beheld the Stepniak—the comrade and confederate of the late Nicholas Paulovitch—leaving the General's quarters.

Save that he wore the scarlet livery of his new trade,—torture and death,—he was unchanged, and was the same hideous and ill-visaged giant— with square shoulders, enormous beard, mouse-like eyes, hair shorn off straight across the beetle-brows, and the pine-apple shaped head—whom Balgonie had seen in the hut where the wretched Podatchkine perished. He was now public executioner of St. Petersburg: under his felon hands had poor Mierowitz and Mariolizza been, and erelong would Natalie be!

* *Western Gazette*, September, 1867.

Weymarn was a grave and stern, yet not unkind, old soldier; and, on perceiving that his young aide-de-camp looked pale, he spoke to him with unusual kindness, and added :—

" I am sorry to say, that I have a new duty of importance for you to perform."

"Thanks, General; any excitement is better than—than idleness."

" True. You will have to ride to Schlusselburg with an escort, composed of six Cossacks of the Imperial Guard, and bring hither in a kabitka the sum of eighty thousand roubles, which are there in canvas bags, *sealed*. They have been levied on the estates of the Count Mierowitz. You will receive them from the officer commanding there: give a signed receipt, and deliver them into the Imperial Treasury."

Balgonie bowed in silence.

The General, who, of course, knew well the corrupt venality of the Russian service, added :—

" If the sum is brought *entire* to the Treasury, Carl Ivanovitch, a reasonable gratuity will, of course, be paid you."

" Excellency, I require none for doing my duty, either in this or any other matter," replied Balgonie coldly, even haughtily.

" As you please, sir,—as you please. Some among us might be less particular," said the old General, tugging his grisly mustaches. " And stay; by-the-bye, there is a prisoner in Schlusselburg, whose sentence is to be executed to-morrow,

in presence 'of the assembled troops and people
here——"

Balgonie thought of but *one* prisoner there; and
an icy chill came over him, as Weymarn said—

"With the escort and the kabitka, Captain,
you will, at the same time, bring the culprit
here."

"And—and this pris—on—oner, Excellency?" faltered the poor fellow.

"Is Jagouski, the Cossack, who so severely
wounded Colonel Bernikoff when in the execution
of his duty."

Charlie breathed more freely.

"An order will be necessary for you—a special
order: since the affair of that wretched young
fellow Mierowitz, we cannot be too particular, so
take this :—

" ' *To the officer commanding in Schlusselburg.*

" ' You are hereby directed to deliver to
Captain Carl Ivanovitch Balgonie, of the Smolensko Regiment, the prisoner who is to be
executed to-morrow.

" ' WEYMARN, *Lieutenant-General.'*

"For the delivery of the money, here is a
separate order from the Treasurer—adieu."

CHAPTER XXIII.

WILL HE SUCCEED?

As Balgonie left the presence of General Weymarn, a sudden light broke through the darkness of his mind—an unlooked-for thought and hope suddenly inspired him, and a prayer of thanks to Heaven rose to his lips therefore. No prisoner was actually designated by *name* in the written order of the General!

Thus, in lieu of the Cossack Jagouski, he would demand that Natalie Mierowna be given into his custody; and with her he would escape, quit Russia and the service of the Empress at all risks.

He had no papers—no leave of absence, or passport; but, as the epaulette is an all-powerful badge in Russia, his uniform and his sabre would be passports enough. For the rest, he must trust to his own love and courage, and to his knowledge of the country. But then there was the Cossack escort—how was he to rid himself of it? The same kind Heaven which favoured and inspired him now, would not fail to do so, he hoped, when the crisis came.

While his best horse was being saddled and

accoutred, and even when the escort was at the
door, he consulted, till the last moment, the map
of Russia, and also that of Finland, which was not
ceded to the latter till forty-four years after ; and
he made notes of his proposed route. Escape by
sea, by the Lake of Ladoga, or by the shores of
the Gulf, were alike impossible.

There was no way for it but to ride, at all
hazards, towards the frontier of Finland, or the
shores of the Lake of Saima ; they would there
be safe beyond pursuit—safe among the hospit-
able Swedes, who are always hostile to the grasping and aggressive Russians. And so for nearly
an hour he sat, compass in hand, calculating the
chances and measuring the distances, while his
brain grew giddy, and his heart was sick, with
mingled hope, anxiety, and a love that was full
of terror and compassion.

At last he saw his way clearly, as he thought,
through Viborg, from Schlusselburg, north-west-
ward, in safety. He put all the money he possessed—not much, certainly—about his person in
gold; filled his cartridge-box with ammunition,
and buckled on his sabre.

"By this time to-morrow," he muttered, as he
glanced at his watch, "the game will have been
won or—lost !"

He then mounted, with a resolute heart, and
set forth, having with him a light kabitka, or
covered waggon, drawn by a single horse, and attended by his escort—six Malo-Russian Cossacks

who wore the uniform of Hussars, and who were all stout, athletic, and noble-looking fellows, whose clean-limbed, active, and hardy little horses, unmatched for strength and speed, made Balgonie speculate painfully and anxiously on his slender chance of outstripping them, if pursued.

It was considerably past the noon of an October day—a dark, lowering, and ominous day—when they set out for Schlusselburg, and erelong the rain began to fall heavily, soaking the Hussar finery of the Cossacks of the Guard; but Charlie Balgonie rode silently on at their head, heedless of the blinding torrents and the bellowing wind; though he little knew that as the darkness increased, and the early night drew on, that the waters of the lake and river were rising fast, and that a peril, of which he had no conception, already menaced the existence of Natalie.

But her voice seemed to be ever whispering in his ear—

"Carl, Carl—my beloved Carl, come to my aid—save me—help me, if you love me!"

When they were mid-way to Schlusselburg, the kabitka driver, who was either sleepy or tipsy, fell awkwardly from his seat, and broke his right arm. What was to be done now?

No Cossack of the Guard would condescend to supply his place, and for more than an hour the party remained halted in a desolate spot, near a pine wood, while looking about to capture the first peasant, serf, or civilian of any kind, whom they might meet, and press him into the service, as a temporary whip, in the employ of the Empress.

A skulking and somewhat sulky boor, in a fur cap and canvas caftan, leather leggings and bark shoes, who had been smoking his pipe under a great tree, was, erelong, discovered, dragged forward, and, with sundry oaths and threats, commanded to mount the shaft and act as driver, which he did, with a reluctance he was at no pains to conceal.

Knowing how necessary it was to control or to conciliate this new acquisition, Balgonie asked him a few questions, with sternness, but yet with politeness.

The serf was a singularly handsome young man, with eagle-like eyes, and an aquiline nose, that was almost hooked; he was without his mustache, which seemed to have been recently shaved off; but he had a curly red beard, with a complexion of well-nigh Asiatic darkness.

"Trust me, dear Carl Ivanovitch," said he, in a low and impressive voice, that was strangely familiar to Balgonie. "My disguise, I find, is complete indeed, when it deceives even you; but speak in French."

" Your disguise—yours ? "

" Yes,—I am Apollo Usakoff," he added through his teeth.

" Heaven be blessed for this new omen of

success ! " exclaimed Balgonie, in French. " And you were not drowned ? "

" No ; I swam down the Neva, under water, escaping many a bullet—got ashore, and reached the old place in the wood, where Olga, the gipsy, stained my face, trimmed and dyed my beard, as you see. She is quite an artist, that girl ! Even Mariolizza would not know me now."

Balgonie sighed as the poor fellow spoke. Mutilated and disfigured as she was now, would he have known *her* ? He evidently knew nothing of the barbarities to which she had been subjected, so Balgonie resolved, mercifully, to keep him in ignorance ; and they proceeded at an easy pace together, he keeping his horse close by the shaft of the kabitka, on which the pretended peasant rode ; and, as they spoke in French, a language unknown to their ignorant and half-savage escort, Usakoff, in referring to the late event and its failure, poured out all the bitterness, the hate, and fury of his soul, against the Government, the Councillors, and the rule of the Empress ; and, of course, entered with fervour into the scheme of an escape with Natalie. But still their ultimate plans were undecided, when they saw the red flash of the evening gun, as it pealed from Schlusselburg, amid the murky haze of a wet and stormy sunset ; and erelong they saw the lights that glittered at times from amid the massive towers and black outline of that old castle (the scene of so many terrors, sufferings, and atrocities) streaming and wavering on the turbulent waters of the lake, and the wet slime of the sluices and ditches.

When, all dripping and jaded, the escort halted and dismounted under the castle arch, Balgonie found that some changes were taking place in the executive of the fortress.

Bernikoff, whose wounds had been inflamed to gangrene, by passion, rage, and vodka, was at that moment actually on his death-bed, with Father Chrysostom kneeling by his side. The old sinner was in all the agonies and terrors of reviewing his past life on one hand, and anticipating the coming change on the other. Many pounds of perfumed wax candles were flaming now round the effigy of St. Sergius, whom, in weak and querulous accents, he implored for intercession, alternately with the Chaplain, to whose cassock he clung tenaciously, and to whom he was mingling threats of punishment, if he permitted him to fare ill in the other world, or omitted masses for his soul's repose. And that superstition and absurdity might not be wanting amid this solemn but repulsive scene, from which Balgonie hurried away with more disgust than pity, Bernikoff was dying in the habit of *a friar*, with cowl, cord, beads, and sandals, hoping even on his death-bed, as Ivan the Terrible hoped, when similarly arrayed and disguised, to cheat the devil, if that dread personage came for his sinful soul.

The cowl and other paraphernalia he had obtained from the Chamberlain, or wardrobe-keeper, of the Troitza monastery near the Louga—a cowl that had lain on the mummy of the uncorrupted saint in the silver shrine;—and almost with his last breath, he threatened Father Chrysostom with a drum-head court-martial for venturing to hint that this attempt to mask his past life was vain without true repentance.

Leaving this scene, Balgonie presented the order of General Weymarn and that of the Treasurer, to Captain Vlasfief, who was now in command, and to whom he stated that "the prisoner referred to was Mademoiselle Natalie Mierowna."

"Carl Ivanovitch," said the Captain, "you cannot think of leaving to-night in such a storm of wind and rain?"

"I've seen worse in Silesia," said Balgonie, looking to the locks of his pistols.

"What of that?"

"But the *verbal* order of the General was most peremptory."

"Ah!—and you have brought a kabitka for the money?"

"A kabitka for the prisoner also—so be quick, Captain."

"'Tis a large sum in roubles," mused the other.

"I am in haste to be gone!—the prisoner—you hear me, sir?" said Balgonie impatiently.

"By all the devils, you seem more anxious about the prisoner than the treasure!" responded

Vlasfief sulkily, as he knocked the ashes from his pipe, but still delayed to move.

"You have my orders—I come in the name of the Empress—let there be no delay, Captain Vlasfief," was the curt reply.

"Bring in two Cossacks of the escort; the money is here in seventy bags, each containing a thousand roubles."

"Excuse me, but the order of the Imperial Treasurer says expressly *eighty* sealed bags of a thousand each," said Balgonie, trembling with anxiety, yet compelled to appear to take an interest when he really felt none.

"Ten thousand are missing," said Vlasfief, leisurely, refilling his pipe.

"Missing !"

"Yes. Suppose," he added in a whisper, "suppose we divide the lost sum between us, and offer a thousand to the Treasurer."

"Impossible, sir !" said Balgonie, with a fiery and impatient manner.

"Well, well—there are the other ten sealed bags," added Captain Vlasfief, with a dark and stealthy frown of greed and hate, as the Cossacks tossed the whole among the straw of the kabitka : "it matters little; but I hope you may not find the road *beset*, and so lose the whole."

"To be forewarned, sir, is to be forearmed," said Balgonie, touching his pistols; for he quite understood the treachery implied, and only trembled lest it might mar his dearest plans. "And now, sir, for my prisoner."

"If she be not drowned; for the lower vaults are apt to be flooded on such a night as this," said Vlasfief spitefully.

Writhing under the keen glances of this low-born Muscovite, Balgonie felt that all now depended upon his outward and assumed bearing of coolness and carelessness. Night favoured him in this, and his face was almost concealed. Could any one then have read his heart, as he, Usakoff, two Cossacks, and two soldiers of the main-guard made their way down, down through dark and slimy passages and stairs, till they were foot deep and then knee deep in the water that flooded the low and humid corridors, off which were the arched doors of numerous cells—corridors where spiders spun their webs, rats were swimming, and terrified bats flew wildly to and fro !

Erelong they reached the door, through the crannies of which despairing cries and painful gaspings had been heard, and, after unlocking, forced it open by main strength.

"A great flood of water poured from the aperture amid the darkness," says the *Utrecht Gazette*, "and with it came the body of the poor lady, who was well-nigh drowned."

So the red light seen by Natalie was no fancy, but that of the lamp which was borne by one of those who came just in time to save her from the same terrible death by which the Princess Orloff perished.

Lest all might be perilled by a recognition, Balgonie was compelled to retire and leave her in the Chaplain's hands till she was restored to consciousness, to warmth, and till she was habited anew; and he passed three dreadful hours of doubt and anxiety, while pacing to and fro in the cold and gloomy archways of the fortress, and having to conceal his face when she was brought forth and supported into the kabitka, to which two *fresh* horses were now traced. Usakoff sprang on the shaft and flourished his whip; then the Cossacks and Balgonie put spurs to their chargers, and clattered over the wet drawbridge, just as the passing bell for the departure of Bernikoff's tortured spirit rang ominously and solemnly on the stormy gusts of that black and gloomy night.

Balgonie, instead of proceeding by the way he had come, avoided the town of Schlusselburg, and wheeled off to the right, committing himself partly to the guidance of Usakoff, and quite in ignorance that, about an hour before, Vlasfief, who could by no means let so many roubles escape without paying toll, had beset two of the roads by chosen followers of his own—men whom he hoped might pass for some of the adherents of the late Prince Ivan, rescuing the daughter of the exiled Count Mierowitz.

A strange incident occurred before the interment of old Bernikoff, who had a pompous military funeral. The bottom of his grave was found to be on fire!

A Scottish doctor (named Rogerson, we believe) at Catharine's Court attempted to explain this phenomenon, as resulting from a species of ironstone which was saturated with the phosphorus supplied by the bones of old interments, and which had been ignited by the friction of the sexton's shovel; but the superstitious Russians took a very different and much more diabolical view of the matter, and laughed to scorn the learned opinion of the Scottish pundit.

CHAPTER XXIV.

CONCLUSION.

THEIR horses were tolerably refreshed by the halt at Schlusselburg, and the nags which drew the light kabitka had been quite unused, so the whole party pushed on at a brisk pace, by the road towards the frontiers of Finland, the Cossacks of the escort, whatever they thought, making neither remark nor inquiry, as they trusted obediently and implicitly to the officer who led them ; but the darkness of the October morning, the deep and muddy, stony and rough, nature of the roads, and the violence of the storm, erelong began to have a severe effect upon their cattle, and, to the great satisfaction of Balgonie, two of the troopers gradually dropped to the rear, and were seen no more.

Now the Corporal of the Cossacks ventured to hint, that "perhaps they were not pursuing the way they had come, as the lights in St. Isaac's Cathedral must have been visible long ago ;" but Balgonie replied, haughtily and briefly, that he " had *special* orders."

Then the Corporal urged a short halt, as the

horses were sinking; but again Balgonie replied, that he "had peculiar orders, and must push on."

After passing a little village with a windmill, several miles from the shore of the Lake of Ladoga, the road dipped down into a dark hollow, between impending crags of granite, the grey faces of which were already beginning to brighten in the first light of the lagging October sun. The rain and wind were over; the hollow way was full of rolling and perplexing mist; but Usakoff affirmed with confidence that he knew the country well.

Out of the grey vapour, from both sides of the path, there flashed, redly and luridly, five or six muskets! One bullet struck white splinters from the kabitka eliciting a shriek from its occupant; another whistled through the mane of Charlie's horse; and a third killed one of the Cossacks, who died without a groan, for it passed fairly through his temples.

The way was beset by armed men, whose numbers and disposition the dim light, or, rather, the darkness and the mist, alike served to conceal.

"Make way, in the name of the Empress!" cried Balgonie, dashing forward, with his sabre drawn; "Nay, I command you, on your peril and allegiance!" he added, as the threatening words of Vlasfief occurred to him; and, to his astonishment and dismay, he saw that personage actually appear, mounted and armed, wearing a regimental hat and plume, with a kind of dark green tunic, or patrol jacket, richly braided with gold, and trimmed heavily with black fur. His party, who seemed all on foot, were clad like peasants, but were armed with muskets, which they were rapidly casting about and reloading.

"Halt, in the name of the Empress—halt, I command you! for this is *not* the way to St. Petersburg, whither the prisoner and treasure were to be conveyed. Treason! treason!" shouted the Staff Captain Vlasfief.

Balgonie fired a pistol at his head; but the Captain's horse reared, or was compelled to do so by bit and spur, for the bullet pierced its throat; and with an oath, Vlasfief fell on the pathway, entangled in the stirrups as the animal sank under him.

The three remaining Cossacks, who were somewhat bewildered by the attack, by the appearance of Vlasfief, whom they knew, and whose confident bearing confirmed certain gathering suspicions that something was wrong as to their route, now drew their sabres, aimed several blows at Usakoff's head, and endeavoured to cut the reins of his horse, or stab it between the shafts, as he lashed the animal almost to racing speed, and the light kabitka jolted, rolled, and bounded along the rough road behind it.

By another pistol-shot Balgonie rid himself of the Cossack Corporal, whose bridle arm he broke, while facing about and galloping in rear of the kabitka; and now with wild hallooes, the entire party of armed men followed it on foot, with all speed, up a steep slope, over which the path wound.

Usakoff ground his teeth, for he was without weapons, and passive in the flying combat; but, being fertile in expedients, he tore open a bag of roubles, and scattered them on the upland road with a ready and reckless hand.

The bright silver coins proved too exciting for the cupidity of the pursuers, who loitered to pick them up, tumbling, scrambling, rising and falling over each other, with shouts, curses, and male-dictions, their fire-arms sometimes exploding the while; and so the whole were speedily left behind, as the kabitka, guarded now by Bal-gonie alone, was driven along a lonely and unfrequented road, that led to the little town of Pomphela.

"Thanks, dear Usakoff—thanks for your presence of mind," said Balgonie; "I had forgot all about those roubles."

"Silver has achieved for us what neither our lead or steel would have done!"

"But, to lighten the kabitka, let us throw out those remaining bags—this perilous lumber, the intended recapture of which has nearly cost us our lives—honour—all, at the hands of Vlasfief."

"Nay, nay, never! Lumber, say you? The roubles are Natalie's—hers and mine—hers and yours, when you wed her; they have saved us once, and may do so again," replied Usakoff cheerfully, as the sun burst forth in his clear October splendour, and they saw the dome-shaped cupola of the Church of Pomphela rising with a golden gleam from amid the white morning haze.

There Balgonie's uniform and a display of gold and roubles operated powerfully on the Postmaster, who, without asking for passports or other papers, at once, and in the name of the Empress, supplied them with fresh horses for the frontier, towards which, after procuring some proper nourishment and restoratives for Natalie, they pushed on without a moment of unnecessary delay.

"Ah," thought Balgonie, with a shudder and a prayer; "had Jagouski's name *not* been omitted in that order of Weymarn, where would she have been now?"

Pale with sorrow and long suffering, her face was still beautiful, though sorely wasted; the deep thoughtful eyes had yet a wealth—a world of tenderness in their liquid depths; and the long dark hair was thick, soft, and wavy as ever, as it fell in masses behind the small, compact, and finely-formed head.

Yet withal, her wretchedness had been extreme, having been so suddenly and rudely rent from all those habits of luxury and tender nurture, which had become, as it were, a second nature; and often, very often, had it occurred to her in her later misery of soul "that the repose of the grave is sweet, and that there cometh after death a levelling and making even of things which would at last cure all her evils."

But all was changed now; and, as she laid her head on Charlie's breast, she felt content—almost happy; and the horrors that hung over her family alone prevented her, as yet, from being completely so.

No trace of pursuers were behind them now, though their flight must by this time have been known both in the capital and at Schlusselburg. But in those days there were neither railroads nor electric telegraphs; so, riding on more leisurely, Balgonie changed horses again near Viborg, and erelong the great Lake of Saima appeared before them, with the distant hills of Swedish Finland beyond its friendly waters.

A boat was procured there; the kabitka was abandoned; and, with a shout of joy, Usakoff assisted the Finnish boatman to hoist the great lug-sail to catch the breeze of a balmy and beautiful evening, as they bade a long farewell to Russia and all its terrors.

In a quaint old Church of Finland, by the eastern shore of the Lake of Saima, and in view of its little archipelago of granite isles,—a lonely little fane, buried amid groves of plum and cherry trees, built of wood and painted red, with a little holy bell jangling in its humble belfry,—Charlie Balgonie and his fugitive bride were united by the old Curate, with the consent of the Lutheran Bishop of Heinola; and there a thousand roubles spent among the poor spread in the primitive district a happiness, the tradition of which is still remembered with many a grateful exaggeration.

After this, poor Usakoff, finding himself perhaps, as a third person, rather in the way, left them to become a soldier of fortune; and he is supposed to have perished in one of the Polish struggles for freedom; at least, they heard of him no more, after their final journey to Scotland.

Two years before these events, it would appear that Charlie's uncle, "the godly and upright" Gamaliel Balgonie, merchant, magistrate, and elder, had departed in peace to sin no more, leaving the lands and possessions of Balgonie unimpaired; and a long tombstone in that famous city of the dead, the Howff of Dundee, records at length all the virtues which his contemporaries in general and the Presbytery in particular believed him to possess.

So Carl Ivanovitch became once more Balgonie of that Ilk; and the roubles of Natalie added many a turret and many an acre to his patrimonial dwelling in beautiful Strathearn.

L'ENVOI.—ILLUSTRATIVE NOTE.

To convince the reader how nearly History has been followed in the previous pages, we shall take the liberty of inserting the subsequent manifesto, published with reference to the death of Ivan IV.

> "By the Grace of God, we, Catharine the Second, Empress and Autocratrice of all the Russias, &c., &c., to all whom these presents may concern:

When by the divine will, and in compliance with the unanimous desires of our faithful subjects, we ascended the throne of Russia, we were not ignorant that Ivan, son of Anthony, Prince of Brunswick-Wolfenbuttel, and of the Princess Anne of Mecklenburg was still alive. This Prince, as is well known, was immediately after his birth unlawfully declared heir to the imperial crown; *but*, by the decrees of Providence, he was soon after irrevocably excluded from that high dignity, and the sceptre was placed in the hands of the lawful heiress, Elizabeth (daughter of Peter the Great), our beloved aunt of glorious memory.

"After we had ascended the throne, and offered up to Heaven our just thanksgivings, the first object that employed our thoughts, in consequence of *that humanity which is so natural to us*, was the unhappy situation of that Prince, who was *dethroned* by *divine Providence*, and had been unfortunate since his birth

"To prevent, therefore, ill-intentioned persons from giving him any trouble, or from making use of his name to disturb the public tranquillity, we gave him a guard, and placed about his person two officers, in whose fidelity and integrity we could confide. These were Captain Vlasfief and Lieutenant Tschekin, who by their long military services deserved a suitable recompense, and a station in which they might pass quietly the remainder of their days. They were accordingly charged with the care of the Prince, and were strictly enjoined to let none approach him. Yet all these precautions were not sufficient. . . .

"A *Put-parooschick* (a sub-lieutenant) of the Regiment of Smolensko, a native of the Ukraine, Basil Mierowitz (grandson of the first rebel that followed Mazeppa), took it into his head to make use of this Prince, to advance his fortune at all events, without being restrained by a consideration of the bloody scene that such an attempt might occasion. In order to execute this detestable, dangerous, and desperate project, he con-

trived, during our absence in Livonia, to be
upon guard in the fortress of Schlusselburg,
where the guard is relieved every eight days;
and the 15th of last month, about two in the
morning, he called out the main guard, formed
it in line, and ordered the soldiers to load with
ball. Bernikoff, Governor of the fortress, came
out of his apartment, and asked Mierowitz the
reason of the disturbance, but received no other
answer from this rebel than a blow with the
butt-end of his musket.

"Captain Vlasfief and Lieutenant Tschekin
seeing that it was impossible to resist such a
superior force, and considering the unhappy consequences that must ensue from the deliverance
of THE PERSON who was committed to their care,
after deliberating together, took the only step that
they thought proper to maintain public tranquillity, which was to *cut short the days of the unfortunate Ivan.* Mierowitz, on seeing the dead body
of the Prince, was so confounded by a sight he so
little expected, that he acknowledged his temerity
and guilt, and discovered his repentance to the
troops, whom, about an hour before, he had se-
duced from their duty, and rendered the accom-
plices of his crime.

"Then it was that the two officers who had
nipped this rebellion in the bud, joined the
Governor of the fortress in securing this rebel,
and bringing back the soldiers to their duty.
They also sent to our Privy Councillor Count

Fanin, *under whose orders they acted*, a relation of this event, which, though unhappy, has nevertheless, *under the protection of Heaven*, prevented still greater calamities. This Senator despatched immediately *Pulovnick* (Colonel) Caschkin, with sufficient instructions to maintain tranquillity on the spot (or where the assassination was committed), and sent us, at the same time, a circumstantial account of the whole affair. In consequence of this, we ordered Lieutenant-General Weymarn, of the division of St. Petersburg, to take the necessary information on the spot; and the confession of the villain himself, who has acknowledged his crime.

" Sensible of its enormity and consequences with regard to the peace of our country, we have referred the whole affair to the consideration of our Senate, which we have ordered, jointly with the Synod, to invite the three first classes and the Presidents of all the Colleges to hear the verbal relation of General Weymarn, who has taken the proper informations, to pronounce sentence in consequence thereof, and to present it to us, for confirmation of the same.

" CATHARINE."

By a singular species of sophistry, the guilt of Ivan's death is thus, by a subsequent document, transferred to Basil Mierowitz :—

"As the violent death of the unfortunate Prince Ivan was the immediate consequence of the desperate attempt of Mierowitz, so must this officer be considered as the principal cause of this assassination—nay, even regarded as *the murderer of that unhappy Prince.*"

To this, five Russian Bishops appended their signatures.

Vlasfief was made a General, and his Lieutenant a Colonel, in the following year, with a pension of ten thousand roubles each.

THE END.

PRINTED BY W. H. SMITH AND SON, 186, STRAND, LONDON.

9—8—69.

WORKS OF CHARLES LEVER.

Reprinted from Blackwood's Magazine.

THE name of Charles Lever is still chiefly associated with those novels by which his popularity as a writer was first secured, and by which, perhaps, his subsequent literary reputation has been in some measure overpowered. These works have prob-ably met with a more cordial reception from the public than from the critics. Their author may, in a certain sense, defy criticism, by exclaiming like Horace, " *Pueris canto!*" He has been the biographer of boyhood. In all his earlier works he especially addresses himself to that happy portion of mankind whose digestion is yet unimpaired, whose nerves are unshaken, in whom the breath of life has no resemblance to a sigh, and who (as he himself portrays them) are ever ready to risk, with unabated ardour, a broken neck or a broken heart at every turn in the joyous chase of existence. To the verdict of such an audience Mr. Lever has every right to appeal as gaily and as confidently as Anacreon appealed to the Loves. It would undoubtedly be as ungracious to reproach the author of 'Charles O'Malley' with the absence of those pretensions to literary dignity which he himself disclaims with so merry a laugh at dignities of every sort, as to denounce the Greek lyrist for his resolute refusal to celebrate the exploits of Atrides. To the most captious critic Mr. Lever may fairly say,—

"Non potes in nugas dicere plura meas
Ipse ego quam dixi."

And he that can follow the adventures of HARRY LORREQUER, CHARLES O'MALLEY, JACK HINTON, and TOM BURKE, without

A

the frequent interruption of hearty laughter, has probably survived all sense of enjoyment in the society of the young. In any case he is not a man to be envied. To us, indeed, there is something of pathos in the reperusal of these books. It is like reading one's old love-letters, or hearing an old friend recount the frolics of one's own youth. We turn the pages with a certain tender incredulity, and there steals over us a sensation like that

> "Smell of violets hidden in the green,"

which the poet declares to have

> "Poured back into his empty soul and frame
> The times when he remembers to have been
> Joyful, and free from blame."

Mr. Lever's blooming young heroes, if not invariably blameless, are at least exceedingly joyful. Like the first mariners, they launch into the sea of life with breasts fortified by oak and triple brass : their constitutions are Titanic. To watch them from the beaten high road of tame and ordinary experience, dashing and glittering through a stupendous steeple-chase of astounding and never ending adventure, literally takes away our breath. We cannot but sigh as we ask ourselves, "Was life indeed, then, at any time, such an uncommonly pleasant holiday?" Has not the world itself grown older and colder since those jaunty days when the dazzling Mr. Lorrequer drove his four-in-hand through all the proprieties? Is it possible that Mr. Lorrequer's son and heir, whom we presume to be now a hopeful cornet in the Blues, can be such a merry dog as we all remember his father to have been? Would not any such artless, but not invariably harmless, ebullitions of youthful mirth as those recorded with infinite gusto in the biography of the elder gentleman, be now visited with the severest penalties at the disposal of Bow Street, and denounced with the angriest eloquence at the command of the 'Times'? We suspect that the younger Mr. Lorrequer is a man of much sadder complexion. It would not, alas ! surprise us to learn that, notwithstanding a prudent regard for his health, he is occasionally not altogether free from low spirits, especially when his natural hilarity is tempered by the prospective shadow of a competitive examination, or vexed by the aggressive attentions of the Civil Service Commissioners. The fact is, that times are changed with us. Napoleon's Paladins are *quivis et umbra*. Beau Brummel has paid his last debt. Duelling is a thing forsworn. Notwithstanding Dr. Parr's celebrated receipt for the gout, consisting of " prayer, patience, and port-wine," this latter source of human comfort is all but extinct. The epitaph of it is already written by Mr. Cobden in the French Treaty. The Union is an historical reminiscence. The Encumbered Estates Bill has done its work. " After life's fitful fever," O'Connell agitates no more. And Harry Lorrequer, and Charles O'Malley, and Jack Hinton, and Tom Burke, and Bagenal Daly, look down upon us from the distance of an age no longer ours. We have no hope ever again to meet them cantering in the Phœnix Park or swaggering down Sackville Street, or dancing at Dublin Castle. They are all " gone *proiapsui* to the Stygian shore." Like Achilles, and Ajax, and all the *fortes ante Agamemnonem*, they rest in an elysium of which the beatitude appears to us shadowy and unreal But they have quaffed their last bumper, and shot their last shot—

" They lie beside their nectar, and their bolts are hurled."

And although their glittering hosts yet hover about the fading splendour of the " good old times," as the Scandinavian warriors are said by the Swedish poet to hover in the light of sunset over the horizon of the Baltic, yet we can no more recall them to tangible existence than we can renew the race of the Anakim.

Mr. Lever has himself survived his first progeny. That in growing an older, he has also grown a wiser, and in some respects a sadder man, his more recent writings bear witness. Job's second batch of sons and daughters, who were, doubtless, a much steadier set of young people than the first, could not have differed from that jovial crew who were overwhelmed in a whirlwind whilst " eating and drinking wine," more strongly than Mr. Lever's later works differ from his earlier ones.

The author of ' Harry Lorrequer ' has given unquestionable proof of powers matured by time and enriched by cultivation. His more recent novels evince a greater mastery in the craft of authorship, a larger experience, and more skilled faculty of construction. But whether these qualities exist in so great a

A 2

degree as entirely to compensate the reader for the absence of that vivacity, freshness, and continuous flow of high animal spirits, which have rendered Mr. Lever's first books so widely and so justly popular, is a question which we shall presently have occasion to consider. Meanwhile, to say of such novels as 'Harry Lorrequer' and its immediate successors that they abound in extravagance, is to detract nothing from the merit of them. Youth is in itself the grandest of all extravagances; and these books are an emanation from, and the embodiment of, all the joyous audacity of young manhood. We cannot too largely estimate the extent to which Mr. Lever possesses the merit most essential to popularity in narrative composition—viz. *gusto.* He relates incidents with a relish, and accumulates them with a fecundity of invention and a rapidity of movement that never flag. Of all qualities in the genius of an author, this is the most necessary to the successful conduct of narrative interest; and we must the more admire it, wherever it is displayed, because it is innate, and neither to be acquired by labour, nor replaced by experience. It is to this rush and flow of vigorous animal life that we must attribute the indescribable attraction exerted by Homer upon the sympathies of all ages and conditions of men; and we accord to the Father of Verse a supremacy felt to be unattainable by any other poet, in recognition (which is perhaps partly unconscious) of the completeness with which he has expressed the high spirits and dauntless health of the boyhood of mankind. A recent poet, who deserves to be better known, has said that " the old gods were only men and wine." Their godship is certainly the extravagant idealization of the merely human faculties at their highest pitch. The same extravagance gives to the Homeric heroes their colossal proportions. Achilles and Hector will, to the end of time, be a head-and-shoulders taller than all other men, because it is impossible that any man should realize so intensely, or define so distinctly, as Homer, the supernatural dimensions of all natural faculties and sensations. To represent human beings precisely as they are, is not a necessary condition of art of any kind. A deformed saint by Massaccio may be truer in art than a correct anatomical study by Mr. Etty. Nor is there any reason why that extravagance of design which dilates either human actions or human emotions, or even the situations of human life, to perfectly impossible proportions should be in itself a defect. For what is impossible in fact may be proper in art. Ariosto is undoubtedly one of the greatest narrative poets, and it is probably in his extravagance that we shall find the secret of his indefinable power. The humour of Quevedo is often most irresistible when it consists entirely of what might be called pure extravagance of expression. And such extravagance as is tob e found in Mr. Lever's earlier novels is occasioned by the overflow of that exuberant vitality which constitutes their special excellence. The plan and character of these books are obviously panoramic rather than dramatic. It is by the narration of humorous incident that the interest of the reader is to be carried on. For this, rapidity and gusto are the best of all qualifications. No great writer of narrative fiction has ever been wholly without them. Le Sage possessed them largely; they are to be detected in the sadder and more profound genius of Cervantes; they are not wanting to the elaborate minuteness of De Foe; they give vigour to the most envenomed creations of Swift; they are remarkable in Sir Walter Scott, than whom, certainly, there is no happier master of the art of telling a story. Fielding, though his genius philosophizes while it frolics, was far from neglecting those means of exciting interest which depend upon the rapid movement and striking effect of incident. But Smollett certainly possessed the gift of high spirits to a pre-eminent degree. The extraordinary impulse and animation of his genius is such, that his narrative, though often extremely digressive, always rushes away with the reader, and carries him, like a runaway horse, over every obstacle, "*turbine raptus ingenii.*"

In this respect Mr. Lever, of all modern novelists, most resembles the author of 'Roderick Random.' There is, indeed, not only much similarity of character between the works of Charles Lever and those of Tobias Smollett, but also no inconsiderable coincidence in the circumstances which may possibly have given to the genius of both authors something of the same tendency.

The Irish humorist, like his great Scotch predecessor. was, we believe, brought up for the medical profession, and foç some years practised as a doctor. Whether indeed Mr. Lever found his profession as little profitable to him as it would appear to have proved to Dr. Smollett, or whether he was simply impelled to abandon so sober a career by the consciousness of those powers of humour and that facility of composition which he evinced at an early age, we do not know; but it is difficult to believe that the pen which wrote 'Charles O'Malley,' or that which wrote 'Peregrine Pickle,' would have been equally well employed in signing prescriptions. To the experience of medical life, however, to the opportunities for the study of character thereby afforded, and the quickness of penetration and habits of observation thus acquired, it is highly probable that both Smollett and Lever have owed much excellent material for humorous fiction. Both authors appear to have early evinced, and long retained, an extreme predilection for a military life. Smollett, indeed, never forgave his grandfather for thwarting his inclination to enter the army; and he never omits an occasion for introducing into his novels some description of martial scenes and events. There is fair reason to attribute to both Smollett and Lever some carelessness, not so much of composition, as of writing. They both appear to have written hastily. Of Smollett it is told that (whilst writing the 'Adventures of Sir Launcelot Greaves') "when post-time drew near he used to retire for half-an-hour or an hour to prepare the necessary quantity of *copy*, as it is technically called in the printing-house, which he never gave himself the trouble to correct, or even to read once." And we may assume that Mr. Lever, speaking through the mask of Harry Lorrequer, is not very wide of the truth when he says, "I wrote as I felt—sometimes in good spirits, sometimes in bad—always carelessly—for, God help me! I can do no better." Smollett is, indeed, the more correct writer of the two; his style, though often hasty, is never inaccurate, and, for the most part, his English is very pure. Mr. Lever's language, on the contrary, is in places so heedless that the grammar of it is sometimes more conventional than correct. In one place he speaks of "purchasing a boon," and in another he describes an Irish member waiting "till the House was done prayers." Nevertheless he has great powers of description. He represents objects and actions with a touch that is always vivid, often masterly. He is always happy in the open air; in his love of nature and hearty relish of out-of-door life, as well as in the force and fidelity with which he depicts them, he is certainly unsurpassed, and perhaps unequalled, by Smollett himself. The veracity, freshness, and power with which he describes scenery is deserving, we think, of higher appreciation than it has yet received. His pictures of Irish landscape, sea scenery, and all effects of wind and weather, are full of the truth and intensity which belong to poetry. It is for such reasons all the more to be regretted that an author entitled on so many grounds to hold a permanent place in literature should ever be forgetful of the duty which is owed by eminent writers to the language they bequeath to posterity. Some expressions throughout Mr. Lever's works, so incorrect as to be obvious oversights, have passed through so many editions that we must believe the ὃ γέγραφα γέγραφα sentiment to be in him unusually strong, and that what he writes he never revises. The bent of such minds as those of Mr. Lever and Dr. Smollett is instinctively conservative, loyal, and inclined to the maintenance of institutions which have been tested and endeared by time. On the one hand, a shrewd appreciation of life as it is, and a keen sense of the ludicrous and incongruous, indisposes them to indulge in the dreams of democracy; whilst, ou the other hand, a certain chivalry of disposition induces them to side with a cause which, by the very nature of it, must always be that of the party attacked. Conservatism, therefore, has found in each of these writers a warm and ready adherent. To continue any further this passing comparison between the two authors would be tedious and pedantic; but if we turn to the books themselves, we cannot but remark a resemblance which in many respects is striking.

The merits as well as the defects of both writers are, for the most part, of the same kind. Their humour does not always rise above fun, their fun sometimes degenerates into farce. Criticism, which is applicable to such books as 'Harry Lorrequer' and 'Charles O'Malley' may equally be applied to 'Roderick Random' and 'Peregrine Pickle.' We can feel little sympathy for the heroes themselves, and still less for

the greater part of the personages by whom we find them
surrounded. Roderick Random is a low-minded, selfish,
unamiable character. Harry Lorrequer is not much more
thoughtful of the feelings of others, and his various misdeeds
are only not amenable to the gravest censure because they
render gravity impossible, and compel the reader himself to
become an accomplice in their impish frolic.   Peregrine
Pickle is a brutal savage, indulging an almost fiendish delight
in the prosecution of the most barbarous practical jokes.
Charles O'Malley, though much less repulsive, is certainly a
brawling mischievous fellow, whose acquaintance we, for our
own part, must confess we should little desire out of a book.
The female characters are often too merely animal, or else too
shadowy and indistinct, to inspire much interest.   Of the
rest of the *dramatis personæ* the larger portion is often made
up of adventurers, blacklegs, practical jokers, and such oddi-
ties and odds and ends of humanity as seem only made to
furnish material for practical jokes.   The heroes ramble from
page to page, through scenes and situations almost uncon-
nected, and characters which crowd one portion of the book
hardly appear in another.

Yet, when the critic has summed up all such apparent
grounds of objection, he will find that they constitute no real
defect in the art of these romances, which can only be
criticized in accordance with the laws which they themselves
create.   The fact is, Art does not make Genius, but Genius
makes Art.   "Genius," says Kant, in his 'Analysis of the
Sublime,' "is the talent to produce that of which one cannot
give the determinating rule, and not the ability that one can
show in doing that which one can learn by a rule.   Hence
originality is its first quality."   Every writer of original
genius has his own object, and his own way of carrying it out;
and his success or failure can only be fairly estimated by
reference to the object which he has himself had in view, not
that which the critic expects him to have had in view.   The
barbarous conduct of the clown in the pantomime, the elfish
perversity and duplicity of the Pierot in the French Harle-
quinade, and the excessive profligacy of the Don Juan in the
play, inspire no disgust, outrage no moral sentiment, revolt
no sympathy, but only excite innocent and hearty laughter.

When a clown trips up a baker in the street, wheels him off in his own barrow, trundles him into his own oven, and there bakes him alive, the fate of the baker excites no pity, and the inhumanity of his persecutor no indignation. And when Harry Lorrequer initiates his proceedings in Dublin, by gratuitously detailing to a perfectly inoffensive stranger an elaborate falsehood, and afterwards shoots the man he has insulted, without the least consciousness of any reason why he should fight him at all, we laugh at the drollery of the misdeed described, without for a moment attributing either to ourselves or the author any participation in the immorality of the conduct which causes our merriment. We know beforehand that all such victims are only men of straw, purposely so contrived as to minister to the fitting spirit of mischievous fun which presides over that entirely fantastical world wherein all that passes is too impossible in fact to come within the jurisdiction of any moral law, and yet sufficiently real in art to enthral attention and create pleasurable emotion. It is in securing this result that the art and genius of the author consist ; and we believe it is no less an authority than Sir Walter Scott who has said, " If it be the highest praise of pathetic composition that it draws forth tears, why should it not be esteemed the greatest excellence of the ludicrous that it compels laughter ? The one tribute is at least as genuine an expression of natural feeling as the other." Certainly, in the power of producing effects irresistibly ludicrous, and instantaneously destructive of all gravity, Mr. Lever is pre-eminent, and may challenge comparison with any writer, living or dead. Nor is even the broad fun of Mr. Lever's earliest novels destitute of passages which indicate powers of thoughtful humour and subtle irony. Sparks's story, in ' Harry Lorrequer,' and the description in it of the man who loves a mad girl—his sensations on discovering her insanity, and hers on finding that he is not the Ace of Spades, and that she has taken "the nephew of a Manchester cotton-spinner, with a face like printed calico, for a trump card, and the best in the pack," is told with an irresistible drollery which only partially conceals a depth of grave sad satire and pathetic allegory. The story of the Knight of Kerry's conversation with the Irish tenant, who earns his "rints" by personating a wild man in a London showroom, has in it much more than the merely ludicrous. The origin of the story would undoubtedly appear to be Hibernian, but it has also been told by Paul de Kock, with little more alteration than that of substituting Frenchmen for Irishmen, and Paris for London. Mr. Lever's version of the story, however, is far more humorous, and in all respects infinitely better than that of the French novelist.   But of all the characters in Mr. Lever's earlier romances, that which affords most evidence of this higher kind of humour, is undoubtedly Mickey Free; and the story (as recounted by himself) of how he got his father's soul out of purgatory, is so excellently well told, and is so admirable a specimen of that sly wit which is characteristic of the Irish peasant, that it is with great reluctance that we refrain from extracting it.

The whole character of Mickey Free is indeed inimitable. We have no hesitation in affirming it to be the most perfect type of Irish humour that has ever been given to the world. It is perfectly sustained from first to last, and nothing in the conception of it is exaggerated or incongruous. Mickey Free is the Irish Sam Weller. He has, in fact, this advantage over Sam Weller, that he is the more thoroughly national and comprehensive type of the two. It is impossible but what this creation, which is in many respects the most felicitous of all Mr. Lever's creations, should live for ever as a distinct embodiment of national character. It must always have a historical value; and it is indeed so truthfully and so comprehensively drawn, that whoever has since attempted to describe in future the Irish peasant, has appeared to copy rather from Lever than from nature. Mickey Free, however, is but one (although, to our thinking, the best) picture in Mr. Lever's large gallery of Irish portraits.

The KNIGHT OF GWYNNE is another equally characteristic; and it is perhaps more delicately, although less vividly, delineated. Nothing can be more complete than this elaborate picture of a character which has ceased to exist—the high-bred, ill-starred Irish gentleman of the days before the Union. It is a strange anomaly, combining all the courtly grace and refinement of a Sir Charles Grandison with the rude, half-civilized life of a Rob Roy; at once splendid and spendthrift; chivalrous in all things, careful in nothing; alienating prosperity, yet elevating misfortune, and always *débonnaire* in the midst of disaster ; every inch a gentleman, yet just such a gentleman as seems destined by Providence to ruin himself, and hasten the ruin of the class to which he belongs. The Knight of Gwynne is certainly one of the most lovable characters that Mr. Lever has ever drawn ; and he monopolizes so much of our sympathy, that we hope to be forgiven for extending less of it than he probably deserves to Bagenal Daly, notwithstanding the vigour with which that character is drawn, the remarkable originality of it, and the fidelity with which it represents and sustains a most peculiar combination of qualities, intellectual as well as moral.

We may, however, note here by the way that this singular character is the first of Mr. Lever's earlier creations, in which he has given evidence of that shrewd experience of mankind, that practical worldly wit, and power of philosophical epigram, into which his natural humour has developed itself in more recent works ; and there are passages of dialogue between "the Howling Wind" and his Irish Scot which not unfrequently remind one of the dry humorous wisdom which abounds in such creations as Dalgetty and Sancho Panza. This work is indeed a most complete and varied picture of Irish life and manners. The book is written with a profound knowledge of the subject of it ; and, without overloading the narrative with political or philosophical discussion, the author never loses sight of a thoughtful purpose ; he penetrates beneath the surface of the society which he describes, and lays bare, with the ease and accuracy of a skilful anatomist, all the minutest causes and remotest effects of those social and political phenomena which in Ireland preceded the Union. The Castlereagh policy is sketched with the masterly hand of a man who has thoroughly comprehended both the nature of the measure itself, and that of the country to which it referred. The whole epoch of that time is indeed reproduced, investigated, and criticized by Mr. Lever, with an accuracy of delineation and depth of reflection which show him to be not only an admirable novelist, but something also of a philosophical politician. What is especially to be noted in this book is, that all the principal

characters therein are the representatives of *genera* rather
than of *species*—that is to say, they image and embody large
aggregates of national character rather than individual and
special peculiarities.   Creation of this kind necessitates
many high powers of thought as well as of fancy ; and
although Mr. Lever has not attempted it so often as he gives
us reason to wish, yet, wherever he has done so, his success
cannot be disputed.   The old ᴌrish proprietor, the old Irish
domestic, the petty usurer, the Irish attorney, founders of a
new race of landlords ; the Irishman of the north, and the
Irishman of the south—are all admirably described in the
'Knight of Gwynne.'   Freeny, the robber, is also a very
well-drawn character ; and the escape of Freeny from the
burning jail is a scene which in power and terror fully justi-
fies the admiration of it formerly entertained by Miss Edge-
worth.

Mr. Lever has, indeed, given many proofs that he is by no
means deficient in the faculty of exciting terror, and some of
his night-rides, his battle-scenes, and robber-meetings have
about them a palpability and intensity which may fairly en-
title them to compete for praise with Smollett's much admired
sea-engagements.   It is as having given the completest and
most intense expression to Irish humour, and furnished familiar types of almost every distinction of Irish character, that
Mr. Lever, whatever may be his other merits, will, in our
opinion, maintain a solid and permanent reputation as a
humorist.   Scenes which, in such novels as ' O'Malley ' and
' Hinton,' may perhaps appear to Cockney critics as simple
impossibilities, are truly facts of Irish life ; and Mr. Lever
has so little caricatured or exaggerated the habits and characters of Irishmen, that those parts of his Irish novels which
appear absurdly unreal are only ridiculously *true*.   It would
be entirely beyond the scope and purpose of these remarks
to discuss the relative value of any really original conception ;
but we see no reason to doubt why Mickey Free, and Major
Monsoon, and Kerry O'Leary, and Baby Blake, Mary Martin,
and Kate O'Donoghue, and Kenny, and Mrs. Dodd, should
not live as long as Jeanie Deans, or Matthew Bramble, or
Squire Weston, or any other distinctly-recognized type of national character.

That conviction which is entertained by Irishmen, not without a certain self-satisfaction, that their characters are all but incomprehensible to Englishmen ; the humorous enjoyment which they derive from the consciousness that their ways and habits are a continual source of dismay and bewilderment to their fellow-subjects over the water ; and a certain sense of not unnatural resentment, with which, some years ago, the Irish people must have been disposed to regard every attempt on the part of Government to shape out or constrain the pattern of their national life into formal accordance with the modes and manners of an alien and dominant race —have furnished Mr. Lever with many opportunities for drollery at the expense of Cockney critics. An amusing piece of good-humoured caricature in this sense occurs in the story of the gentleman who never saw daylight in Ireland, which occupies the twenty-fourth chapter of 'Jack Hinton.' Equally comical in its way is the quiz upon Mr. Prettyman, the "intelligent traveller."

As instances of easy and natural Irish humour, we may refer, by the way, to the oration delivered by Kerry O'Leary over the ruins of the doctor's gig, in the fourteenth chapter of 'The O'Donoghue,' and the priest's moonlit ride in 'Jack Hinton.' Mr. Lever has also shown, in the death of Mary Martin, that he can, when he pleases, be pathetic as well as humorous. His female characters are seldom very refined or very interesting. In depicting a romping "wild Irish girl," a wily adventuress, a Continental demirep, or a pretentious petticoated parvenue, he is never at fault ; but his women are for the most part either *rouées*, romps, or Xantippes ; and the majestic visions which animate old Chaucer's 'Legend of Good Women,' and inspired Wordsworth's picture of the "perfect woman, nobly planned," never flit across his pages. If, indeed, modern mothers and daughters are only half as knowing, vigilant, and unscrupulous in their designs upon that portion of humanity, who have not only breeches but breeches pockets, no batchelor can have a chance against the female foe ; all unmarried men are marching through an enemy's country, in which they must expect at every step to have their flank turned by some astute matrimonial manœuvre.

We cannot, however, sufficiently praise Mr. Lever for his

evidently hearty abhorrence of all sentimentality and false writing. The most tempting occasion never betrays him into this—he is always manly, simple, and sincere in his treatment of sentiment and passion. This is no small virtue in a modern novelist—many of our modern writers, like our modern singers, are always in *falsetto ;* and the public is in both cases always entrapped into applause.

Nor can we pass from the consideration of Mr. Lever's earlier romances without according our cordial approbation of the admirable ballads, fighting songs, and drinking songs, which are interspersed throughout the pages of those books. These songs are full of spirit—they have all the drollery, dash, and devilry peculiar to the land of the shamrock and shillelah. If they have here and there a flavour of poteen, the scent of the heather and the breath of the mountain breeze are equally strong in them. It is almost impossible to read them without singing them, and almost impossible to hear them sung without wishing to fight, drink, or dance. They bubble forth without premeditation from the depth of a most joyous conviction in the

> " Nunc est bibendum, nunc pede libero
> Pulsanda tellus."

We believe that Mr. Lever's later novels are, on the whole, less generally popular than those by which his reputation as a writer was first acquired. This is natural, for many reasons quite independent of the merits or defects of the works themselves. The public is seldom of one mind with an author in comparing the relative merit of his works, especially where such comparison is between early and subsequent efforts. The author is naturally inclined to esteem most highly those of his works upon which he is conscious of having expended most labour ; the public, on the contrary, are inclined to prefer those to the enjoyment of which they have given the least labour. The first works of an original writer take us by surprise. They issue unexpectedly from the unknown, our enjoyment of them is spontaneous, and the delight occasioned by the freshness of feeling with which the author writes is increased by the freshness of sympathy with which the public reads. Every man's favourite poet is the poet he

first learned to love under the summer trees in his boyhood.
New poets only address new generations. The authors which
most agreeably impress us are those which we read when
most capable of receiving agreeable impressions; that is to
say, in youth. We cannot even entirely renew for the subsequent works of the same author those sensations of delight
which we derived from our first acquaintance with him, when
he was young to us, and we were young to ourselves; and
in proportion as we experience this difficulty on our own part,
we are inclined to resent more naturally than justly the inability of the author to overcome it. Long familiarity, moreover, with the name of an author, often indisposes the public
to expect much novelty from increased familiarity with the
mind of him. Nothing is so reluctantly conceded to a popular
writer as superiority to *himself*. The more readily his claim
to attention and sympathy has been admitted in one direction,
the more resolutely is it resisted in every other. A previous
success is often the greatest hindrance to a subsequent reputation. People are sometimes startled into applause by the
first revelation of an original mind; they are generally on
their guard against any inconsiderate approval of a second.
And as the process by which the mind of an author passes
from one phase into another is usually gradual, and marked
by various stages of development more or less imperfect and
unsatisfactory, the advance made is not always immediately
noticeable, and the recognition accorded to it is naturally
slow and dubious. This must be especially the case with an
author who has introduced himself to the public rather as a
boon-companion than a moralist. We have often heard it said
of Mr. Lever that he is much less funny than he used to be ;
which is indeed true. But when it is asked why he does not
resort to the style and matter of his early novels, and implied
that he should write nothing but 'Harry Lorrequer's' and
'Charles O'Malley's,' we must express the conviction that
compliance with any such demand, even if it were not purely
impossible, would be altogether unadvisable. We could not
ourselves bring to the perusal of repeated 'Harry Lorrequer's' an undiminished capacity to be amused by them.
Consuetudine vilescunt. The piper might pipe as of old, but
who would dance to his piping ? *Non eadem est ætas, non*

B

mens. We cannot blame Mr. Lever for abandoning a vein of humour which he has the merit of having exhausted ; but it is nevertheless obvious, that in relinquishing that particular kind of fiction in which he is allowed to have excelled, Mr. Lever has withdrawn from a territory of which he was sole and undisputed proprietor, and entered upon one in which, whatever the acquirements he may bring to the cultivation of it, he is not without competitors.

It must be conceded that what we miss in Mr. Lever's later publications is that freshness, vivacity, and exuberant wealth of animal spirits, which gave to his earlier novels their chief charm. Although the relative merit of his recent works is decidedly unequal, some of them being much better than others, and all of them being better in one part than in another ; yet there is in the majority of them a sameness of subject and material which does not give fair play to the powers employed upon them. Upon this point we shall speak more fully by-and-by ; but whatever objections we may presently have to make in detail to some of Mr. Lever's last books, we have no hesitation in expressing the opinion, that amongst these books are to be found proofs of a genius richer, maturer, and more pleasing than any which is apparent in the earlier works of the same author. Indeed, 'The Dodd Family Abroad,' which has not been published many years, is in our opinion the best of all Mr. Lever's works. He has written nothing at any time comparable to the letters of Henry Dodd ; nor could there be any better evidence than what is afforded throughout the pages of this delightful and good-humoured satire, that the genius of the author, if it has lost much of that physical animation which is the arbitrary gift of youth, has acquired with years that thoughtful and more pleasing humour which is the result of enlarged experience and deeper sympathy with mankind. This chronicle of the adventures of 'THE DODD FAMILY ABROAD,' like 'The Expedition of Humphrey Clinker,' Smollett's last and most pleasing fiction, is a narrative thrown into epistolary form, and related by the actors themselves, who are thus made with great skill to be, as it were, the unconscious exponents of their own characters, follies, and foibles, as well as the historians of their own fates. We do not desire to suggest even a critical comparison between this clever romance and that master-piece of Smollett, which will doubtless remain unrivalled as long as the English literature endures. But the most conspicuous merit in 'The Dodd Family' is, that each character in the story is so contrived as to evoke, in the most humorous form, the peculiarities of all the others, without any violation of the individuality assigned to itself. The book, which is a sort of prose 'Fudge Family,' deeper, broader, and more comprehensive than Moore's clever satire, is a good-humoured but unsparing mockery of "false pretences" all over the world. If the dramatic power exist in the capacity to realize and express with an accuracy, too great for mere conjecture, other people's habits of thought and feeling, Mr. Lever has shown in this book more of such power than in anything else he has ever written. The humour of his earlier books is almost entirely superficial. It deals purely with external things, and is little more than any extraordinarily acute sense of the ludicrous in situation and circumstance. In this book the humour is of that rarer kind which plays less with external and accidental peculiarities than with men's modes of thought, and the manner in which different minds are impressed by the same facts, or operated on by the same influences. The difference of the result in each case is great. The highest humour is inseparable from a profound sympathy with human nature, and is therefore always tinged with sadness. For man is too grand a subject, after all, for eternal practical jokes, and even the most defaced and misfeatured humanity should be safe from unmitigated laughter. The fun which abounds, however, in Mr. Lever's more youthful writings, ignores the existence of sorrow in any sense but that of hateful deformity, to be contemplated as little as possible : and consequently this sort of fun, incompatible as it is with any deep sympathy, is never quite free from a certain element of cruelty, inherent to the strong animal life of early youth. But what is most delightful in the letters of "K. I." is that loving, tender capacity to feel for and with humanity in all the forms of its imperfection and weakness—that tendency to live in the life of others, and to draw from the various thoughts and acts and manners of mankind constant food for reflection, which breathe through the playful satire, and furnish material to the genial humour of those charming letters. And though the author appears to have given fuller scope both to his own sentiments and his own experience in the letters of "K. I.," yet the same spirit of kindly humour, and the same shrewd appreciation of social characteristics, are apparent in all the epistles, even where the drollery most approaches to caricature, as in those of the Irish servant-girl who complains to her friends at home of being like "a pelican on a dissolute island."

Of all Mr. Dodd's numerous misfortunes, those under which his patience is most pathetic, and which enlist our warmest sympathies, are certainly his domestic and conjugal afflictions. Who that remembers or anticipates matrimonial experience can read without a cold shudder this description of the household tactics adopted on great occasions by Mrs. Dodd ?—

"For the last week Mrs. D. had adopted a kind of warfare, at which she, I'll be bound to say, has few equals and no superior—a species of irregular attack, at all times and on all subjects, by innuendo and insinuation, so dexterously thrown out as to defy opposition ; for you might as well take your musket to keep off the mosquitoes ! What she was driving at I never could guess, for the assault came on every flank and in all manner of ways. If I was dressed a little more carefully than usual, she called attention to my 'smartness ;' if less so, she hinted that I was probably going out 'on the sly.' If I stayed at home, I was waiting for somebody ; if I went out, it was to 'meet them.' But all this guerilla warfare gave way at last to a grand attack, when I ventured to remonstrate about some extravagance or other. 'It came well from *me*,' she burst forth with indignant anger—'it came well from me to talk of the little necessary expenses of the family—the bit they ate, and the clothes on their backs.' She spoke as if they were Mandans or Iroquois, and lived in a wigwam ! "

Poets, we are told by one of them, "learn in suffering what they teach in song," and philosophers acquire wisdom from their own afflictions. Mr. Dodd, in the true spirit of the philosophy preached by Æschylus, παρ' ἄκοντας ἦλθε σωφρονεῖν, thus moralizes on his own misfortune :—

"Ah, Tom, my boy, it's all very good fun to laugh at Keeley, or

Buckstone, or any other of those diverting vagabonds who can con-
vulse the house with such a theme, but in real life the Farce is down-
right Tragedy. There is not a single comfort or consolation of your
life that is not kicked clean from under you ! A system of normal
agitation is a fine thing, they tell us, in politics, but it is a cruel
adjunct of domestic life ! Everything you say, every look you give,
every letter you seal, or every note you receive, are counts in a
mysterious indictment against you, till at last you are afraid to blow
your nose, lest it be taken for a signal to the fat widow lady that is
caressing her poodle at the window over the way ! "

But his greatest trial of all is the prospect of a sudden
accession of fortune to the ambitious partner of his bosom.
His excessive alarm at the possibility of a contingency so fatal
to domestic happiness is very humorous, and his opinions
upon the subject of legacies to married ladies in small circumstances are evidently the result of profound and painful
experience.

"To tell you the plain truth, Tom, I don't know a greater misfortune for a man that has married a wife without money, than to
discover at the end of some fifteen or twenty years that somebody has
left her a few hundred pounds ! It is not only that she conceives
visions of unbounded extravagance, and raves about all manner of
expense, but she begins to fancy herself an heiress that was thrown
away, and imagines wonderful destinies she might have arrived at, if
she hadn't had the bad luck to meet you. For a real crab-apple of
discord, I 'll back a few hundreds in the Three per Cents. against all
the family jars that ever were invented.

"Save us, then, from this, if you can, Tom. There must surely
be twenty ways to avoid the legacy ; and so that Mrs. D. doesn't hear
of it, I 'd rather you 'd prove her illegitimate, than allow her to
succeed to this bequest. I 'll not enlarge upon all I feel about this
subject, hoping that by your skill and address we may never hear
more of it ; but I tell you, frankly, I 'd face the small-pox with a
stouter heart than the news of succeeding to the M'Carthy inheritance."

The adventures of a vulgar Irish family abroad in search
of economy combined with pretension and display, afford Mr
Lever a good opportunity for satirising the social and political
condition of a great number of foreign States. In doing
this he has shown not only an affluent experience of Continental life, and a quick perception of all social phenomena,

but also a very uncommon amount of shrewd common-sense and sound political judgment. We must say the satire is well deserved and unerringly aimed. Nothing escapes. The state of society, the conduct of government, the foreign and domestic policy, the administration of justice, the civil and military jurisdictions, the morals and manners of Continental capitals, are sharply canvassed. The character, too, of Kenny Dodd, in its strange admixture of childishness and wisdom, ignorance of the world and knowledge of mankind, and that subdued humorous consciousness which it betrays of the utter worthlessness of those influences to which it is ever an easy victim, greatly facilitates the indulgence of that moralizing vein in which Mr. Lever reviews almost every possible aspect of society. From the moment in which K. I. discovers that "shamelessness is the grand characteristic of foreign life," and that "one picks up the indecency much easier than the irregular verbs," the wisdom of his private reflections keeps pace with the folly of his public proceedings.

We extract the following passage from Mr. Dodd's reflections upon geology and the sciences, viewed in their relation to education and politics, because it is a favourable sample of a particular kind of humour in which Mr. Lever's later writings, and especially the work from which the passage is taken, are equally fertile and felicitous. It is a humour which consists in turning some indisputable truth upside down or inside out when the reader is least expecting it. The effect is often irresistible.

"For a man who has daughters abroad, my advice is—stick to the sciences. Grey sandstone is safer than the polka, and there's not as dangerous an experiment in all chemistry as singing duets with some black-bearded blackguard from Naples or Palermo. Now mind, Tom, this counsel of mine applies to the education of the young, for when people come to the forties, you may rely upon it, if they set about learning anything, they'll have the devil for a schoolmaster. What does all the geology mean? Junketting, Tom—nothing but junketting! Primitive rock is another name for a Pic-nic, and what they call Quartz is a figurative expression for iced champagne. Just reflect for a moment and see what it comes to. You can enter a protest against family extravagances when they take the shape of balls and soirees, but what are you to do against botanical excursions and anti-

quarian researches? It's like writing yourself down Goth at once to
oppose these. 'Oh, papa hates chemistry; he despises natural history,' that's the cry at once, and they hold me up to ridicule just in
the way the rascally Protestant newspapers did Dr. Cullen, for saying
that he didn't believe the world was round. If the liberty of the
subject be worth anything—if the right for which these same Pro-
testants are always prating, private judgment, be the great privilege
they deem it—why shouldn't Dr. Cullen have his own opinion about
the shape of the earth? He can say, 'It suits *me* to think that I'm
walking erect on a flat surface, and not crawling along with my head
down, like a fly on the ceiling! I'm happier when I believe what
doesn't puzzle my understanding, and I don't want any more miracles
than we have in the church.' He may say that, and I'd like to know
what harm does that do you or me? Does it endanger the Protestant
succession or the State religion? Not a bit of it, Tom. The real
fact is simply this : private judgment is a boon they mean to keep for
themselves, and never share with their neighbours! So far as I have
seen of life, there's no such tyrant as your Protestant, and for this
reason : it's bad enough to force a man to believe something that he
doesn't like, but it's ten times worse to make him disbelieve what he's
well satisfied with ; and that's exactly what they do. Even on the
ground of common humanity it is indefensible. If my private judgment goes in favour of saints' toe-nails and martyrs' shin-bones, I have
a right to my opinion, and you have no right to attack it. Besides,
I won't be badgered into what it may suit somebody else to think.
My opinion is like my flannel-waistcoat, that I'll take off or put on as
the weather requires ; and I think it very cruel that I must wear mine
simply because you feel cold."

When Mr. Dodd moralizes on the field of Waterloo, his
words are the words of wisdom. Could Mr. Mill himself be
more logical on the subject of Divine Right? All the political
philosophers in the world could add but little to this pithy
summary of the case, as between kings and peoples :—

"I know you'll reply to me with your old argument about Legiti-
macy and Divine Right, and all that kind of thing. But, my dear
Tom, for the matter of that, haven't I a divine right to my ancestral
estate of Tullylicknaslatterley ; and look what they're going to do
with it, to-morrow or next day! 'T is much Commissioner Longfield
would mind, if I begged to defer the sale on the ground of 'divine
right.' *Kings are exactly like landlords ; they can't do what they
like with their own, hard as it may seem to say so. They have their
obligations and their duties ; and if they fail in them, they come into*

the Encumbered Estates Court just like us—ay, and just like us, **they** 'take very little by their motion.'

"I know it's very hard to be turned out of your 'holding.' I can imagine the feelings with which a man would quit such a comfortable quarter as the Tuileries, and such a nice place for summer as Versailles ; Dodsborough is too fresh in my mind to leave any doubt on this point : but there's another side of the question, Tom. What were they there for? You'll call out, 'This is all Socialism and Democracy, and the devil knows what else.' Maybe I'll agree with you. Maybe I'll say, I don't like the doctrine myself. Maybe I'll tell you that I think the old time was pleasantest, when if we pressed a little hard to-day, why, we were all the kinder to-morrow, and both ruler and ruled looked more leniently on each other's faults. But say what we will—do what we will—these days are gone by, and they'll not come back again. There's a set of fellows at work, all over the world, telling the people about their rights. Some of these are very acute and clever chaps, that don't overstate the case ; they neither go off into any flights about Universal Equality, or any balderdash about our being of the same stock ; but they stick to two or three hard propositions, and they say, ' *Don't pay more for anything than you can get it for—that's free trade ; don't pay for anything you don't want—that's a blow at the Church Establishment ; don't pay for soldiers if you don't want to fight—that's at a 'standing army ;' and above all, when you haven't a pair of breeches to your back, don't be buying embroidered small-clothes for Lords-in-Waiting or Gentlemen of the Bedchamber.' But here I am again, running away from Waterloo, just as if I was a Belgian.*"

K. I. has certainly no pretension to be a faultless philosopher, but he is a very pleasant one. Montaigne would have chosen him for a companion. Molière would have sympathised with and loved him. He has so large a sympathy for human nature, that his own claim upon that of the reader is irresistible ; and so kindly and compassionate a feeling for the imperfections of mankind, that we follow him with undiminished affection through all the faults and follies that he so frankly attributes to himself. He so innocently pleads guilty to the occasional "delight of doing wrong ;" there is something so natural in the touch of envy with which he remarks that "India-rubber itself is not so elastic as a bad character," and so sly an appeal to commiseration in his candid avowal, "I don't want to disparage principle, no more than I do a great balance at Coutts's, or anything else that I don't possess myself," that all such good-humoured self-accusations are at once understood to be among the philosophical paradoxes peculiar to that vein of banter which proves all problems by the *ad absurdum* argument, and which he frequently indulges at his own expense. Mr. Lever is, indeed, so happy in the management of dialogue, and in the art of allowing his characters to evolve themselves without interference from the author, that there is every reason to think he would be successful in the comic drama : and were he to exercise his genius in that direction we have little doubt but what he would do much to rescue the English stage from its present discreditable obligation to the charity of third-rate French play-wrights. Our extracts from 'The Dodd Family' have extended over a larger space than we could well afford, because it is our sincere opinion that Mr. Lever has written nothing comparable to this book ; and without ample reference to the work itself, it was hardly possible to justify the opinion which we have not hesitated to express about it.

The 'Dodd Family' is an elaborate denunciation of the folly of " people living upon false pretences ;" and 'Davenport Dunn,' which deals with the crimes rather than the follies of society, exposes with considerable power, and an extraordinary knowledge of the dark side of modern civilization, the innumerable " fraudulent pretences " of roguery in every rank of life. The character of Dunn himself, which is that of the brilliant commercial swindler, the Robert Law of these days, whose roguery is on a magnificent scale, is carefully drawn; and Mr. Lever has certainly the merit of never allowing himself to be tempted into conventional exaggeration of this character. Davenport Dunn is a rascal of genius, and throughout all his roguery he remains sufficiently human and natural (the good being never entirely obliterated by the evil in his complex character) to justify to the last the interest which his career excites in the mind of the reader. His ambition, before it comes in contact with distracting and debasing influences, is legitimate, and even noble ; and the gradual deterioration of a character whose power is uncontrolled by principle, is finely worked out. But the best and most powerful character in this book—a character in which Mr. Lever has shown, in addition to his ordinary knowledge of the world, no ordinary knowledge of human nature—is that of Grog Davis, the professional "sporting swindler." This man, a vulgar blackleg, and in all his dealings with society a most unmitigated scoundrel, nevertheless affects us with a sense of power, and secures from us a degree of interest which it would be impossible to feel for a character of which the delineation was less true to the deepest realities of nature. The whole conception of this character is, indeed, of the highest order. The one redeeming point in the much-defaced humanity of this man, and the secret of the strong dramatic interest which he excites, lies in his devoted and absorbing affection for his daughter.

Whatever he has in him better than the fiend, or above the brute, is concentrated in this affection, of which the pathos is all the more poignant from the power of nature which it indicates, and the contrast which it suggests with the prostitution of that power in the habitual life of the man. The professional associations of Grog Davis with the turf and the fashionable gambling-houses of Europe, bring him into daily contact with the most worthless and demoralized members of the upper ranks of society. Their ambition to be knaves renders them only the dupes of a knavery more practised and audacious than their own ; and the contempt of the professional swindler for those who, though his superiors in social rank, are only his equals in infamy, and his inferiors in the dexterity which renders infamy partially profitable, is embittered by his haunting consciousness that they are by birthright the inheritors of what a man may desecrate but cannot transfer, and that the sphere from which they descend into connection with him is one into which, by no possible connection with them, is he able to elevate himself. His dreary and restricted experience teaches him that there is no moral degradation which men will not incur for the sake of money, and from this he argues to the conclusion that there is no social disability which may not be overcome by that all-powerful agent. He therefore labours to accumulate wealth dishonestly, in order that he may make his child rich enough to be honest. What matter though his own hands be soiled ?— hers shall be stainless! What matter though he heap infamy on himself, if it be to bequeath to her the purity and innocence which, the further it is removed from the depths of his own degradation, the more he delights to contemplate and revere in the future of his child? The profligate gentlemen who are his boon companions may laugh away, in the course of a night's debauch, the reputation of every duchess in England; but where is he, so bold of tongue, or so sure of his pistol-practice, as shall dare to find a spot on the character of the daughter of the "infamous Grog Davis?" Whilst he, for her sake, is plotting nefarious plunder, in the company of men whose presence is pollution, she, an innocent happy girl, in her convent at Brussels, shall be learning all that can refine and elevate life—the associate of spotless maidens, and the pupil of the most accomplished teachers that money can secure. And in all this notable scheme nothing is overlooked save that alone which involves the inevitable failure of it. It never occurs to the remarkable natural shrewdness of a man whose experience, however varied, is limited exclusively to evil, that in this world, where the consequences of evil are endless, the sins of the fathers are visited upon the children, and that, in the eye of society, the daughter of the "infamous Grog Davis," were she wise as Sheba, and pure as Ruth, can never be other than the child of infamy, and the inheritor of shame. And so complete is his inability to realize or comprehend any but social distinctions between right and wrong, that although there is no self-sacrifice of which he is not capable to secure the happiness of his child, and no barbarity in which he would scruple to indulge his vengeance on the man who should injure her, yet he is himself a conspirator to sell her in marriage to the most abjectly worthless and contemptible of all his infamous associates, simply because that man is brother and heir to a peer of the realm. That the daughter of Grog Davis should be a peeress, for this Grog Davis schemes to secure as his son-in-law a man whom he knows to be guilty of forgery, and whom he himself despises as a poltroon. This is the summit of his ambition. And how a theory of life which insults human nature is defeated by human nature itself; how the human heart vindicates its inherent birthright to the control of its own destinies, and avenges upon itself the wrongs inflicted by itself upon its better aspirations; how, out of the utter wreck, and failure of

all that unscrupulous ingenuity can devise for the attainment
of unworthy desires, arises at the last, in the mere might of
man's common instinct to be good, something which recon-
ciles the fact of human sin to our faith in human nature, and
seems to vindicate the hope of a distant but ultimate sal-
vation,—is shadowed forth in the development and destiny
of these two characters, with a masterly power and depth of
insight which not unfrequently reminds us of Balzac.

Before we pass from the consideration of this work, we
may remark, as regards the entire conception of it, that considerable skill is evinced in the mechanism by which Mr.
Lever contrives to show that every rogue is limited, in his
power to do mischief, to the use, as it were, of a single engine,
and that he who assails honest men with one kind of weapon
is liable to be himself overthrown by his ignorance of the
fence peculiar to some other species of rascality. Thus, for
instance, the amateur blackguard Annesley Beecher, is no
match for the professional blackleg Grog Davis ; and Grog
Davis, in turn, with all his craft and audacity, is no match
against the more astute tactics of Davenport Dunn, the refined and comprehensive rascal ; whilst even Dunn is over-
reached at last by the combined common-sense of the honest
portion of society ; so that, with this species of vermin, as
with all others, the rhyme holds good, that

" Greater fleas have little fleas,
 Upon their legs to bite 'em ;
And little fleas have lesser fleas,
 And so *ad infinitum*."

There are some admirable characters in Mr. Lever's last
novel. Mrs. Penthony Morris is excellent. So, in another
way, is Mr. Ogden, the bully of a public office, the sycophant
of secretaries of state, and the tyrant of junior clerks, the
pedant of Downing Street, and the bore of all society. There
is nothing more delightful than to see a bully cowed ; and
the absolute terror and anguish of Ogden when he unexpectedly encounters, on the Continent, the fascinating wife
from whom he has been divorced, the groan of positive pain
into which his pompous compliment is suddenly converted
by a single glance at the person for whom it was destined

witu the most approved conventional gallantry, is inimitable. There is something even which claims our sympathy in the capacity for common human suffering thus revealed beneath all the small formalities of the man. Layton, the lost man of genius, is of a higher range, and there is considerable power, and not a little pathos, in Mr. Lever's vigorous sketch of this character. But, perhaps, the best-sustained character in the book is that of the Yankee, Leonidas Shaven Quakenboss.

In the delineation of this character Mr. Lever has evinced one merit, for which, perhaps, he can hardly hope to receive due appreciation from the majority of readers. Quakenboss is, so far as we know, almost the only Yankee of English manufacture in whose figures of speech the purely Yankee idiom, peculiar to the New England States, is not constantly confounded with the slang of the South and West. Mr. Lever is also deserving of approval for not having allowed the merely ludicrous in a subject so obviously open to coarse caricature, to overpower his finer perception of what are the better and worthier qualities of the Yankee character. In this respect, however, he has been anticipated by Sir E. Lytton.

There is certainly no lack of power in Mr. Lever's later novels. On the contrary, they contain writing of great power, and evince qualities which belong to a genius of a higher order than we discover in his earlier, and still, perhaps, more popular books. Had he never written anything but the 'Dodd Family,' that work alone would have entitled him to take undisputed rank among the humorists of England ; and had that work been the first of a hitherto unknown writer, the sensation it would have excited must have been very great. But familiarity, if it does not breed contempt, often induces indifference. If Aristides had taken to rope-dancing, perhaps he would not have been ostracised by the Athenians. Popularity is an alms which, the more cheerfully it is accorded to a first appeal, the more churlishly is it conceded to a second from the same quarter. When we see a boy in the street standing on his head, if we are in a good humour we fling him a penny, but the next time we see him turning a somersault, we only say, "There's that boy again!" and button up our pockets. Still, there are undoubtedly

drawbacks to the claim of Mr. Lever's later works on general
sympathy and approval for which he is himself responsible ;
and we have reserved to the last the few remarks which
we have to make of an unfavourable nature in reference
to these works, because the cordial recognition which we have
already expressed of their author's ability will be the best
guarantee for our sincerity in objecting to the subjects on
which that ability is sometimes exercised.   There is a sameness of subject about the majority of Mr. Lever's younger
novels which is partly counterbalanced by the fact that such
sameness lies at least within the sphere of a more or less
national interest, such as the portraiture of Irish life.   But
the continued repetition of scenes representative of a kind of
society which is neither familiar nor pleasing to a large
class of English readers, which is the characteristic of nearly
all Mr. Lever's later works, is under any circumstances a mistake.   The frivolity of Continental society, the vulgarity and
mistakes of English travellers abroad, and the tricks and
deceptions of sharpers and adventurers, is a very legitimate
subject for satire ; but it has really been exhausted with
great success in the 'Dodd Family,' and we regret to see
it enter so largely into the staple material of Mr. Lever's
subsequent novels.   However excellent may be the cookery,
and skilful the arrangement of the dishes, we object to
continual invitations to dine off the leavings of any feast,
however good ; it is not hospitality, but thrift, which would
force us to drain the last flagon and swallow the last crumb.

> " The funeral baked meats
> But coldly furnish forth the marriage-feast."

In such works as 'DAVENPORT DUNN,' and ONE OF THEM,'
the genius of the author carries everything before it.   But
the subject of such a story as 'The Daltons' can, we should
think, have little interest for the mass of the public.   We
need not defend these remarks from the imputation of a false
and vulgar morality which would exclude from fiction its
legitimate sources of interest in the delineation of crime and
the analysis of evil.   Nothing in human nature can be alien
to art, which derives from nature all its materials.   All we
ask from an author is to preserve the balance and proportion

of the emotions to which he appeals. To be continually poring over the blots and failures of humanity, or the vices and corruption of any social state, is neither profitable nor pleasant. And the perusal of a series of fictions which present to us only the deformities of nature, and detain us without relief or intermission in the society of sharpers and vagabonds, and all manner of vicious or vulgar persons, becomes fatiguing and painful. As we close one after the other of such books, we feel like men returning from a hell. Our gains are not equivalent to the unpleasurable process of their acquirement, and we long for some more wholesome intercourse with mankind. The highest and most truthful art must occasionally hold intercourse with evil, but it is a mistake in art to make that intercourse habitual. When an author continually presents to our view one side only, either of society or of man's heart, and that the most unpleasant of all, he appears to imply—not that this is to be found in society or human nature, and is worth looking at—but that nothing else is to be found in society or human nature, and that this is worth looking at; and we revolt from acqui escence in any such view of a cause which is, after all, our own. Our estimation of the genius of Le Sage would be much lower if he had written half-a-dozen small 'Gil Blas; and if Fielding had written many 'Jonathan Wilds,' we should be disposed to think less highly of the mind that made 'Tom Jones.' We attribute this defect to what is, perhaps, in itself a conscientious quality. We think that Mr. Lever is apt to be content to draw his materials for fiction too exclusively from *observation.* Human nature is indeed inexhaustible, but no one man's observation of human nature can be so. The widest experience is limited, and the limit of it must be reached at last. There is only one inex haustible source for fiction, and that is the Imagination.

But the imagination itself is an engine which cannot be kept in frequent operation without being frequently supplied with fuel. It cannot act without being first acted upon. And the fault we are inclined to attribute to the majority of our modern writers of romance is, that they give out too much and take in too little. Let men say what they will about native originality, man is not really a creator. He changes,

improves, and extends, that is all. *Ex nihilo nihil fit ;* and
the best new ideas are the product of a large accumulation
of old ones. Those authors who rely chiefly upon personal
observation and experience for the materials of fiction, cannot
be too careful to vary their point of sight pretty often.
Every imaginative writer must at some period have experienced
the feelings expressed by Cowley, when he wrote—

> "The fields which sprang beneath the ancient plough,
> Spent and outworn, return no harvest now,
> And we must die of want,
> Unless new lands we plant."

If Mr. Lever is disposed to dispute the justice of these observations, or, at any rate, their special application to himself,
he may certainly refer to the extraordinary sameness of a vast
number of his contemporary novelists, who do not seem, on that
account, to enjoy less popularity. One set of writers can talk of
nothing but governesses, tutors, and athletic curates, who love
fly-fishing and abhor Strauss. The domestic novel happens
to be in fashion, and we certainly have enough of it. Others
are never happy out of the precincts of Pall-Mall and the
clubs, unless it be at a fashionable watering-place ; and some
can give no flavour to English fiction without importing it from
Florence or Rome, or borrowing their intrigue from the secret
societies, and their sentiment from Mazzinian manifestoes.
But Mr. Lever is immeasurably richer in imagination and
power than all such writers ; and if he would occasionally
emigrate to "fresh fields and pastures new," he has already
all that is needful in the way of stock and capital. He may
be contented with his present reputation, which is extensive and likely to be permanent ; but we believe that it is in
his own power to elevate and enlarge it.

" Count no man happy till he has ceased to live," says the
Greek proverb. Sum up the attributes of no genius till
it has ceased to act or to write. The last work of an author
may sometimes be the first which gives a just idea of his
mind as a whole.

www.ingramcontent.com/pod-product-compliance
Lightning Source LLC
Chambersburg PA
CBHW030616030726
47497CB00006B/1527